They were a wonderful mix of fun, friendship, and fearlessness. I wasn't quite ready for the story to end.

—Mary Davis, author of *Mrs. Witherspoon Goes To War* (Heroines of WWII), and the award-winning Quilting Circle series (Mountain Brook Ink)

Patty Smith Hall's novel, *On My Honor,* sheds a spotlight on the Outer Banks of North Carolina during WWII. Readers may not realize the enemy's activities right off our own coastline, which Smith Hall incorporates into a suspenseful mystery.

—Carrie Fancett Pagels, author of *Behind Love's Wall* and *My Heart Belongs* on *Mackinac Island, Maude's Mooring.*

≡ HEROINES OF WWII ≡

ON MY HONOR

PATTY SMITH HALL

BARBOUR
PUBLISHING

On My Honor ©2022 by Patty Smith Hall

Print ISBN 978-1-63609-432-8

Adobe Digital Edition (.epub) 978-1-63609-433-5

All scripture quotations are taken from the King James Version of the Bible.

This book is a work of fiction. Names, characters, places, and incidents are either products of the author's imagination or used fictitiously. Any similarity to actual people, organizations, and/or events is purely coincidental.

Cover image © Mark Owen / Trevillion Images

Published by Barbour Publishing, Inc., 1810 Barbour Drive, Uhrichsville, Ohio 44683, www.barbourbooks.com

Our mission is to inspire the world with the life-changing message of the Bible.

 Member of the
Evangelical Christian
Publishers Association

Printed in the United States of America.

DEDICATION

To my troop—Lisa, Virginia, Janet, and Ivie. I'm so glad I get to live life with you! God blessed me with wonderful life-long friends when He gave me you!

To my Outer Banks girls—Jodie, Laura, Mesu, Hope, Carole and Terri—the 'spies' we saw coming out of the sound found a home! Love you all!

To Rebecca and JoAnne, thank you for your insight and patience. You make me a better writer. Thank you!

⚍ CHAPTER 1 ⚎

January 18, 1942
Atlantic Ocean near the Outer Banks Coast

Timothy Elliott breathed in a chilly breath of salty air and closed his eyes. Water lapping against the tanker's hull washed away his worrisome thoughts. In this moment, he felt at peace. He'd forgotten what peace felt like in the two years since Germany had invaded Poland and the United Kingdom had declared war. Almost as quickly, the bombs rained down on London, turning the once beautiful city into a pile of rubble. War had come to their doorstep. Tim glanced at the lights twinkling along the Outer Banks of North Carolina. Did the Americans realize war knocked at their door right here, right now?

It had been an uneventful voyage on the *Allan Jackson* thus far, and Tim hoped it remained that way. At least the captain had taken his advice and called for blackout conditions, his only exception being the ship's standard red and green lights that shone from the mast. Tim had tried to convince him that seventy-two thousand barrels of crude oil were an attractive target to the Germans, but the man refused to listen. There had been no attacks off the Eastern Seaboard yet, and he saw no reason to believe his ship would be the first.

Tim leaned against the railing. New York Harbor couldn't come soon enough.

The metal hinges of a door squeaked behind him, followed by the slow, steady sound of footsteps. "I thought I would find you here."

He shifted slightly as Rolf Schmidt joined him. An officer in the German *Kriegsmarine*, he'd escaped when he was ordered to fire on his own men rather than risk them being captured. Tim stole a quick glance at the man. Not that he cared. One Nazi in the world was one too many. The only thing that kept Schmidt alive was his claim to have the navy's battle plans for the war in the Atlantic. Once they were secured, Rolf could rot in prison for all he cared.

Rolf struck a match, then lifted it to his cigarette. "Choppy seas. Still, we're an easy target."

Information Tim knew and had informed the captain of. "You rooting for the fatherland?"

"I love my country, Elliott. I simply don't agree with the führer's vision for it." The officer's jaw tightened. "Once this war is over, I intend to return."

"I wouldn't make any plans just yet." Tim pulled the edges of his coat tighter. He didn't trust the man. Schmidt had personally overseen attacks on British ships, killing hundreds in His Majesty's Navy as well as destroying dozens of ships. Not once had he considered the lives of those lost defending their freedoms. He'd grown a conscience too late, in Tim's opinion.

Not that it mattered what he thought. His job was to get Schmidt to New York. But with German submarines seeded in the waters along the Eastern Seaboard already, an attack was imminent.

Schmidt must have shared his thoughts. "If they catch me. . ."

"They won't," Tim assured him. Assurances were flimsy when it came to war, but Tim would do whatever he could to see the captain delivered safely to his commanding officers. Then Tim would be off to his next assignment. There had been rumors of him being sent to infiltrate the German army in Paris. Or maybe he would visit his underground sources in Stockholm. After almost a year of writing propaganda pieces to convince Americans to join in the war, he was ready to enter the fray. This was his first real assignment since being recruited, and he would not fail. Serving king and country was his calling, just as the sea had been his father's.

A low hum, almost like a whistle, jerked Tim from his thoughts. His eyes trained on the horizon, he searched the choppy waters as the intimidating sound grew louder.

"There!" Rolf pointed into the watery depths.

Tim followed the line of his finger, then saw it, a torpedo cutting through the waves like a hot knife through butter. Without thinking, he grabbed Schmidt by the arm and pulled him down. "Stay close, and no funny business."

The words were barely out when the world around them exploded, the dark sky replaced by bright light. The floor beneath them lifted, then bowed. Metal and wood splintered like dry timber, shooting sparks like falling stars in every direction. Boots drummed against the cracked floor as men hurried to their posts. The smell of oil thickened the salt-laced air. Tim glanced over the side. Water flowed into the ship through a large gaping hole.

The ship was sinking.

There was only one alternative. "Come on." Tim pulled off his jacket, then toed off his boots. "We're going in."

"I've never been on a boat that was sunk before." The man glanced around, a look of astonishment in his eyes. "It's very different than I imagined. Or maybe my men were trained to behave much better than this."

The ship was sinking, and Schmidt was waxing poetic about his crewmen? Tim grabbed him by the lapel and jerked him close.

"There's seventy thousand barrels of oil beneath us. You can stand here and talk, or you can go over the side."

Schmidt hesitated, then unbuttoned and threw off his coat. "At least this way we have a—"

Tim didn't let him finish. With his shoulder in Schmidt's midsection, he hoisted the man up, then tossed him over the railing, following quickly behind him. The world exploded a second time, then receded into a dull moan as he hit the icy water. He'd swum in cold water before, but nothing like this. Salt stung his eyes as he forced them open. Overhead, an eerie glow swept the surface like the fire and brimstone his father preached to him as a child. He swam away from the light, only surfacing when darkness filled the sky around him. Turning, he surveyed the damage. Flames licked the night sky, illuminating what was left of the tanker. She would sink soon, the tanker listing to one side. Screams from the injured and dying echoed against the darkness. If help didn't come soon, many would die before morning.

Dear God, please send help to us.

Praying was all he could do at this point. That, and finding Schmidt. Tim glanced around the place where the captain had gone in. Nothing but fire there now. Cupping his hand to his mouth, he called out, "Rolf Schmidt!"

There was no response, and then, over the moans and yelling, "Elliott?"

"Keep talking!" Tim zeroed in on his voice, then saw the man, a circle of burning oil surrounding him. If Schmidt didn't move, he would burn away to nothing. A fitting ending to the man. But if he died, the Allies would lose their opportunity to win this war in months rather than years.

That couldn't happen. Tim started toward him, but as he raised his right arm, pain shot through every nerve from his hand to his shoulder. Holding his arm close to his body, he paddled toward the man. "Go under and swim toward me."

"My arm."

Tim saw the odd angle of his shirtsleeve. Broken. Still, if they didn't get away from the boat, they would die. "You can do this, Schmidt. You must do this. It's the only way to end this war."

The man's jaw tightened; then he gave a slight nod, drew in a deep breath, and slipped under the water.

Please, God, don't let me lose Schmidt. He's the only one who has the answers. A high-pitched whistle jerked Tim around. Another torpedo. It plowed through the ship's compartments, the explosion ripping the boat in two. More lives lost, but there was nothing Tim could do. He had one job—to deliver Schmidt to his superiors—so he'd best get to it. He sucked in a heated breath then slipped under the icy depths, uncertain when or if he'd ever resurface again.

"All right, everyone, let's get our compasses and gather around the map," Ginny Mathis instructed the band of girls circled around the wooden picnic table. "It's important that we learn this skill so we can help the coast guard if called upon."

"I'd rather keep an eye on the guardsmen," her sister, Belle, whispered, sending the other girls into a cascade of giggles.

Ginny rolled her eyes. What was with her sister all of a sudden? Belle's interest in the opposite sex shouldn't bother her. She'd noticed boys for the first time when she was thirteen, so it was perfectly normal for her sister to follow suit. But with the war going on, Seabees and guardsmen just a couple of years older than Belle would be pouring into their tight-knit island community, and that was a recipe for disaster. The last thing Ginny needed was a cow-eyed sister mooning after some boy.

That's why she had to keep Belle and her friends occupied

with the war effort if only to keep them out of trouble. "During the Great War, several ships were sunk off Hatteras by the Germans, so there's every reason to believe they'll do it again."

"Daddy told us the explosions were so close, Grandma's entire house shook and some windows broke." Ruthie Rogers glanced around, concern lining her young face. "Back then, they were worried the Germans would come ashore."

Clara, Ruthie's twin sister, turned to Ginny. "Is that something we need to worry about?"

She glanced around the picnic table. The girls' expressions mirrored her own concerns. In the weeks since Pearl Harbor, there had been no sign that the German U-boats that had wreaked havoc during the Great War were lurking around the island again. The explosion Ginny had seen off Diamond Shoals last night changed all that. An invasion by the Germans was a very real possibility. All she could do was prepare them for what might come. "What have we been doing the last few weeks during our Girl Scout meetings?"

Belle glanced around. "Well, we learned how to stitch someone up if they've been hurt, and how to set broken limbs."

"We started collecting fat to make bullets." April Smith wrinkled her nose. "Which I find disgusting."

"And you've been trying to teach us how to read maritime maps, though for the life of me, I don't know why," Clementine Yancy added, looking vaguely bored.

Ginny had to stifle a chuckle. "We've been doing all these things to prepare us for the possibility of the war coming to our shores. Because what is the Girl Scout motto?"

All six girls answered. "Be prepared!"

"That's right, and it's up to us to be prepared to protect our families and friends for whatever may come." Not that Ginny believed the Germans would actually come ashore, but being ready fell more in line with her personal motto: *Expect the worst and hope for the best, and it usually falls somewhere in the middle.*

"Then let's learn how to read these maps," Belle answered, handing out the list of coordinates.

As the girls settled into work, Ginny strolled over to the first set of sand dunes. She had worked late into the night on this assignment. Sleep had evaded her as usual. She wasn't sure why. Yes, she worried about her father and the responsibilities he'd left her with. The problem was he'd never told her why he'd asked her to come home in the middle of her last year of nursing school, just that she was needed. Well, the boys on the front line needed her too, but she was stuck here until her dad returned home.

But that wasn't the reason for her insomnia. Between her job at the Oregon Inlet Ferry and volunteering at the coast guard infirmary, she was on the run from sunup to sundown. But once she laid her head on her pillow, it was as if her brain wouldn't shut off. At first it didn't bother her. She'd rest until sleep claimed her in the early hours of the morning. But as the days dragged into months, she wondered if she'd ever sleep through the night again.

Maybe that's why she'd sought refuge in the lighthouse. The Cape Hatteras Lighthouse had been deserted for years, yet it offered her a place of peace and quiet, away from a world in constant motion—and since Pearl Harbor, a world at war. It gave her a place to pray in secret, away from her sister and mother. A place where she could unload all her worries, even if it was just to the walls.

"Gin, we're having a problem with this one," Belle called out from the huddled group.

Walking over to the table, Ginny leaned over Clementine's shoulder and glanced at the worksheet. "Which one?"

"Here." Ruthie pointed to a red dot someone had made on the

map. "If our calculations are right, this one's out in the middle of nowhere."

"Hmm." Just as Ginny thought. The flash of light that had caught her attention last night had come and gone so quickly, she wasn't certain it had even been real. She'd stopped by the coast guard station this morning on the way to work and reported the incident to the guardsman at the front desk. It was up to Officer Chapline and his men to coordinate a search and rescue. She could only hope they had gotten there in time. "It's in the shipping lanes, so we need to plot it out."

The girls exchanged glances and then went back to work.

Ginny watched them. A hodgepodge of personalities, yet they were totally devoted to one another and their friendship, some of which started in the cradle. They were devoted to her too. Without their help, she never would have found her footing after being gone for four years. All the friends she'd grown up with had left the island like her, wanting to be more than a fisherman or a boat builder. Her troop had made things easier for her, even finding a decent car to get her to work every morning. The six of them were Girl Scouts in the truest sense of the word, and one day they would grow into fine young women.

Climbing the sand dune, Ginny breathed in a comforting mixture of salt and brine, then closed her eyes against the jangle of nerves. Before last night, the war had been just a newsreel before the main feature at the movies. Yes, the images had troubled her, but it was "over there" away from everyone and everything she held dear. Last night changed all that. It was here, threatening her family and the island, and she would protect them any way she could.

She drew in another lungful of air, then coughed. What was that smell? It reminded her of her father and the time he built a motor for his boat. He would come home in the evening, grinning like a cat who ate the canary, wearing oil-stained clothes that stunk to high heaven. Momma had made him take off his clothes in the kitchen rather than have him stink up her clean house. Ginny walked up another dune, the noxious odors growing stronger with each step. As she reached the crest of the last dune, she fell to her knees.

High tide had stained the creamy-colored sand dark gray close to the dunes. Closer to the water, the beach was pitch black as if something had bled out on the sand. The blue-green ocean they'd played in during the summer was gone, replaced by a slimy film that seemed to weigh heavy on the water. Broken wood lay splintered in piles, pillars of steel buried deep in the sand. Farther down the beach, people gathered tin cans, most likely food or other provisions they could use.

If she'd had any misgivings about the explosion, they were wiped away. A ship had been attacked and, from the looks of the beach, blown to bits. Uncertainty overwhelmed her. What could she do? She needed to speak to Officer Chapline. As she hurried over the dunes, the pussy willows and seagrass slowed her, her boots sinking in the shifting sand. By the time she reached the girls, she could barely breathe.

"Ginny, what is it?" Belle ran up to her. "You look like you've seen a ghost."

It felt like she'd seen one. She bent over, her shirt sticking to the perspiration running down her back. "I must go to the coast guard station. There is an oil slick on the beach they need to investigate."

"You think maybe one of those German subs ran aground on the shoals and the current tore it apart?" Ruthie asked as the rest of the girls joined them. "That would be something to see."

"It can't be as bad as all that." Belle started past Ginny. "I want to see."

Ginny reached out and grabbed her sister's arm. "That's not a good idea."

"But I want to see it." Belle's stubborn chin lifted. "I've seen the beach after a shipwreck, you know."

This was different. Their beach, the one filled with memories of their childhood, had turned into a battlefield.

"Are you worried I might find a body on the beach?" Belle asked, all wide-eyed amazement. "Because I've seen one before."

That was news to her. She glared at her sister. "When was that?"

"When Miss Arnold, the librarian, passed away. Momma took me to the funeral." Belle turned to her friends. "They laid her out in her nightgown for everyone to see."

"This is different." Ginny had only seen one person wash up onshore, a swimmer who'd been caught in the riptide. The memory had caused her to have nightmares for weeks after, and it took her a year to go back into the water. No, Belle didn't need that memory. "There's probably not even anyone on the beach."

"Then don't you think we should go and find out if anyone needs our help?" Belle pulled out of her grasp. "You've been preparing us for this since you came home last summer. Let us use what we've learned."

Ginny couldn't argue with her sister. Helping where they could was exactly what she'd trained them to do. "All right. But let's all go together, okay?"

Belle's eyes sparkled in triumph. "Well, don't just sit there. Come on!"

As the other girls stood, Ginny felt what was left of her control slip through her fingers. They needed to know what they were walking into. "Girls, the beach looks very different from what we're used to seeing. Whatever was attacked was full of oil, so the sand is soaked in it." Ginny grimaced. "And it's possible you may come across a body. If you do, please let me know so that I can inform the coast guard."

"We should partner up." Belle sided up with Ruthie.

Ginny nodded. It was good seeing Belle being logical for a change. Most times, she was as flighty as one of the loons they watched as it dived for its supper. It was typical teenage stuff. Ginny hadn't been much better when she was that age. She'd had the luxury of growing up in a time unmarred by war. Their experiences would be so different from hers. So many things they would miss, the types of occasions teenage girls looked forward to like homecoming and prom. Their future would be put on hold. They wouldn't have time to learn from their mistakes. They'd be forced to grow up fast.

As they topped the last dune, they stood and stared in silence.

"It's worse than I thought," Lucy stated, her eyes wide as saucers. "And with my imagination, that's saying a lot."

"This ship didn't just sink. It was destroyed," Clementine whispered.

Belle pointed farther down the beach. "What are those people doing?"

"They're searching for canned foods or things they might use." Ginny glanced around. The atmosphere felt thick with grief. Those poor people on the ship. Probably never knew what hit them. And if they did? Ginny closed her mind to that thought.

"Isn't that stealing?" Ruthie asked. "Shouldn't we collect it and return it to its rightful owner?"

Clara gave her a little nudge. "Don't you read? When a ship wrecks or sinks, its possessions go to whoever finds them."

Belle snapped her fingers. "You got that from Mrs. Langley's English class." She glanced at Ginny.

"I see," Ginny replied. Well, it was nice to know the girls learned something. "If we're going to help, we need to get started."

But how? Ginny scoured the beach. Not too far from them, an oil-covered pelican sat. It tried to stand, but it sank back to the ground. "Why don't we find the birds that have been soaked in oil and clean them up? The oil prevents them from flying so they're unable to search for food."

"We're going to need some cages," Lucy suggested. "Gloves and aprons too."

"Why?" Clementine playfully pinched her chin. "Don't you like to get dirty?"

Lucy smiled sweetly. "Not if I don't have to."

"Do any of you have a bird?" Ginny asked, stepping between the two girls.

No one answered, then Clem raised her hand. "Lobster cages might work."

"Crab traps too," April piped in.

"I'm certain everyone has those at home." Ginny glanced down at her watch. They only had a couple more hours of sunlight left. "While I run to the coast guard station, everyone else run home and grab whatever cages you have. We'll meet back here in thirty minutes."

"We won't need that many cages this afternoon, so why don't Lucy, April, Clementine, and Clara grab some cages while Ruthie and I look for birds? By the time you get back, we would have rounded up a few birds." Belle looped her arm with Ruthie's, then glanced over at Ginny. "Is that a good plan, sis?"

Ginny gave her a reluctant nod but couldn't help feeling her sister had gotten the better of her. For now, it didn't matter. She needed to report her findings to the coast guard. It was her duty as a secret coastal watcher to keep them informed. Twenty minutes there and back, and the girls would never miss her. If she timed it just right, she'd be back in time to help load the cages. As the girls scattered to do their assigned jobs, Ginny headed back over the dunes, praying she wasn't too late.

———— ≋ ————

"What is going on with your sister?" Ruthie asked as they each went their separate ways. "She's acting more squirrelly than usual. It's like she's hiding something from us."

Belle found a driftwood pole, then stuck it into the sand. She didn't usually like it when her friends talked about Ginny, but Ruthie Rogers was her best friend in the entire world, so she'd let it pass. Besides, her big sister was most definitely hiding something, but what? Between her job at the ferry and her volunteer work at the infirmary, she didn't have much of a life. Which left only one conclusion, and Belle hated to think it was that. "I think she's mad at me."

Ruthie's brow wrinkled. "She didn't seem mad. Why do you think she's angry with you?"

"I don't know." Belle trapped a can of peaches under her boot and picked it up. "Maybe because Daddy forced her to come home to take care of me and Momma while he went off building boats for the military."

"I thought she came home on her own."

Belle shook her head. "He told her he wouldn't help pay for her final semester of nursing school if she didn't come home immediately." She kicked at a pile of rubbish. "I don't know why Daddy thinks we need Ginny home to take care of us. Momma and I can manage perfectly fine by ourselves. We don't need someone to watch us like we're children or something."

"Fathers are always the last to realize their little girls have grown up." Ruthie lifted her hand and touched the back of it to her forehead. She glanced at Belle. "I heard that at the movies. Do you think people really talk like that?"

"I swear you have the attention span of a gnat sometimes,

Ruthie. I've got a real problem here."

"I know. Ginny's angry, and your daddy treats you like a kid." She patted Belle's hand. "Does that about sum it up?"

Belle sighed. If only she could tell Ruthie everything that was bothering her, but her dad had sworn her to secrecy. Why he thought they had to keep Momma's condition a secret didn't make sense to her. Not that she'd actually seen one of the episodes Daddy had described, but really, it couldn't be that bad if this was the first time she'd heard about it. Maybe if Ginny didn't sneak off at night, she wouldn't be so worried.

Ruthie stopped in her tracks and gawked at her. "Ginny's sneaking off at night. Why didn't you tell me?"

Oh dear, had she said that out loud? Belle shook her head. "I'm sure it's not as bad as it sounds."

Her friend's eyes widened. "You don't think she's got a boyfriend, do you?"

"Ginny?" Belle burst out laughing. "She's never been one to date much, and when she did, they were always the boring types. You know, a real wet blanket."

"Hey! She dated my older brother!" Ruthie laughed about that with her. "So, I understand exactly what you mean. But really, why would she sneak out like that? She doesn't seem like the type."

Belle had her suspicions, and none of them were good. "Let's talk about something else." She stopped and glanced around. "This doesn't even look like our beach anymore."

"How could those stinkin' Germans do this?" Ruthie put her hand over her mouth, her face suddenly somber. "We've never done anything to them. Why do they even want to be in a war in the first place? It changes everything."

Belle studied her friend's expression. Ruthie usually took everything with a grain of salt, but since her brothers had joined up—Nathan in the army and Tom in the navy—her friend had changed. Still carefree at times, but there were moments when Belle didn't recognize the serious person she'd become. The thought of losing the girl she'd grown up with troubled her.

They were still thirteen, and there was adventure to be had. Belle bumped her shoulder against Ruthie's, then smiled. "Let's see if we can find some oily birds."

Ruthie laughed. "I'd give you my babysitting money to see you pick up one of those filthy things."

"Be ready to hand over your wallet then." Belle picked up another piece of driftwood that could double as a cane and handed it to her. "You're going to need something to help you balance in this sludge. It's like quicksand."

"Thanks." Ruthie jabbed it into the blackened sand. "Where do we start?"

"Momma always says to start where you are." Belle pointed toward the Hatteras Inlet. "You go that way, and I'll head toward Avon. We'll meet back at the picnic table in fifteen minutes."

"Sounds like a plan," Ruthie answered, her seriousness gone as quickly as it came. "Holler if you need me, okay?"

Like anyone could hear anything over the waves. But Belle just nodded, then worked her way down to the water. Ruthie had every right to her feelings. Belle didn't know what it was like to send someone she loved off to war, much less two. And now the Germans wanted to destroy their island. How could anyone want to do that to such a beautiful place like the Outer Banks? So many memories were made here. Daddy teaching her to fish. The walks with Ruthie and her friends after school. Shooting off firecrackers on the Fourth of July. This place was a part of her, and she'd protect it any way she could.

Broken piles of wood littered the beach where the tide had brought them in. Belle knelt and carefully pushed the smaller planks out of the way, using her makeshift pole to check for a bird or turtle that might need help. When she found nothing, she moved to the next pile, then the next. The work was slow, the mixture of oil and sand pulling at her boots with each step. Beneath her sweater, she felt hot and sticky. Taking a break, she sat back on her haunches and covered her nose with her coat sleeve, the scent of petroleum so strong she could taste it.

"This is going to take forever," she muttered to the wind. But if there was one thing she'd learned as a Girl Scout, it was that they never gave up. Pulling herself up with her cane, she trudged her way to the next pile of rubble. Grasping her pole, she stuck the tip into the wreckage.

"Mmmm."

Belle jerked her hand back. That didn't sound like any bird she knew. She poked at it again, deeper this time. In one swift movement, the cane was yanked out of her hands and tossed into the water. Belle swallowed, then tried to scream, but the tiny noise was lost in the waves.

"Don't do that again," the voice growled at her.

A man? Or was her overactive imagination playing tricks on her? Belle kicked one corner of the debris. An oil-covered hand rose out of the pile of rubble and grasped her ankle. Her other foot stuck in the sludge, and she lost her balance and fell bottom first into the water.

"What part of 'don't do that again' do you not understand?"

"I didn't mean any harm." Water seeped into her pants. "You scared me."

His grip loosed. Reclaiming her leg, she crouched on her knees and pushed the pieces of wood and debris away until she finally uncovered his legs. What had Ginny said, something about keeping an injured patient talking? "Are you okay?"

There was movement under a large piece of plywood. "I think so. My shoulder hurts."

If that was all he'd injured, he should praise the Lord. "I'm going to try and move this piece of wood covering you. It may take me a couple of times, but I will get you out of there."

He mumbled a response, but Belle couldn't understand it. She stood, then turned, waving her hands frantically in the air. "Ruthie!"

Her friend's head whipped around, then she turned and started slowly to make her way back to Belle. With Ruthie on her way, Belle crouched down again and began to remove the small pieces of wood and debris in the way. "What's your name?"

There was nothing but silence. Had he slipped into unconsciousness? Belle began to pray. *Please don't let him be dead. Please, God, don't let him die on me.*

"Tim." His voice sounded like he'd swallowed gravel. "What's your name?"

"Belle, though why my parents named me that is a mystery to me," she rattled on as she continued to work. "Why not something like Claudia or Greta? I'd even take Bette."

"You talk a great deal."

"My sister—she's training to be a nurse—she told me to keep someone who has been injured talking. Something about keeping their mind off their situation."

"I see." Did he just chuckle?

Ruthie came up alongside her, sucking in great gulps of air. "I feel like I've run a mile." She popped Belle lightly in the shoulder. "You scared me to death."

Belle nodded her head toward the rubble. "That's because he scared me to death."

"Hello."

Ruthie blinked in surprise. "Who is he?"

"Tim, but that's not important right now." Belle stood, eyeing the large sheet of wood. What would be the best way to pick this up without hurting the man any further? "Grab that side over there, and I'll get this one. If we work together, we can both lift it."

"All right." Ruthie got into place, then grabbed the end. "Got it. You ready?"

Belle nodded. "On the count of three. One. Two. Three."

They lifted it, angling the wood toward his feet, then flipped it off him. Belle glanced at the man. He laid on his side, his legs drawn up as if in pain. His right arm hung across his body as if disconnected from the rest. His clothes were drenched in oil, and a slimy ash covered his face and hands. But it was his blood-stained shirt that drew her attention. Kneeling, she took the small pocketknife she carried and cut a small hole in the fabric, then tore it with her hands.

"Where did you get that?" Ruthie asked beside her. "I thought your mom said a pocketknife wasn't ladylike."

"I think Momma will make an exception this time." Belle opened another section of his shirt to find clotted blood around a two-inch cut. "This cut on your side is pretty deep. You're probably going to need stitches."

"What about my shoulder?"

"No broken bones." Ruthie skimmed her hand across his clothed back, then nodded. "Your shoulder is out of place."

"I thought as much." He closed his eyes, his expression a mask of frustration.

Ruthie took a long look at him, then glanced up at Belle. "His name is Tim, but does he have a last name?"

"For Pete's sake, I was doing good to get his first name." But Belle knew Ruthie's stoic expression meant she wasn't about to let this go. Belle gave the man an apologetic smile. "What's your full name?"

The man's lips tightened, reminding her of Ginny when her

patience had run thin. "Captain Timothy Elliott."

"He has an English accent." Ruthie bent closer to him. "I just love English accents. They're just so romantic." She gave him a dreamy smile. "Say something else."

"Leave the man alone." Belle glared at her friend. "There are more important things for us to think about right now than his accent."

"Thank you." He grimaced as he pushed himself up on his left hip, holding his right elbow with his hand. "Is there a doctor on the island?"

"The coast guard has an infirmary in Roanoke." Ruthie sat back on her haunches and pointed down the beach. "If you want me to, I can call and get them to send an ambulance out to pick you up."

"Don't do that," he snapped, then closed his eyes and drew in another deep breath. "I don't want to take up a bed with something as trivial as a dislocated shoulder. Is there a doctor or even a nurse who could stitch me up and put my shoulder back into place?"

Belle and Ruthie exchanged glances. Something wasn't right. Why didn't the man want to go to the infirmary and get checked out? Ginny had warned them that there could be Germans passing themselves off as Allies, even going so far as to learn the language and accents, but Belle had scoffed at the idea. Everyone knew everyone else in Buxton and along the coast. Wouldn't someone new be suspicious enough?

But Ginny had never spoken about shipwreck victims. Belle lowed her gaze to meet his. "Why don't you want us to call the coast guard?"

His stern eyes met hers. "There were hundreds of people on the tanker that sank last night, some badly injured. The staff at the infirmary will have better things to do than stitch up a cut and set my shoulder to rights."

The man had a point. Ginny had given up her only day off to process patients in the infirmary this morning. Then why did Belle have this feeling that Mr. Elliott was holding something back? Maybe she simply needed to ask more questions. "You're a captain. What branch of the service?"

"The Royal Navy," he answered grudgingly.

"Then why aren't you on one of their ships instead of here? Ruthie studied him for a long moment, then gasped. "Are you a deserter and the ship that sank was taking you away to start a new life?"

"I am not a deserter." The captain cradled his head in his good hand and muttered, "Dear God above, save me from this."

But Belle wasn't put off by his request. "Look, if you go to the infirmary, my sister is there. Not only is she a whiz with stitches, she's also kind of pretty. Maybe you'll be her patient."

"I'm not going to the infirmary," he growled.

"And I can't help someone I don't trust," she growled back.

Ruthie tugged at Belle's sleeve. "What are you doing?"

"He's not being honest with us, and one thing my daddy told me before he left for the shipyard was to be careful whom I helped. He said not to trust anyone, especially people I don't know." Belle met his gaze again. "I want to help you, Mr. Elliott, really I do, but Daddy made me promise, and I won't break a promise to him."

His expression tightened and his skin went pale underneath the grime. "I can't believe I'm being held hostage by a teenage girl."

"Believe it, mister." Ruthie glanced from Belle to the man. "When Belle sets her mind to something, she's like a dog to a bone."

"If you want our help, you need to come clean. It's as simple as that," Belle announced. His gaze turned murderous, and for a moment, fear threatened to make her back down. But she couldn't back down. Elliott could be a German for all she knew, here to invade her home. Well, she would do anything to protect it, even if it meant being rude. Belle lifted her chin. "I can sit here all day waiting."

"You're a stubborn little brat, aren't you?" Elliott pushed out through gritted teeth, then huffed out a chuckle. "You remind me of my sister, Iris." He drew another deep breath. "All right then. I worked in the galley on the tanker."

Belle nibbled her lower lip. She'd met a lot of her dad's friends over the years, including some who worked on the bigger ships. None of them looked like this man. "I don't believe you."

"Belle!"

She glanced up at her friend. "Well, I don't."

"Just because you don't believe him doesn't change the fact he needs help," Ruthie replied. "He's just been through something horrible."

"If he worked in the galley, then why all the secrecy?" She shook her head. "No, something else is going on here, something Mr. Elliott feels the need to keep secret. And why is he here instead of England?" An outlandish thought came into Belle's head. "Unless you're a spy."

"Belle, really." Ruthie laughed. "You've been listening to too much *Little Orphan Annie.*"

"Stop! The two of you are giving me a headache." The man rubbed his forehead with his good hand. "My cover is already blown, so there's no need to use it anymore." He lifted his head and glared at them. "You're correct. I work with British Intelligence."

⚊ CHAPTER 2 ⚊

"British Intelligence."

Tim almost expected the two teenage girls at his side to break out in giggles. Dealing with girls of this age had never been his strong suit. His younger sister had certainly given him enough grief. Girls in general, really. He simply didn't understand them. But he doubted he could get to his feet on his own, and these two were his only option at the moment. He cleared his throat, then glared at Belle. "Is that truthful enough for you?"

Shoulders slung back, she nodded. "I wouldn't have pressured you if I'd known."

He seriously doubted that. Still, he admired the way she held to the promise she'd made to her father. People these days broke more promises than they kept. Belle must think a lot of her father. That was rare these days too.

But he had other concerns right now. "Does that mean you're going to help me?"

"Of course we are," the one who called herself Ruthie answered brightly, then glanced at Belle. "We are, aren't we?"

"Yes. I'm just figuring out how we're going to do this." Belle tapped her finger against her chin. "The only person I know who can stitch a cut like that is Ginny, and she had to go to the coast guard offices. We can't take him to my house. It would call too much attention to him if we dragged him to the other side of the village."

"Oh my goodness, Mom would blow a fuse if I brought him home. If he'd only go to the infirmary." Ruthie glared at him.

That couldn't happen. News that he was laid up with his shoulder would be the opening the Germans were looking for to find and kill the former German captain. That is, if he was still alive. He had to be. An extended battle along the United States Eastern Seaboard would be a difficult fight for the Americans and a tragic one for those in Great Britain who depended on American goods to survive. Once his shoulder was put back into place and his side stitched up, he'd be back out and start his search for the German.

"That's out of the question. Mr. Elliott must have a good reason to avoid the infirmary, so we'll have to figure something else out." Belle knelt beside him. "Do you think you can stand up on your own?"

"I'll try." Tim pulled his right leg underneath him, using his left for leverage. But as he pushed upward, his shoes dug deeper into the sand. He fell on his hip, the jolt sending pain cascading in a fireball from his shoulder down to his fingertips. "I'm going to need help."

"Would a cane help?" Ruthie handed him a pole that had washed up nearby.

He glanced at Belle. "Is this yours?"

She gave him an impish smile. "Not anymore."

Tim tried again, this time putting his full weight on the pole. When he was almost standing, Belle slid in under his good arm for support. "We need to get you off this beach." She glanced at Ruthie. "The picnic table?"

"The other girls will be back by now."

There were more of them? Tim glanced down at Belle. "Are these other girls your friends?"

She nodded as she watched her step. "Most of us have known each other since we were in diapers. We had a Girl Scout meeting today. That's why we were here on the beach. Ginny was teaching us how to read maritime maps when we found the beach in such a mess."

"We were looking for oily birds when we found you," Ruthie added. Her smile dimmed slightly. "We're going to have to tell the other girls. The only way we're going to be able to supply him with enough food is if we all pitch in."

"We don't even have a place for him to stay yet." Belle glanced along the sand dunes. "There are a few abandoned beach shacks you could hole up in until you're feeling better."

"That would work." Not that Tim intended to be there long. Still, it would give him a base if his search for Rolf lasted longer than he expected.

They cleared the sand dunes. As they walked past the black-and-white-striped lighthouse, Tim noticed the small cottage a few hundred yards away. "Who lives there?"

"That used to be where the Carruths lived. Mr. Carruth was the lightkeeper for a while, but then they shut down the light-house. They stayed for a while, but Mr. Carruth wasn't a fisher-man, so they packed up and moved back to the mainland," Ruthie answered as if giving a history lesson. "It's a pretty place, or at least my mom said it was."

Tim glanced around. It was perfectly located near the beach, yet far enough from the main roadway to remain out of sight. "Let's look at it."

The girls exchanged glances but didn't argue with him. Hobbling to the walk that led to the house, Tim paused to look. The weeds had been mowed down, the yard flat except for the occasional small rise. A small stand of trees blanketed his view of the road, giving him the privacy he needed to carry out his assignment. The house was quite large, made for a large family, with crackled whitewashed boards and a door that was once trimmed in red. The outbuilding, once the home of chickens, pigs, and cows, sat quietly to the side.

"I'd like to stay here."

Belle glanced at Ruthie, then him. "I guess that would be all right. No one's lived here in years, so I'm not sure what the inside looks like."

"We'll have to jimmy the lock," Ruthie said. "Isn't that considered breaking and entering?"

"He's with British Intelligence. And who's going to report us?" Belle nodded toward Tim. "Him?"

"I suppose you're right."

But Ruthie didn't sound too convinced, and Tim was determined that this was the best location for him. "Why don't you go and get the rest of the girls in your troop?"

"Don't you go anywhere yet," Belle ordered Ruthie. "I may still need you." Then she glanced up at him. "Do you think you can handle walking from here?"

"Certainly." Yet even as he replied, a wave of dizziness roared through him. Grabbing onto the porch's handrail, he closed his eyes. "Give me a minute. I've still got my sea legs." Tim concentrated on his breathing. In, then out. The dizzy feeling dissipated and he let go of the railing. "I'm fine now."

There was no need to jimmy the lock. The door clicked open with a twist of the knob. Tim went in first, followed by Belle. The former lighthouse keeper must not have vacated too long ago. Only a thin layer of dust covered the wooden furniture, and there were aged logs in the fireplace ready to be lit.

"I'll go get the girls," Ruthie announced from her place just outside the door. "We'll be back in a few minutes. What do I tell Ginny if she's back?"

"Tell her the truth. Mr. Elliott's shoulder needs to be put back into place, and he needs to be stitched up," Belle replied as she fluffed up the pillows on the couch, then led him over to sit down.

"She's not going to like this." The door slammed shut with Ruthie's pronouncement.

Tim slowly sat on the couch. The slightest movement sent jarring pain all the way down to his fingertips. He hoped Ginny was there so that she could put his bloody shoulder back in place. Finally, the pain subsided, and Tim relaxed. "I'm ruining someone's couch with these wet clothes."

"We'll worry about that later. Right now, we need to immobilize your arm." Belle tugged at the scarf she was wearing. "This will have to do for now."

Tim braced himself as the girl gently threaded the material under his forearm. "How do you know so much about giving aid? You couldn't be any more than what? Twelve?"

"I'm thirteen," Belle answered as she laced the scarf around his neck and tied it off. "And my sister taught our troop first aid right after Pearl Harbor. She believes we should be prepared for whatever happens in this war." She sat back and studied her handiwork. "Looks like she was right."

"Hmmm." If only the United States military was as prepared as Belle's sister. Despite daily news of the war, the Americans had been totally unprepared when the Japanese bombed their naval fleet at Pearl Harbor. Now they played a game of catch-up, building ships and planes and enlisting men for the battle. In the meantime, their coastline was prey for the German war machine.

"You're bleeding again."

"I am?" He stretched to one side but couldn't see the cut.

"Stop before you make it worse." Standing up, Belle glanced

around, then headed toward the back of the house. Whatever she was doing, it was nice to have a few minutes to think. Where could Rolf be? If Tim was lucky, he'd been picked up by the navy ship he'd seen from the beach this afternoon. Not that he believed the captain would tell anyone about the deal he'd made with the British government. Besides, he was the only one Rolf trusted to deliver him safely to his superior officer's hands.

"I found something that will help." Belle returned, waving a dish towel in her hand. She took her seat beside him again, then folded the towel into a neat square. Pulling his shirt away, she pressed the cloth into the wound. "I couldn't find a needle or thread, so it's going to be a while before Ginny can close up your cut."

"What does your sister do for a living?"

"Right now, she sells tickets at the Oregon Inlet Ferry." Belle took his good hand and pressed it into his wound. "You mind if I start a fire? It's kind of chilly in here."

He hadn't realized how cold it was. Probably the shock of the last twenty-four hours. "Please."

She smiled, then stood and walked over to the fireplace. "But Ginny doesn't want to work at the ferry. She's in her last year of nursing school in Chapel Hill, or at least she was until Daddy made her come home." After checking that the flue was open, she found a box of matches on the mantel. Lighting one, she pressed it into the dry tinder. "What about you? Did you always want to be a spy?"

"I hadn't even thought about it until six weeks ago." Tim chuckled. After another day of writing articles, he'd been called into his editor's office. It was there he met Commander Maxwell Adair with British Intelligence, and the plan to extract Rolf and bring him to the States by way of South America was conceived.

A plan that hadn't counted on a bombing.

"What were you doing before that?"

"Writing articles." The puzzled look on Belle's young face pressed him on. "I'm a reporter."

She came over and sat down beside him on the couch. "Then what were you doing on a boat in the middle of nowhere?"

She was an inquisitive little brat, and stubborn too. All the earmarks of a good reporter. Not what he needed right now. He removed the cloth from his side. "How does it look?"

Belle glanced down. "It stopped bleeding."

"Good." He tossed the towel on the coffee table.

"You're not going to tell me, are you?" Belle nudged. "About why you were on the boat?"

Commander Adair had told him he could share the details of his mission if necessary, but telling a thirteen-year-old girl didn't fall into that category. Tim shook his head. "You don't want to get me in trouble on my first assignment, do you?"

A battle raged inside of the girl between her need to know and her desire to help him. Finally, there was a victor. "No, I don't want that."

There was a knock on the door, and then it opened. "We're back." A cold wind blew through the room as Ruthie, followed by four other girls, stepped inside. "Ginny must have got held up at the coast guard offices, because she's not back yet."

Which meant there was no one to put his shoulder back into place. Tim tried to move to a more comfortable position but bumped his arm. Bile filled his throat from the pain. He thought about going to the infirmary, but that would be like admitting defeat. A blow to the male ego, and in front of six very impressionable teenage girls.

"When do you think her majesty will be here?" Tim asked through gritted teeth. "I'm sorry, it just hurts. That's all."

"I can do it," an unidentified girl behind Ruthie said. She

glanced at the disbelieving looks on the other girls' faces and continued. "My dad knocked his shoulder out of place the last time he went fishing, and I put it back in place. Of course, I talked to Ginny about it, to make sure I'd done it correctly, and she told me I did." She glanced at him, meeting his gaze. "Would you like me to try?"

Tim didn't see as he had much choice. He nodded. "Yes, I would."

"All right."

"First," he blurted out, "what's your name? I think it's only proper I know who's going to pull my arm out of the joint and put it back in again."

The girl's smile took up her whole face. "I'm Clementine. You know Ruthie and Belle. This is Clara, April, and Lucy. Clara and Ruthie are twins."

Tim nodded to each one. "Nice to meet you. My name is Tim Elliott." He glanced up at Clementine. "You may proceed."

"All right. It's best if we do this standing up."

Belle gently removed the pillow, then helped Ruthie get him on his feet. Once he stood, Clementine took charge. "I need a couple of you to hold him. He can't move much. Mr. Elliott, if you can pull your body away at the same time I'm pulling your arm, it makes things easier." She whispered so only he could hear her. "It's going to hurt for a second, but you'll feel a lot better after I'm done." The girl grabbed hold of his hand and elbow, sending pain down his arm again. "All right. One. Two. Three."

She yanked hard, then set the arm back in the joint. Instant relief flooded through him as Belle put the scarf back into place.

A gentle hand took his. "Do you feel better now?"

Tim opened his eyes to find Clementine, her bright blue eyes dimmed with worry. He patted her hand with his good one. "You did an excellent job. A couple of days, and I'll be as good as new."

Any doubts about her work faded into a relaxed smile. "I'm just glad I could help." She helped him sit down, then straightened. "Is there anything else we can do for you?"

"I bet you'd like some tea and maybe something to eat," the silvery blond–haired girl—April—said. "Though I don't know if there's even a pot in the kitchen, but I can go and find out."

"I'll go with you." A dainty, auburn-haired girl followed her out of the room.

Belle sat down beside him. "We have to figure out everything we're going to need to take care of Mr. Elliott for the next few days." She took a shallow breath and grimaced. "Clothes, for one."

"A comb and some soap," Clara said, then added. "And a razor."

Tim rubbed his hand across his mouth and chin. The rough edges of his beard scratched him. "It's not that bad. Besides, I shave with my right hand."

The girls looked at each other, then back at him. Belle grinned. "Then one of us will shave you."

Tim grimaced. Not if he could help it. Besides, he looked good in a beard. "Why don't you concentrate on getting me food and clothing for now? And a blanket if I decide to stay here for a while."

Ruthie studied him. "Why would you do that?"

Belle nudged her friend. "He won't tell you. He hasn't been a spy for that long, and it might get him into trouble with his superior."

And yet the idea didn't seem like such a bad one now. Tim mulled over the idea. He wouldn't have to tell them everything, but he could give them a description of Rolf. It never hurt to have another set of eyes on the lookout. Once the man was found, they could get to New York and the mission would be finished.

Tim cleared his throat. "I was on the boat with a friend. We were traveling from Honduras to New York where he was going to be interviewed. After the boat was torpedoed, we somehow got separated once we were in the water. The last time I saw him, he had gone under to get away from the flames." He swallowed as the memory flooded back. The ocean of fire that surrounded him had felt like the fire and brimstone his father preached between his times at sea. It was only later when Tim and his sister went to live with their grandparents that he learned about God's abundant grace and love. His father had died before he'd had a chance to share Christ with him. An opportunity that was taken away from him by Rolf Schmidt. Did hell come to the German's mind as he floated in that ocean of fire? Tim certainly hoped so.

He shook the memory away. "If he survived, I need to get him to New York as soon as possible."

"And if he drowned?"

Tim stared into the fireplace. The same question had haunted him during the hours he'd clung to the life-saving ring he'd found. *"God's providence,"* he could hear his sister say. But he didn't believe that. God's justice, maybe. Rolf had the blood of many innocent lives on his hands, hundreds, maybe thousands of them. God's punishment would be far worse than any prison they would put him in.

"Mr. Elliott?"

He blinked. "I'm sorry. What was it you wanted to know? Oh, if my friend drowned. Well, then there wouldn't be an interview, I guess."

The girls glanced at one another, seemingly at a loss for words.

The smell of strong coffee preceded April and Lucy into the room. Lucy cleared the coffee table, tossing the used dish towel on a nearby chair while April set down the tray. "I'm sorry, Mr. Elliott, but there was barely enough coffee to make a pot, much less any tea. I did find some old crackers, and once we scraped the mold off some cheese Lucy found, we had the makings for cheese and crackers."

Reaching over, Belle poured a cup of coffee, then handed it to him. "Just drink the coffee for now."

Wrapping his fingers around the cup, Tim blew on it, then took a long sip, ignoring the pain as the liquid burned his throat.

"You might not want to drink that so fast. It's the last of the coffee, and I don't know when I can bring you more," April said as he took another gulp. "There's barely anything in the kitchen. Just some old pots and pans."

"Well, it's been a while since anyone lived here," Belle replied. "We'll just have to bring in supplies for Tim."

"And how do you propose we do that? It's not like our momma has extra groceries lying around." Ruthie sat down on the hearth. "I've been thinking about this, and I think we should take him to the coast guard office."

"Ruthie, you're such a scaredy-cat." Clementine shook her head. "Besides, he's perfectly fine here. He can heal and get some rest before he has to do whatever it is he has to do."

"He's looking for his friend." Belle glanced at him. "You never did tell us what he looks like."

He hadn't, had he? "Well, he's about my height. Older than me with dark blond hair. A little silver at the ears." He thought for a moment. "I never noticed his eyes, but if I had to make a guess, I'd say blue. Very pale."

"What about his build?" Clementine bent over a small notebook in her lap. "Is he thin? Or about your size?"

"Smaller than me." Tim set his cup down. With his shoulder back in place, he felt somewhat like himself again. Or maybe it was the thought of having more people on the lookout for Rolf. These girls probably knew everyone in the small island community. A new face would send up warning bells.

"All right." The girl shut her notebook, tucking her pencil in her jacket pocket. "I'll write this up and have it to everyone tomorrow."

"Let's check and see if there's anything else we might need." Belle rose, and the others followed. "I'll check the bedroom. Can someone else check the bathroom?"

The girls scattered, leaving Tim to nestle deeper into the couch. His clothes had dried, and for the first time in days, the frigid cold that had settled in his bones had dissipated. Maybe everything wasn't lost as he'd thought. If he could survive last night, so could Schmidt. He only had to locate him and get him to New York City to be debriefed.

He closed his eyes. All this spy stuff wasn't what he'd signed up for when he'd gone to university for a journalism degree. Yet it made sense in some twisted way. Reporters were allowed access to areas others would be denied. They could dig into a problem without drawing attention to themselves. They could even write propaganda articles to change public opinion like he'd been doing for the last year.

His breaths became shallow and slow. He would find Rolf, then go back to writing his usual pieces for the Intelligence Department. Sleep tugged at him, pulling him into its grasp, his last conscious thought before surrendering the sound of the front door clicking shut.

CHAPTER 3

Ginny glanced down at her watch for what seemed the hundredth time since arriving. Where was Officer Chapline?

The guardsman who'd shown her back to the liaison officer's office had said he'd only be a few minutes, but that was over an hour ago. She thought about leaving, but part of her job as a coastal watcher was to report any changes to the coast. What she'd seen today—the blackened sand, the oily residue that puddled on top of the water—hadn't surprised her. Daddy had told her stories about the battles fought with the Germans just offshore during the Great War. It was part of the reason he'd enlisted as soon as President Wilson had declared war. But nothing had prepared her for the magnitude of the damage. It would take years for the beach and the waters that were the lifeblood of their community to recover.

Maybe she and the girls could help. Ginny pulled a notepad out of her coat pocket, but she didn't have a pencil. Glancing over Chapline's desk, she borrowed a pen and began making a list, then stopped. She was so used to making her own plans, but with a troop of senior scouts, it was expected that they would bring things to a vote. Would they even care about saving the beach? She didn't know.

After replacing her pad and pen, Ginny sat back in her chair. She really needed to get back to the girls. Though they had good intentions, that didn't keep them out of trouble. With German submarines offshore, she didn't want their efforts to be targeted.

She should leave.

Standing, Ginny turned toward the door just as Officer William Chapline walked in. Quiet and reserved, he hung his hat on a nail near his desk, then took his place behind it. "Were you leaving, Miss Mathis? I was told you needed to speak to me."

"I did. An hour ago. Now I have a Girl Scout troop that is probably wondering where I've run off to." She continued toward the door. If she hurried, the girls might still be there.

"I'm sorry for the wait, but I've been busy organizing a recovery operation this morning and the weather hasn't been friendly." He motioned to the chair she'd recently abandoned. "Please. Sit."

Ginny walked over and sat back down. "So you've seen the beach?"

"Only as far as Avon." He nodded. "Someone walking their dog there found a survivor this morning. When we started combing the beach, we found several more and a lot of debris. We used the coordinates you gave us this morning and sent a ship to the area."

"How many did you save?" Ginny was at the edge of her seat. It troubled her to think of all those people injured or possibly dying floating around out there, miles from shore, not knowing if they would live or die.

Chapline shuffled some papers, then found what he was looking for. "About half of the crews so far. We had an eyewitness account that said the U-boats appeared to line up for a perfect broadside shot at the tanker." Chapline leaned back in his chair, steepling his fingers over his chest. "It was hit twice before breaking in two. It sunk a few minutes later."

Ginny swallowed. "I saw the explosion. It was just a flash of light, but I was able to see it from the lighthouse."

"But the Cape Hatteras Lighthouse has been closed for years." Chapline eased himself up. "What were you doing there last night?"

Oh dear. Ginny hadn't meant to tell him she'd been at the lighthouse. Now the coast guard would probably change out the locks. "I have trouble sleeping sometimes, so I go to the lighthouse just to watch the ocean or stare out over the island. After I became a coastal watcher, I took my binoculars and a map to figure out the coordinates of passing boats and such. I even started teaching my Girl Scout troop how to read coordinates just in case." She realized she was blubbering on at this point and stopped. "That's what I was doing when I saw the explosion last night."

"Did you see anything else?"

She swallowed, the memory making her stomach knot up. "Not really. It was so far away. When I used my binoculars, I did manage to see a small patch of red. I figured it was flames from the boat, but it seemed to dance across the water, almost like some kind of liquid. It did burn a while."

Chapline nodded. "The ship was carrying thousands of barrels of petroleum to New York."

"That explains the smell and the oily mess on the beach this afternoon. Are you expecting any more survivors?"

The officer's expression suddenly closed off. "A few. I'm waiting for a report from the Ocracoke infirmary, but we could be looking for survivors for days. Even longer for the dead."

Silence fell over the room as they considered the men lost. No matter how much these attacks had been expected, the sudden consequences of war, especially a battle fought close to home, made Ginny question her actions. Was there anything else she could have done differently? Anything that might have saved those men's lives last night? Maybe she should have told the coast guard as soon as she realized what had happened, but what good would that have done? The tanker was already under attack, and sending another boat in the German's path meant another target for them. No, she had done all she could do.

"I should go. I'm taking up all your time." Ginny stood. "Thank you for meeting with me."

"If I could just have another moment of your time, please." Standing, he pointed at her recently abandoned chair. Ginny glanced at him, then nodded. The liaison officer was known around the island as being a man of few words. So what he had to say must be important. Once she was settled, he took his chair. "As you know, we expect these attacks to become more prevalent in the days ahead, Miss Mathis. It's why we've enlisted coastal watchers like you."

"Guardsman Galloway told me that when we went over my responsibilities."

"I have two more responsibilities that I'd like to add." He gave her a reserved smile. "First, I want you to continue your visits to the lighthouse. Your coordinates this morning helped us locate the survivors quickly and saved lives. If you require time off at the ferry to catch up on sleep, I'll arrange it."

"I need my hours at the ferry, sir. And I won't give up my hours at the infirmary either." The words came out more forceful than she'd intended. "I was in my last semester of nursing school when my father asked me to come home. Working at the infirmary keeps my skills honed."

"I understand."

Someone knocked, then opened the door. "Sir, you have a meeting with the Naval Command Post in five minutes."

"Thank you." Chapline gathered up some papers and shoved

them into a folder. "I'm sorry to rush you like this, but I've been waiting for this call most of the day."

"That's all right." Ginny scooted to the edge of her chair. "What's the second thing you wanted me to do?"

"Oh yes." He glanced at a typed paper and stuffed it into the growing stack. "We've had a report from the tanker's captain that two men boarded the tanker in Honduras. One was an English reporter who works out of New York City, while the other is a former naval officer who had defected from Germany. Needless to say, we are looking for these two men."

"Were they traveling together?"

"It appears that way." He stopped fidgeting with his folder and glanced down at her. "One of the men on board reported that he saw the reporter throw a man overboard, then jumped in after him as the first torpedo hit the boat. They were each seen in the water immediately after the explosion but haven't been seen since."

This was all very interesting, but what did it have to do with her in her job as a coastal watcher? "I'm not sure I understand."

"You have eyes all over this island. Between working at the ferry and volunteering at the infirmary, you have the opportunity to see quite a few people throughout your day. That and the fact that you know almost everyone on the island makes it easy for you to pick out someone who doesn't belong. If that happens, if you meet someone with a different accent or who may seem suspicious to you, I want you to come and tell me. It would be a great service to our country if you do."

Ginny felt numb. "Are these men dangerous?"

"Possibly, but I don't want you to confront them. The coast guard will handle the situation once we locate where they are."

His pronouncement didn't do much to settle her fears. Why in the world would Officer Chapline ask her to find these men?

"I can't just leave my job to track you down."

"Do you know why I wanted you to be a coastal watcher? Because you have a keen eye for catching small details about people and for your knowledge of boats and the people around here." Dropping his folder, he leaned forward, his forearms bearing the weight of his upper body. "Ginny, I know that this is a big ask, but you're one of the few people I've shared this situation with. You know the comings and goings of everyone on this island. That makes you a perfect candidate for this job."

The way he made it sound, she didn't have much choice. Still, she wasn't completely sold on the idea. "What do I have to do?"

He drew in a satisfied breath. "Exactly what you've been doing. Keep your eyes and ears open. Then report back to me if you see anything unusual." He hesitated. "I'll have the guardsmen give you a description of the men as well as a new set of maps. Mark the location of every attack you witness plus the coordinates. Bring them back every morning before you go to work."

Great—she already rose before the rooster crowed in the morning. Now she'd have to get up thirty minutes earlier to make it to her job on time. Since the officer seemed to be asking favors this afternoon, maybe it was time she asked for one herself. "Sir, I'd like to share the description of the men with my Girl Scout troop. They roam the island more than I do and would be a huge asset in finding these men quickly."

"Teenage girls?" Chapline shook his head. "I don't know, Miss Mathis. The thought of girls doing this kind of work doesn't sit right with me. I mean, what if one of them gets hurt or worse? The thought of putting a child in danger, even if they wanted to help, is not something I can do. Besides, aren't they busy collecting fat or whatever it is this week? That's a real help to our boys."

It was the same argument they'd had every time she had brought up the girls. But she wouldn't give up. She'd read about the Girl Guides in Britain, how they'd raised money for ambulances and even an airplane. They had played an enormous role in evacuating British children to safer locations during the Battle of London, and Ginny wanted her troop to have the same opportunity to serve their country. "I'll abide by your orders, sir. But know this—since their inception, the Girl Scouts and Girl Guides have proven themselves capable during war and peace time. They want to contribute to the war effort, and I think it's wrong not to let them."

"Duly noted." He rose, grabbing his folder as he walked to the door. "Is there anything else?"

Getting to her feet, Ginny followed him to the door. "No, sir."

"Then get back to your post." With that, Ginny was dismissed.

Forty-five minutes later, Ginny walked along the dirt path that served as the main road into Buxton with a fresh map and a new set of ink pens tucked in her coat pocket. As soon as she'd been dismissed, Officer Chapline had turned her over to his junior staff member, a young man by the name of Brice Fuller. For the next half hour, Lt. Fuller gave her a short lesson in maritime map reading, then instructed her on the ins and outs of U-boats and military boats she would see in the area. By the time she left the coast guard offices, the sun sat low in the water over Pamlico Sound.

The sound of the waves pounding against the shore made her stop and look out over the ocean that she loved. The foul smell of petroleum had grown as high tide brought the waves in, and Ginny found herself missing the tang of the salty breeze. In a couple of weeks, maybe a month, the oil would dissipate, but with the promise of more attacks off the coast, it might be years before the shore returned to its former glory.

She had other, more pressing problems to think about. How did Officer Chapline expect her to find the two men he was searching for? They could be lost at sea or lying on the beach dead for all anyone knew. If he would be patient, he might find them in the morgue in a few days' time. Unless he knew they weren't dead, which would mean they were already on the island somewhere. Ginny reached into her pocket and pulled out a paper with two black-and-white images. Unfolding it, she studied the pictures. The German looked as she'd expected, somber and tight-lipped, a steely glare that made gooseflesh prickle her arms even now. She shifted her gaze to the reporter. Despite the grainy picture, he was handsome with dark eyes and a hint of a roguish smile that reminded her of Cary Grant. She could see him writing articles for the *New York Times* or *Washington Post*. How could someone like him be involved with a German defector?

Ginny was still pondering that question minutes later as she turned down the shortcut to the picnic tables where she'd left the girls. As she walked down the sandy path toward the light-house, she caught a glimpse of her sister and the rest of the troop standing on the porch of the abandoned keeper's home. She'd told them to meet at their usual picnic table. What were they doing loitering around the house?

Taking a slight detour, she walked up the sidewalk to the house. "What are y'all doing over there? We were supposed to meet at our usual spot."

The guilt reflected in their expressions put Ginny on alert. Well, everyone except her sister, who looked at her with such innocent blue eyes, Ginny almost questioned why she'd asked.

Almost.

Belle stepped forward, her gaze meeting her sister's. "Where have you been? We've been waiting for you for over. . ." She glanced back at Ruth.

The girl looked at her watch. "Two hours."

"Two hours," her sister continued. "People can die in that period of time."

"I was delayed at the coast guard offices." Ginny stepped closer. Belle was up to something. She just knew it. "Now, what are you doing over here?"

"Two hours! Was Officer Chapline there?" Belle turned to the other girls. "The man's sweet on Ginny. He sends her notes almost daily and has her to his office at least one day a week."

"He's too stuffy for my taste," Ruthie added. "But I can see why Ginny might like him."

Belle had used this ploy on her parents before, but it wouldn't work on her. "Answer the question. What are you doing here?"

"It's nothing to get all knotted up about. We just went inside to find some blankets." Belle tilted her head, a sure sign she wasn't being completely truthful. "We didn't bring any and thought the birds might get cold."

"Birds don't get cold." Ginny glanced at the discarded lobster traps lining the porch. "There's not one bird in any of these cages. So what have you been doing while I was gone?"

They glanced from one to another but didn't offer any explanations.

"How did you get inside?" Ginny walked over to the door but found it locked. "You do know what you did was against the law, don't you?"

"Breaking and entering," Clara replied. "Though it should be only entering seeing as the door was unlocked."

Ginny mashed her lips together in frustration. Teaching children the difference between right and wrong shouldn't be this hard. "You could have been arrested."

"For Pete's sake, Gin, you're such a fuddy-duddy at times." Belle rolled her eyes in that annoying way that always set Ginny's teeth on edge. "It's not like anyone's living here. The door was open, and we were cold waiting on you."

A slight pang of guilt assailed Ginny. She had left them on their own without any explanation, nor would any be forthcoming. Still, they should have gone home rather than to the deserted house. "No more going into houses that aren't your own, especially after what we saw on the beach today." She picked her next words carefully. "According to the coast guard, we should expect more attacks, which means people being washed up on the beach. There's no telling what side of this war they're on."

Belle exchanged a look with Ruth. "How would we know the difference?"

"You won't. The Germans have trained people to look and sound just like us. They could live amongst us, and we wouldn't know it until it's too late. That's why we must report anyone we find to the coast guard right away." She glared down at her sister. "Is that understood?"

"Makes perfectly good sense to me," Belle agreed with a smile.

Why couldn't she shake the feeling that they were up to more than finding blankets? Well, what was done was done. Ginny gave them a soft smile. "You did good work on your coordinates today even if we did get caught off guard by the beach conditions. We'll meet up again on Saturday to see what we can do to help with the cleanup. Until then, you're dismissed."

Like clockwork, the girls gathered in a circle, held hands, and began to sing.

Make new friends,
But keep the old,
One is silver and the other, gold.

Ginny watched the group as they hugged and then went their separate ways. The girls were up to something. She just knew it, but what it was, she didn't know. All she could do was keep a watchful eye on them and pray. *Lord, please keep these girls safe, and help our community in the dark days ahead.*

≡ CHAPTER 4 ≡

"Why didn't you tell Ginny about Mr. Elliott?" Ruthie asked Belle as they turned down the dirt path to their neighborhood. "It was the perfect opportunity."

"Are you kidding me?" Belle picked up a stick, then ran it along the slats in Mrs. Cooper's fence. "She would have had a conniption fit right before she marched us down to Officer Chapline's office."

"What's so bad about that?" Ruthie asked. "We don't know Mr. Elliott from the man in the moon."

Belle tossed the stick down and turned to her friend. "You heard Mr. Elliott. He doesn't want to go to the infirmary until he's found his friend. There would be zero chance of finding him if Tim is turned over to the authorities."

"I get it. If you were lost, I'd move heaven and earth to find you. You've been my best friend since the cradle, and you always will be." The worried look in her friend's eyes tugged at Belle's heart. "But you heard Ginny. Mr. Elliott might not be who he says he is."

"Maybe," she grudgingly agreed, but her gut told her Tim Elliott was telling them the truth. "Then why tell us he was a reporter or that he was looking for his friend if he was hiding something?"

"Then why was he on an oil tanker? Doesn't that seem odd to you?"

Belle had to admit that did seem suspicious, but she was certain there was a reasonable answer. "I don't know. Maybe it was the only way he could get back to New York. His office is there...."

"Good grief, Belle. Do you hear yourself? Just because a man is nice-looking and has a British accent doesn't mean he's being honest with us. And who is this friend of his? Have you thought about that?" Ruthie turned and took off at a fast clip.

Something was eating her, more than this business with Mr. Elliott, but what? Belle ran to catch up with her. "What's wrong with you? It's like you're a different person here lately."

"Maybe I am."

Belle grabbed her arm and spun her around. "Why?"

"Why?" Ruthie barked. Her expression twisted into a mixture of pain and anger that drove a stake through Belle's heart. "We're at war, Belle. I know that's not a big deal to you. You look at it as some big adventure. But it's not. It's dangerous, and soldiers are dying every day fighting in it."

"I know it's real. My daddy left to build ships in Virginia Beach, remember."

Ruthie scoffed. "You have no idea what it's like. You don't have brothers going overseas to fight." Tears pooled in her eyes. "Momma doesn't think we hear her, but she cries every night as she prays. And my daddy—my brave, sweet daddy—has become an old man right before our eyes." She closed her eyes. "So yes, I've changed. I've had to grow up, and it's time you did too."

Her words felt like needles drawing blood. "I'm older than you by two months."

"You don't get it." Ruthie shook her head, her anger spent, replaced by a weariness Belle didn't understand. "If you've decided to help Mr. Elliott, then count me out."

"Ruthie!" Belle cried out as her friend turned and ran toward her house. She hadn't known Ruthie was so worried about her family, but then, she'd always been one to keep things close to the chest. It was a lot to take in, two brothers suddenly off to war, but she couldn't go through life living in fear. What Ruthie needed was some time to calm down. If she didn't want to help Mr. Elliott, then no one was twisting her arm.

By the time she'd reached the back gate to her yard, she'd moved on to Mr. Elliott. Despite how Ruthie felt, Belle was certain the man was telling the truth, and if he was hiding something, didn't most people? Not her, of course. She was an open book, completely unlike her sister. Ginny never took off in the middle of the night before she left home to go to college, nor had she questioned every little thing Belle did. It was annoying really, the way Ginny didn't trust her, especially when she'd never given her any reason to believe otherwise. Sometimes, she just wished her sister had a little faith in her.

The smell of fish frying wafted through the screen door. Catfish, her favorite. Belle threw open the door and stepped inside. And not just catfish but hush puppies and boiled corn too! Her stomach growled softly. All this rescuing had given her a voracious appetite. She hoped Momma had made extra so she could sneak Mr. Elliott some dinner later. The screen door slammed behind her, and she reached to shut the door.

"Don't you dare shut that door," Momma called out. "I'd rather freeze than have that smell in my house."

After shucking off her coat and hanging it up, Belle stepped into the kitchen. "Where did you get the catfish?"

"And a how-do-you-do to you too." Momma stood at the stove, a spatula in her hand. She glanced behind Belle. "Where's your sister?"

"Beats me." Belle lifted the corner of a cloth-covered bowl and beamed. "I thought I smelled hush puppies. What's the occasion?"

"I got your report card in the mail today." Momma nodded toward the table. When Belle didn't move, she smiled. "Go ahead. Look at it."

Hurrying to the table, Belle snatched up the card and studied it, her heart beating at a frantic pace. She glanced up at her mother, her smile so big, it almost hurt her cheeks. "All As?"

"That's what it says." The hot oil popped and sizzled as Momma flipped one fillet over. "I figured those kinds of grades deserve a celebration."

The back door slammed again, and a few seconds later, Ginny walked in, replacing her boots with a pair of fuzzy house slippers. She walked over to Momma and gave her a kiss on the cheek. "Hi, Momma. How are you doing today?"

Momma gave her a knowing glance, then turned her attention to her sister. "I'm fine. Your sister got straight As on her report card."

"Good for you, runt." Ginny glanced at the contents of the frying pan and grimaced. "That's why we're having catfish."

Of course, Ginny didn't like catfish. She never liked anything that was good. Well, she refused to let her sister spoil her celebration. "We're having boiled corn and hush puppies too."

Her grimace deepened. "I think I'll just make myself a sandwich."

"I can make you something else, dear. You need a hot meal after working all day," Momma said. "Just tell me what you'd like."

"You've been watching the Jones children all day, so I can do for myself." Ginny gave Momma another kiss. "How were the kids today?"

"Why are you taking care of the Jones kids, Momma?" Belle bit into one of the sweet pickles Momma had put into a bowl next to the stove. "We don't need the money, do we? Because I can always get a job. Mr. Simmons down at the food market told me he'd hire me to run the cash register if I'm ever looking for work."

"You are not getting a job, and we don't need the money." Momma lightly smacked her hand as she reached for a second pickle. "Ida Jones is fishing the sound to put food on people's tables while our men are off serving our country. The least I can do is watch over her little ones while she does what she can to get by." With the spatula, she forked the last of the fish and laid it on newspaper covering a plate. "It won't be long before fishing is forbidden."

"You think the coast guard will do that?" Belle asked.

Momma shrugged. "Your daddy said it happened the last time we went to war with the Germans."

"No one's going to want to eat anything out of the ocean." Ginny sighed as she leaned one hip against the counter. "There's a mess on the beach from the tanker sinking. It will take weeks to clean it up."

"A tanker sunk? I haven't heard anything about that." Momma removed the corn from the boiling water and slathered them in butter. "Do they know what happened?"

Everyone has secrets. And one of Momma's was about to be exposed if she didn't stop Ginny. Belle grabbed the plate of fish and shoved it at her sister. "Would you take this? I'll grab the hush puppies."

Ginny leaned back. "You know I hate the smell of catfish."

"It's only a couple of steps from here to the table," Belle answered. Really, Ginny could be such a ninny at times.

"I'll get out the plates." Momma opened the cabinet door and pulled out her flour-bag dishes. "Belle, could you get us each a glass of water?"

"Yes, ma'am." She breathed a little sigh of relief as she retrieved three glasses and poured water into each one. Daddy had been adamant that Ginny not know about their mother's spells. He'd said she would try to get their momma treatment, but it would just make things worse. It was their little secret, hers and Daddy's, and she wasn't going to tell anyone, not even her sister.

"You didn't finish telling me about the tanker," Momma said as she put out the silverware.

Belle jerked around and shook her head furiously when she caught her sister's eye. Ginny seemed confused, then shrugged as she sat down. "They think it was attacked by a German U-boat last night. The coast guard picked up some survivors, but there are still people missing."

Belle closed her eyes. *Please, Lord, don't let Momma have a breakdown right here in front of Ginny. Help her to be okay. Amen.* When she opened her eyes, she knew immediately her prayers would go unanswered.

Momma's eyes were wide with panic as she grasped the back of the kitchen chair. "Was there really an attack last night?"

Ginny glanced up at their mother and blinked as if seeing her for the first time. "Momma, are you okay?"

"Answer the question, Virginia." Her grip on the chair tightened. "Was that boat attacked last night?"

Belle had to do something or risk Ginny saying the wrong thing and setting their mother off. She walked over and wrapped her arm around Momma's shoulders. "It could have been. There was a lot of oil and broken wood along the shore this afternoon. But it also could have hit the shoals and broken apart. That's happened before too."

Momma nodded, loosening her grip. "Diamond Shoals has seen a lot of shipwrecks in its time."

"Those shifting sandbars are nasty," Belle added. "Daddy took me out there once. The water just swirls around you, moving all that sand. It's a wonder any boats make it out of there without sinking."

Belle glanced across the table at Ginny in time to see her sister mouth "What just happened?" Well, she didn't have to explain herself or Momma. Why had she even bothered to come home? It wasn't as if they needed her. Even if they did, they wouldn't be able to find her, not with her sneaking out at night. Ginny could do whatever she pleased. She was a grown woman after all.

"I hope you're right." Momma took a deep breath, then pulled out her chair and sat down. "I was about Belle's age when the Great War started, but I remember the bombing raids on London where we lived at the time. Sometimes, they'd be so close, it felt like the world was exploding all around you."

"Hopefully, we won't have to deal with that here." Belle picked up the small plate of sweet pickles and tomatoes and headed for the table. "Are we ready to eat?"

"What?" Momma shook her head as if chasing the dreadful images from the past away. "Yes, we're ready. Belle, would you say the blessing as we're celebrating your report card this evening?"

"Let's let Ginny do it. She's so good at it."

Belle felt Ginny studying her, but she agreed. "Let's bow our heads."

As Belle bowed her head, her thoughts were not on the blessing. Momma was so rattled by the thought of an attack, almost frantic with fear. Would another attack set off one of her spells? And how would she ever keep Momma's breakdowns a secret from her sister? Not for the first time, Belle wished that her father had left Ginny in Chapel Hill. Instead, everything was changing. Had this war affected her family like it had Ruthie's?

Suddenly, it all became very real for Belle.

———— ≋ ————

"Do you think he's dead?"

Glancing at Clementine, Belle knocked on the door, this time harder than the last. "He's probably just asleep. He was in the water for a while."

"But what if he is dead?" Even in the dim moonlight, she could see the small worry lines in her friend's expression. "What will we do then?"

First, Ruthie. Now, Clementine. Belle rolled her eyes. When had her friends turned into such scaredy-cats? So maybe the attack last night had everyone on edge, but this was what they'd been trained to do, to "help other people every day, especially those at home." It was a vow they made during every meeting, an oath they made to themselves and one another. She wasn't going to let some war stop her from fulfilling her promise.

A promise that included helping Mr. Elliott. Holding her hand out, Belle turned to Clem. "Give me a bobby pin."

"Why?" She put down the picnic basket and reached into the mass of curls at the base of her neck. Extracting it, she handed the pin to Belle. "Don't mess it up too bad. I don't have many of them."

"You'll get it back." Belle twisted it open, then knelt level to the door handle and pushed it inside the lock. "I saw this in a movie once and wondered if you could really open a door like this."

"Like that stuff is real." Clem tsked. "Momma says they're sinful and straight from the devil."

Belle worked the lock. "She obviously hasn't seen Clark Gable or Cary Grant. And movies aren't bad. You just have to take them with a grain of salt." She heard a light click, then turned the doorknob. Belle extracted the metal pin and gave it back to Clem. "The movies weren't wrong about this."

Clem stuck out her tongue as she bent the pin back into shape. "Why am I here in the first place? You and Ruthie were supposed to bring Ginny back. Why didn't either of them come?"

"Ruthie couldn't." Belle opened the door and stepped inside. There was no reason to tell Clem about the argument she and Ruthie had. Best friends didn't do that. Ruthie just needed some time, that was all. Once she thought about it, they'd be like two peas in a pod as they always had. "As far as Ginny goes, I didn't bother to ask her."

Clem was on her heels. "Then who's going to stitch him up?"

"I am."

"What do you mean, you are?" Clem grabbed her arm. "You pass out at the sight of blood."

"No, I don't. And it was just that one time."

"I'd barely scraped my knee, and you were out cold!" Clem hissed.

"Thank you for that reminder." Belle shook her hand off her arm. "I was barely eight then. I've grown up a lot since then. Besides, Ginny said I was a whiz at stitching."

"We were using oranges."

"Ladies, you would wake the dead." A gravelly masculine voice made both girls jump. They watched as Mr. Elliott grabbed the back of the couch and pulled himself up. He winced as he finally sat up. "I wasn't certain you girls would return."

Belle recovered first. "Sorry about that, Mr. Elliott." Stepping closer, she sat down beside him. "How are you feeling?"

"Exhausted, but the arm feels better." He glanced up at Clem and smiled. "Thank you."

Clem blushed to her roots. "Anytime."

"We brought you some dinner and a few things to get you

through the day tomorrow." Belle motioned to the picnic basket. "I also brought everything I'd need to stitch up that wound."

His brow wrinkled. "I thought your sister who's almost a nurse was going to do that."

"Something else came up," Belle replied, pulling thread, a needle, a pair of cross-stitch scissors, and two small glass bottles of hydrogen peroxide and iodine from her coat pocket. "Besides, I'm a whiz at sewing up cuts."

"You are, are you?"

The disbelief in his voice almost undid her. But she couldn't tell them the truth, that she hadn't bothered to ask her sister. Since she'd come home, she'd acted like she and Momma were nothing more than an inconvenience. Like tonight at dinner. Momma had been rattled by the news of the attack, but instead of dropping it, Ginny had gone on and on about it. Momma didn't need to hear that, but her sister refused to stop talking about it even after she'd tried to change the subject. Well, she didn't need Ginny's help. She could do this herself.

Belle stood. "Clem, why don't you fix Mr. Elliott a plate while I suture his wound?"

Her friend's eyes went wide. "You think that's such a good idea? I mean, I can stick around if you need me."

She glared at her. "Thanks, but I won't need your help."

"Fine. But if you. . ." She glanced at Mr. Elliott, then back. "You know, then don't expect me to pick you up from the floor." Clem turned then, as if washing her hands of the matter, and headed for the kitchen.

Belle turned back to Mr. Elliott and smiled. "Are you ready to get started?"

"Let's get this over with." He drew in a deep breath, then let it out. "What do you need me to do?"

She stood. If she used the coffee table to hold her "instruments," she could crouch between it and the couch. "If you could lay with your left side exposed, it will be easier."

"All right."

While he got comfortable, Belle stoked the fire, then placed another log on the embers. She could stitch up Mr. Elliott. She had to. Without it, he could cut it more, even get infected. She just couldn't focus on the blood. Just the thought of it made her woozy. Maybe Ruthie had been right. Maybe she did need to grow up. This would be a start.

When she turned, Mr. Elliott lay flat on the couch, his lower legs and feet dangling off the end. "You're taller than I thought."

"You only saw me hunched over." He gave her a soft smile. "Are you ready?"

"As soon as I wash my hands." She hurried across the room, then down the hall to the bathroom. A set of towels, as well as a cake of lye soap, was laid out. Belle scrubbed her hands with cold water, then wet a washrag to clean out the wound. Grabbing another towel, she headed back into the living room.

Belle glanced at her patient when she returned to the room. His eyes were closed, and his breathing was slow and steady. Putting a hand on his shoulder, she gave him a gentle nudge. "Did you fall asleep again?"

He shook his head. "Just resting my eyes."

"Well then, let's get started." She undid the last three buttons on his shirt and pushed it to the side. Bits of sand clumped with blood had settled inside the wound. Belle swallowed hard. "I'm going to clean it now, okay?"

Mr. Elliott nodded.

Uncorking the glass bottle, Belle started to pour the liquid, then stopped. "This is going to burn a little." When he didn't answer, she poured the peroxide on the wound.

"Bloody...," he whispered under his breath as he tensed.

"I'm sorry, but this gets all of the germs out so that it doesn't get infected." Belle covered it with the washrag, breathing in through her nose as she gently wiped the area around the cut.

"You doing okay there?"

Her stomach knotted up, but she refused to be beaten by this. Taking the thread, she unwound a strand, then snipped it with the scissors. "I'm not the one getting stitches."

He chuckled softly. "You haven't ever done this before, have you?"

She could have fudged the truth, but she refused to lie. "No, but I have seen my sister do it, and I've stitched up an orange before."

"An orange?" His eyes crinkled at the corners. "Why did you stitch through a perfectly good piece of fruit?"

It did sound nuts now that she thought about it. Belle threaded the needle, then tied the loose ends. "Ginny said that's how she was taught in nursing school. Oranges got everything from shots to stitches before they practiced on the patient."

"So when your sister taught you and the other girls, she used oranges."

"Crazy, right?" It was time to make the first stitch. Belle met Mr. Elliott's gaze. "Are you ready?"

He nodded, then said, "You're going to do fine, Belle."

The way he said it, as if he put all his trust in her, tamped down her fears for the time being. Pushing the ends of the wound together, her needle hovered over the puckered skin before finally breaking the skin. It was softer than the orange, more pliable, which made it easier to make the stitch. "How are you doing? I'm not hurting you too much, am I?"

"I can barely feel it." As if to prove his point, he pillowed his head in his hands.

Belle worked as fast as she could, ignoring the tiny drops of blood that formed along the stitches. By the time she tied off the last knot, she'd broken out in a sweat, her fingers shaking as she clipped the loose ends. Finished, she fell back on her knees, her head on her legs, willing herself not to toss up her dinner.

The smell hit her before she heard Clem's footsteps. "Ready for dinner?"

Covering her mouth, Belle jumped up and ran, almost missing Mr. Elliott's words as she turned the corner toward the bathroom.

"That's one brave girl."

▓ CHAPTER 5 ▓

The back door made a soft click as Ginny closed it, then hurried across the yard to the fence gate, the cold metal like ice against her gloved hands. A full moon and clear skies made the sandy path that led to the main road luminous and easy to see in the dead of night. After staring at the ceiling for an hour, she'd figured she might as well get up and do something useful. She gathered up the map and pens the coast guard had given her and headed for the lighthouse.

Why couldn't she sleep? Usually, she didn't have an answer, but tonight she knew why. Momma had been a mess at dinner. Every conversation turned to the attack last night and what it could mean for the island. Belle had tried to change the topic, but Momma went on and on about how they needed to watch themselves and lock all the doors at night. Never once in her life had they locked the doors to their house. If her mother was this worried now, how would she respond as the attacks worsened?

It didn't take long to reach the lighthouse once she made it to the main road. As usual, she stopped and admired the black and white beacon of hope for thousands of seafarers over the years. The lights had been dimmed for years, and probably would remain so if the rumors about blackouts were true. Still, it served to protect the people of this island again, against those who wished to take their freedom and destroy their way of life, replacing it with a system of government best described as evil.

As she walked down the sidewalk past the lightkeeper's house, a flicker of light caught her attention. She stared at the house for a long moment. Maybe it was just her imagination, what with everything that had gone on the last twenty-four hours. Besides, the girls wouldn't have lit a lantern, not with the afternoon sun lighting the house. Why they had gone there in the first place was something she'd like to know. All of them had been taught to respect others' property even if it was an abandoned old house. Of course, if her sister thought jumping off a bridge was a good idea, the rest would follow without thinking.

Assured there were no lanterns lit in the old house, Ginny turned toward the lighthouse. What was she going to do about Belle? That girl had a talent for trouble and a way of dragging her friends along with her. Her sister had changed so much since Ginny had last been home. Gone was the little girl who curled up in her lap and listened as Ginny read to her. She'd been replaced by this brazen girl with a knack for adventure and chaos. If only she could tame her sister, even if just for a little bit. How much good could Belle do then?

A loud rumble made the ground shake beneath her. Ginny opened the lighthouse's door and hurried inside. The explosion vibrated through the walls, shaking her from the inside out. Finding her footing, she grabbed the iron railing and pulled herself up the stairs. The map and pens in her pocket would be of no use if she didn't get eyes on the explosion. By the time she reached the lantern room, her legs felt heavy, her muscles hurting from the exertion. Breathing deep breaths, she coughed, the smell of ash and oil heavy in the air. Her heart thundered beneath her breast, her pulse pounding in her ears. She opened her coat, the cold air a relief against her heated skin.

Wiping the perspiration out of her eyes, she glanced over the perimeter. Right off the coast of Avon was the target. Ginny grabbed her binoculars and brought the scene into focus. It was a large ocean cruiser, or what was left of one. The torpedo had ripped through the center of it, leaving two mirror-image sides listing toward the island and sinking fast. She glanced over the water. People were still on the deck, struggling to get lifeboats over the side. Liquid fire replaced the chilled ocean water, circling a group of men and a woman as if hunting for prey. She wasn't sure if it was her imagination or not, but she could swear she heard a woman scream. One by one, the men descended, whether to swim their way out or give up, she didn't know. Finally, only the woman remained, clinging to a life float as the fire crept closer. A high-pitched scream rent the air.

Throwing the binoculars on the table, Ginny slammed her eyes shut. Knots formed in her throat, but she pushed the words out. "Dear heavenly Father, help the men and women who are trying to survive tonight. Please just lift them up and bring them to safety. Be with the coast guard and the navy as they work together to help these people. Please wipe the evil of this world away so that we may live in peace again. In Jesus' name, I humbly pray. Amen."

Raising her head, she glanced at the wreckage. The fire had died down some, but there were more people in the water now, and some in rowboats. It would be hours before the guardsmen could attempt any kind of rescue, but she could do something to help. Lighting the small lantern she'd stored away, Ginny unfolded her maps over the table, then reached for her protractor and a pen. Lifting her binoculars, she homed in on what remained of the boat then glanced around for a buoy. If she could get the number on the buoy, she'd have a good start on the coordinates. There, not a mile from the wreckage, was the buoy she'd been searching for. Using her protractor, she pinpointed the attack site, then worked on the coordinates. The Germans had enclosed the mainline, not like in the attack from last night. She studied the waters around the sinking ship. If the U-boat had surfaced, light from the moon should reveal the metal body of the submarine. If the Germans were there, she couldn't see them.

Two more ships were sunk before Ginny packed up her things and started the long climb down. Generally, her visit to the lighthouse settled her nerves and she would sleep for a couple of hours, but not tonight. Every nerve in her body felt charged, her mind whirling in different directions. Four boats sunk so far. How many more would there be? If the Germans could safely attack boats right off their coast, what would keep them from invading the island?

As she reached the middle platform, she took a moment to glance out at the sleepy village she called home. Whether they knew it or not, their lives had changed. The welcoming hospitality that was a cornerstone in their community would falter. People would become more suspicious of those they didn't know, and maybe some they did. Just like Momma, more folks would be locking their doors out of fear.

In one day, the island she loved had changed.

She already hated this war, and it had only just begun. Ginny leaned against the window. If Daddy hadn't ordered her home, she would've enlisted. The army was always looking for nurses to work in their field hospitals. She might be a semester shy from graduating, but they'd enlisted others with far less schooling. She knew she could make a difference at a field hospital or on the front. The experience alone would help her care for her patients once she returned home.

But her argument had not moved her father. He needed

Ginny home. But why? Momma and Belle managed everything around the house. Momma had even taken in children while their mothers tried to keep their family fishing businesses afloat. Belle might need a firm hand, but most of her stunts were just annoying. Momma may be nervous, but then, she had always been nervous. So why did Daddy need Ginny at home now?

The sound of a door being opened drew Ginny's attention to the lightkeeper's place. A shadow moved along the front porch, then turned the corner toward the back of the house. Who would be there at this hour? Ginny didn't know, and honestly, she was too exhausted to care at the moment. If she made it home now, that would leave her a couple of hours to sleep before she had to go to work at the ferry. On top of all that, Officer Chapline expected a report first thing in the morning.

The kitchen light was on when Ginny arrived home a half hour later. Climbing the two stairs to the back door, exhaustion overtook her. How was she supposed to keep this up? Granted, Officer Chapline had said he'd arrange a time for her to sleep, but she didn't work like that. And what about her mother? How would she react when she found out what Ginny was doing? Of course, Ginny would tell her if she was confronted.

Opening the door, Ginny couldn't help but notice Belle at the table. "What are you doing up?"

"I could ask you the same thing." Belle smirked as she lifted a mug to her mouth. "Where have you been?"

"Out. Now it's time for you to go to bed."

Belle lifted her mug. "I'm not finished with my hot cocoa."

Ginny gritted her teeth together. When her parents had given her a baby sister the year she turned ten, she'd been thrilled. It was like having her own living baby doll. Belle had always tagged along with her, much to the distress of the few boys she'd dated. But after she'd left for college, things changed between them.

What, Ginny didn't know, but she wished her relationship with Belle would go back to how it was.

"A cup of hot cocoa sounds good." Taking off her coat, Ginny hung it by the door, then headed to the cabinet for a mug. She set down the mug and gallon of milk she'd collected, then dug around in the cabinet for a small pan.

"Why are you sneaking out at night?"

Ginny stared absently into the cupboard. Belle had always been an inquisitive kid. Why would she expect her to be any different now? The fact that she couldn't be completely honest with her sister grated on Ginny. She gave her the only explanation she could. "I'm a grown-up, Belle. I can go out whenever I feel like it."

"I don't believe you."

Ginny sighed. There was a great deal of hurt and anger in Belle's reply, but what could she do? Officer Chapline had been very clear in his directions. The members of her troop weren't to know that Ginny was working with the coast guard or that she was searching for two men from the first attack. Better to hurt Belle this way than put her in danger. "You don't have to believe me. Now, go to bed. You have school tomorrow."

Belle lifted her stubborn chin, an action so reminiscent of their father. "I'll tell Momma what you're doing."

"You don't know what I'm doing, but go ahead and tell her if it makes you feel better," Ginny shot back. "Now, go to bed."

She took the warmed milk off the stove, then added two spoonfuls of cocoa to her cup before adding the steaming liquid. Maybe Belle had given up or maybe she realized she wasn't going to get an answer to her question.

"Momma woke up from the explosion," Belle said softly. "She went to check on us to make sure we were okay, but you weren't there."

Dear heavens. Momma had been nearly frantic after dinner tonight. How had she reacted once she realized Ginny was gone in the middle of the attack? Ginny pulled out a chair and sat across from her sister. "Is she okay?"

"She is now." Belle took another sip of her drink. "I told her you hadn't been able to sleep and that you probably went for a walk. She stayed up until we heard the last explosion, and then I convinced her to go to bed. She's babysitting today."

"Good. And you're right. I couldn't sleep, so I walked over to the lighthouse." Resting her elbow on the table, Ginny leaned her head in her hand. "It's usually quiet there, but tonight it was like New Year's and the Fourth of July all rolled up in one."

"How many boats were sunk?"

"There were three attacked. I don't know if they sank or not."

"Those poor people." Belle stared into her cup. "As many friends as Daddy has who make their living from the ocean, you can't help wondering. . ."

"I know." Ginny covered her hand with hers. The thought of their friends or loved ones being targeted by the Germans had crossed her mind more than once. "After tonight, I wouldn't be surprised if civilians are ordered to stay out of the ocean. I don't know if that would be any better."

"At least they'd be alive."

Yes, they'd be alive, but without a livelihood. "We'll just have to figure out a way to help those folks out."

"Another Girl Scout project." Belle smiled for the first time this morning. "We only have—what? Three or Four?"

Ginny sipped her cocoa. "Well, five is a nice number to start with. I have a feeling we'll be doing a lot of these types of projects for the next two or three years."

Belle grew somber. "You think the war is going to last that long?"

She certainly hoped not, but after what she'd witnessed tonight, she couldn't be sure. "I think the war will last as long as it needs to so we can win."

"In other words, you don't have a clue."

She shrugged. "I'm sorry, honey. I wish I knew, but I don't."

Belle slumped back in her chair. "Then I guess we'll just have to prepare ourselves for the worst and pray."

Ginny smiled into her cup. Sometimes, her baby sister surprised her with her wisdom. "Thank you for helping with Momma tonight. Maybe you can answer a question for me."

"What's that?"

Ginny leaned against the table. "Did Momma seem out of sorts at dinner tonight? All she wanted to talk about was the attack last night, but it seemed to me that was just making her more nervous."

Belle pushed back from the table and stood up, taking her cup with her. "You know Momma. She always has to worry about something."

What her sister said was true. Momma had fought bouts of depression and anxiety for most of Ginny's life. Once, Daddy had told her it had to do with her time in London, then warned her never to speak of it with anyone outside the family. At the time, she didn't understand, but then an episode in nursing school had shown her the horrible stigma of mental illness. Since then, she'd wondered how she could help her parents more.

Still, she thought they should talk about it more. "You're right. She's always been nervous, but tonight seemed worse than usual. She seemed almost wild with worry."

"What are you saying, Gin?" Belle's hackles were up. "Are you saying you think our mother is crazy or belongs in an institution or something? Because I won't let you do that. Do you hear me?"

"Calm down, sis. I was just trying to think of ways we might be able to help her."

"Maybe you should consider staying home at night instead of gallivanting all over Buxton," Belle bit out. "Then she wouldn't be frantic with worry." She didn't wait for Ginny to reply, just quickly deposited her cup in the sink and hightailed it out of the room.

Ginny rubbed her fingers into her forehead, trying to figure out what had just happened. One thing she knew for certain.

Their short truce was over.

≣ CHAPTER 6 ≣

Tim glanced out the window, then let the curtains fall back into place as he grabbed his coat. Seven days had passed since the attack on the *Allan Jackson*. Seven days of wondering if Schmidt had made it to shore alive and, if he had, where he was now. What if the coast guard had picked him up? That would complicate things with Tim's superiors in New York. Or worse, what if German sympathizers had found him? There were many in the States who believed in what Hitler was doing in Germany. What would they do with someone who had defected from the führer's navy? Until he found the man, he couldn't rest.

He shoved his arm into one sleeve, then draped the other side over his injured arm. A quick glance at the clock hurried him toward the door. If he didn't leave soon, the girls would arrive, and heavens knew when they'd leave. Not that he could complain. Belle and the girls had provided him with food and shelter while he recovered. They'd even sat up with him when he developed a fever the day after they'd found him. He'd never be able to repay them for the kindness they'd shown him.

But he was on the mend now. He had a job to do. Grabbing the old map of the island he'd found, he stuffed it in his pocket and walked over to the door. Another quick glance out the window told him the coast was clear. A cold blast of wind crashed over him as he opened the door. Pulling the door shut behind him, he shoved his hand into his pocket. Maybe someone in town sold a hat and gloves. He'd need both if he intended to stay out in these conditions for very long.

"What are you doing out here?"

Tim pressed his lips into a straight line. *Belle.* He turned and came face-to-face with not just Belle but the entire troop. "Hello, girls. What are you doing here in the middle of the day? I thought you had school."

"We got out at lunch." Belle hooked her arm with his as Clem hurried ahead to open the door. "Something about the teachers needing time to plan."

"For what?" Lucy said, coming up alongside him. "They do a pretty good job of torturing us as it is."

"You should appreciate school more. It's preparing us for the future." April switched the hamper she carried from one arm to the other.

Clara blew a raspberry. "What future? All anyone ever talks about is the war."

"Is that really what you think, Clara?" Tim asked. He'd been holed up in a newsroom, writing articles about the war. He'd never considered what young people thought. "Because if anything, this fight is for our future, both yours and mine."

"That's what Mrs. Wynn, our history teacher, says," Belle replied. "But then she starts crying and doesn't finish telling us why it's so important."

They were almost to the house. If he didn't put his foot down now, he'd never find Schmidt. Tim stopped in his tracks. "Ladies, I have some work to do, so if you'll excuse me."

Belle glanced up at him. "You going to look for that man?"

Tim's stomach knotted. How could she know he was looking

for someone? "What man?"

"You know, that man Rolf you're supposed to take back to New York." Lucy glanced at her friends. "He did say that, didn't he?"

"He probably doesn't remember because of the fever." Clara eyed him sympathetically. "You were pretty out of it."

Some spy he was. He'd only had one job to do—get Rolf Schmidt to New York unharmed. Now, the man not only was missing, but he'd also spilled the beans about this mission to a bunch of Girl Scouts. Tim pressed his fingers into his forehead. "Girls, you need to forget whatever I said when I was incapacitated. Is that understood?"

The girls glanced at one another, then back to him. Finally, Belle spoke. "I'm sorry, but we can't do that."

"What?" Tim sputtered. "Why not?"

"Because we've already been looking for this Schmidt fellow." April smiled.

He was confused. "Did I give you his description too?"

That brought a giggle from the girls. Belle and Clara herded him into the house, then shut the door. Clem grabbed the basket and headed toward the kitchen. After they dispensed with his coat, April pulled him down beside her on the couch while Clara propped a pillow under his arm.

"I want to know." Tim tossed the pillow to the floor in frustration. "How do you know whom to look for?"

"You don't know much about our island, do you?" Clara answered, sitting on the hearth.

"Of course I do." He searched his brain for something, anything he might have heard about the Outer Banks. "First, it's a group of islands off the North Carolina coastline. Birthplace to aviation, thanks to Orville and Wilbur Wright, and the supposed hiding place of Blackbeard the pirate." He grew serious. "It's also been a target for Germany in both the Great War and this one."

"I would have aced the test on Outer Banks history Mrs. Wynn gave us if you'd been around," Clara muttered. "But that's not what I meant."

"What she means," Belle interrupted, "is that there's not a lot of people on the island. A little over a hundred people live in Buxton, so it's easy to spot an outsider. We didn't need a description. We just needed to look for someone we didn't know."

It made sense, but still, what an idiotic thing to do, telling them about Rolf. His actions could have put them in danger. "So have you seen anyone you didn't know?"

April shook her head. "At least, not here in Buxton."

"And Ginny said that everyone riding the ferry are residents so there's no one who's come on the island that way," Belle added.

"You didn't mention your uncle, April," Clem teased, then glanced at Tim, her eyes dancing with mischief. "None of us have seen him yet, but he's supposed to be very handsome."

April turned a deep shade of pink. "I told you that in confidence. Besides, Tom is my uncle."

"I'm sorry. It's just too easy to tease you," Clem replied, her voice sincere.

Things were getting out of hand. It was time to rein the girls in. He turned to April. "This uncle of yours. He's visiting from where exactly?"

"Michigan. He has a farm there. Why do you ask?"

"Why do you think he asked? Your uncle is the only new person to arrive on the island for the last week," Belle answered, rolling her eyes. "Don't you think that's strange?"

"Why would it be?" April sat on the edge of the couch and glared at Belle. "It's snowing there now, so it's not like he can do a lot on his farm at the moment."

"So he visits you every winter?" Tim asked.

April shook her head. "Not for a long time. He only bought the farm a couple of years ago. From what Daddy has said, Tom spent a lot of time going from farm to farm over the last ten years. He picked crops that were in season to raise money for his own place."

That would be easy enough to check. All he needed was a telephone. It would probably lead to nothing, but still, he'd like to know for sure.

"It's hard to know how to trust these days."

Tim glanced around at each girl. The grown-ups had spoken nothing but war for so long that they'd forgotten the toll it took on the children. If only he could give them some kind of encouragement, but there was none. Each night, their sleep was interrupted by the Germans waging war off their coast, and each day, they witnessed the aftermath on their beaches. They lived with the knowledge that at any moment, the Germans could invade their home. Each face they didn't recognize was held in suspicion, and some they knew were accused of being sympathizers. They lived under the cloud that at any given moment, their beloved home could be invaded.

"I guess we'll have to hold on to what Pastor Clint said about trusting God through the hard times." Clara sighed. "It's just hard sometimes."

Clementine opened a thermos and poured out a cup of coffee. "Especially when you're worried you'll wake up one night and there's a German soldier at the foot of your bed."

"That's not going to happen," Belle said as she took the coffee mug from Clem and handed it to him. "I know it won't."

Lucy chuckled. "You sound sure of yourself."

"That's because I am."

April shook her head. "How can you know?"

"Because it's in the Bible. If God is with us, then who can stand against us?"

The group fell silent, but Belle's words pierced Tim. It was so easy to forget God when battles raged all around. Yet God was an absolute in this war of uncertainties, and from now on, he would do his best to remember that. He turned to Belle. "Thanks for reminding us of that."

Belle shrugged. "It wasn't me. It was Ginny. She makes us read the Bible every morning."

"Really?" The more Tim heard about Belle's sister, the more he was intrigued. He'd seen her once or twice, going into the lighthouse late at night, but had never taken a second look. Would Ginny live up to her sister's descriptions of her? Or would she be like most women he'd known—vain and self-important?

Maybe it was time to change the subject. "Have you heard any more about the boat I was on?"

"They're all kind of running together now," Clara answered solemnly. "There've been several more attacks since yours."

"The night after we found you on the beach, three boats were sunk not far from here. Ginny said they were covered up at the infirmary. She said there were so many people waiting to be taken care of, they were laid out in the hallways." Belle bit her lower lip. "But it could have been worse. They were only able to save about seventy people from the ocean liner that sank. There were over three hundred on board."

Dear Lord, have mercy on them. Two hundred and thirty souls were lost on that one boat. This couldn't go on, and he knew a way to stop it. Once he found Rolf.

Clem stoked the fire, then added another log. "Mom says I'm not allowed down at the beach anymore. She thinks it's too dangerous."

Tim agreed. No telling what would wash up onshore. The last thing he wanted any of the girls to find was a body. It was time to find Rolf Schmidt. With the Germans' battle plans, the Allies would be able to come up with a defense of their own. And he knew just where to start his search. "Are they still taking the survivors to the infirmary here on the island?"

Belle nodded as she picked at her fingernails. "They've sent some of the more injured people to the hospital in Chapel Hill, but most are still being treated here. Ginny said they must work double shifts just to keep up. As long as it keeps her out of the house, I don't care what she does."

"Come on, Belle," Clara cajoled. "Your sister's not that bad."

"You don't know her like I do." Belle slumped back into the cushions and crossed her arms over her waist. "She sneaks out at night and won't tell me where she's going."

"Maybe she just needs some time to herself," April suggested. "She is basically working two jobs."

"That's no excuse."

This was the first Belle had ever bad-mouthed her sister. She obviously loved and admired the woman as much as she talk-ed about her. It was probably a misunderstanding, something he was very familiar with, having a younger sister himself. Still, he'd hoped to wrangle an introduction out of Belle. With Ginny working at the infirmary, she could be an asset in finding Rolf. "Is there any way you could introduce me to your sister, Belle?"

Belle shot up from her seat. "Why on earth would I do that?"

"Because I need to get into the infirmary. If my friend was picked up by the coast guard, he might be there."

"No." She shook her head violently. "Ginny would turn you over to the coast guard in a heartbeat."

Clara stood, then walked to the coffee table and sat down in front of her friend. "Come on, Belle. This man Tim is looking for must be important if he was supposed to keep it a secret. If Ginny can help him, you know she would."

"We can help him just fine without her."

Clem laughed. "We can't get him into town, much less the infirmary. Besides, someone's going to notice smoke coming out of the fireplace soon and come to check it out."

"No." Belle's expression tightened.

Clara glanced at Tim. "I know how you can meet her."

"Clara!" Belle bellowed. "Don't you dare!"

But the girl continued. "Ginny goes to the lighthouse every night. You can meet her there."

"Clara, you blabbermouth!" Belle glared at her friend. "That was between me and Ruthie."

"What can I say? We're twins and we share everything."

"Hmmm." Belle fell back against the cushions.

He'd seen the girls have silly squabbles, but nothing like what he'd witnessed today. Of course, Belle's argument was with her sister, not these girls who seemed more sisters than friends. Still, he didn't want to hurt the girl's feelings. She'd been a huge help to him over the last week, and mainly, he'd come to like the little brat.

"Do you mind if I talk to your sister, Belle?"

"Go ahead." She swallowed, looking suddenly miserable. "You're going to do what you want to do anyway."

"Ignore her," Lucy murmured. "She just doesn't like to lose."

But Tim wasn't buying it. There was something else going on here, something more than her sister sneaking out at night. It probably was just a family squabble, nothing that concerned him. Tonight, he would start his search for Rolf Schmidt.

And tonight, he would introduce himself to Miss Virginia Mathis.

CHAPTER 7

Ginny slouched deeper into her wool coat, her nose and ears frozen despite her hat and scarf. A gale had blown in late this afternoon, bringing with it a few flurries and freezing temperatures. She'd almost not come, the memory of the slight sway of the lighthouse during the last blow making her queasy. But then the winds died down, and she couldn't think of any reason to stay away. Despite the weather, she still had a job to do.

Not that she had much to report. Ginny opened the door, then once inside, slammed it shut. Leaning back against the cool wood, she closed her eyes and breathed. It had been three days since the last attack, and Ginny was on pins and needles. Officer Chapline was convinced the Germans had returned to Lorient to restock and reload, and maybe he was right. Still, she couldn't help but wonder if tonight they would return and start their attacks again.

Ginny pushed herself off the door and walked over to the spiral staircase where the lantern she'd left sat at the base of the steps. One quick spark and the room was lit, giving the area a cozy feel despite the cold. She lingered. For some odd reason, she dreaded tonight. Maybe it was because the day had been particularly brutal. She had not been at her shift at the ferry for more than an hour before Dr. Stevens called from the infirmary.

None of the hospitals on the mainland could take any of their patients until they had been identified and cleared to travel. With their identification at the bottom of the ocean and families spread out across the southern hemisphere, that was an impossibility for most of these men.

Raising her lantern, she followed the spiral stairs upward. How did these families rest, never knowing what happened to their loved ones? Did they look at every face in a crowd, hoping beyond hope that they would find the one they loved?

Ginny climbed the first step, then the next. It was no wonder she couldn't sleep. Watching a tragedy play out before your own eyes could do that to you. All she could do was pray, even if that felt futile at times. "Lord, I don't understand this war. I don't understand families being torn apart and people dying for no reason. I know You can use this, but for the life of me, I don't see how. Help us, Lord. I beg You."

Her words echoed off the brick walls. Did He even hear her at all?

She sighed, her mind wandering. Then there were the two men Chapline hoped she would find. As if that were possible. Unless they traveled the ferry or were being treated at the hospital, there was no chance she'd find them. No sense looking for them anyway. If they weren't in the infirmary or the morgue, they were probably lost at sea.

By the time she reached the lantern room several moments later, she had to pull herself up using the handrail, her body heated from the exertion. She placed her lantern on the small table nearby and worked on the buttons of her coat. With two sweaters and a pair of gloves she'd cut the fingers out of so that she could work, she should stay warm.

"So you're Ginny Mathis," a low, very British voice said from the shadows. "I've heard so much about you, I thought it was time we met." He hesitated. "My name is Timothy Elliott. I'm a reporter for the *Times*."

Dear heavens! She swallowed the lump of fear lodged in her throat. "You're one of the men the coast guard is looking for."

He didn't seem surprised by the news, nor did he look happy about it. "I've been recovering from injuries after our boat was attacked."

"Do you have some identification?" Ginny could have kicked herself. There had to be more important questions to be asked, but she couldn't think of them. "A driver's license or maybe a passport?"

"My passport went down with the ship, but I do have my press card." He struggled to get his wallet out of his pants pocket, then handed it to her.

"I can't go through your wallet. That's rude."

His brown eyes sparkled with amusement as he motioned to his sling. "It's the only way you're going to find my press card, as I'm unable to retrieve it myself."

"Oh. I'm sorry." She opened the soft leather and found the card. He'd been younger when the picture was made, and it didn't do him justice. Putting the card back, she closed the wallet and handed it back to him. "What's wrong with your shoulder?"

"I dislocated it. It's fine now. One of the people who found me set it back in the socket."

"Would you like me to look at it?" Ginny felt her face go warm. "I mean, I'm one semester shy of graduating nursing school and have some experience with such things."

The corner of his mouth lifted in a roguish smile. "All right then."

Grabbing her lantern, she lifted it enough to get a good look at him. Dear me, but he was handsome with dark blond hair and a strong jaw, and heavens, that accent. Any other girl would melt into a puddle when he spoke.

But she wasn't any other girl, she reminded herself. Was she?

There was no sense ogling the man. He was possibly a spy, albeit an injured one, and she was only looking at him in a professional capacity. Ginny slid his coat from his affected shoulder, then felt along the bones of his arms. "You don't seem to have any breaks. Any numbness or tingling in your fingers?"

He shook his head. "Not since it was put back into place."

"Good." She slipped the makeshift sling from his arm. "Can you lift your arm?"

The man—Mr. Elliott—lifted it slowly, then smiled. "It doesn't hurt a bit."

Ginny couldn't help herself. She smiled back at him. "Everything looks good, so if you want to go without the sling, I think you'll be all right."

He rolled his shoulders. "That feels good."

"Someone who was knowledgeable worked on your shoulder." She picked up his sling, then studied it. It looked familiar, but she couldn't place it.

He held his hand out for it. "I need to return it."

"Of course." She handed it back to him. It was only a woolen scarf. Dozens of people here on the island probably had one just like it. Then why did it seem so familiar to her?

"The reason I wanted to meet you is I was hoping you would help me."

Ginny blinked. Had he just asked for her help? Why would Mr. Elliott think she would help him? "I don't understand."

"You work at the infirmary, correct?" He tucked his arm into his coat sleeve, then leaned on the table next to her. "I need to get inside."

"Why would I help you get inside?" she sputtered. "You could be a German spy for all I know."

Mr. Elliott closed his eyes and gave a little shake of his head as if this wasn't the first time he'd had this conversation. "I'm not a German spy. I'm working as an operative for British Intelligence."

"Do you have. . ."

"No, I don't have any proof." He pushed his hand through his hair. "When did you Americans become so bloody stubborn?"

"Probably around the time we dumped a bunch of your tea in Boston Harbor."

He stared at her for a solid minute, then burst into laughter. "You're funny, and you're not afraid to stand up for yourself. I admire that in a person."

That laugh! It was absolutely the most boisterous laugh she'd ever heard. She wasn't sure why, but it made her feel happy. Not a great reason for doing what she was about to do, and she'd probably live to regret it, yet she wanted to help him somehow. "Why do you need me to help you get into the infirmary?"

"You're going to help me?"

"I haven't decided yet." She leaned back against the table so they were side by side. "You need to answer some questions first."

"All right." Her heart did a little flutter as he gave her his full attention. "I'll answer them if I can."

She drew in a deep breath to steady herself. "What is it exactly you think I can help you with?"

"I'm looking for someone, and he could be at the infirmary or in the morgue."

Ginny nodded. "You mean the German naval officer."

He jerked around to look at her. "How did you know that?"

She couldn't tell him the truth, that the coast guard had asked her to find him and his traveling companion. But she wasn't one to lie either. "I heard it from one of the guardsmen."

The man appeared to accept her answer, so he continued. "Anyway, I must get this man to New York City as soon as possible.

He has vital information for the Allies that needs to be put into the right hands."

"What kind of information?" She knew it was a big request, but no bigger than what he had asked of her.

He pushed off the table and took a short walk around the room. Outside, the ocean was eerily quiet, the plug and tug of their conversation the only battle tonight. Finally, he looked at her and she knew his answer. "I can't tell you."

Ginny never liked secrets, even though she understood their purpose, especially during these times. But if he expected her to help him, he was going to have to do better than vague answers. "If you can't tell me, I can't help you."

Elliott muttered something under his breath, then turned to her. "I don't know why the intelligence department thought I could do this. I'm just a bloody reporter."

She didn't know the man, only the details he'd shared and what Chapline had told her about him. Yet she hated seeing him discouraged. "Someone must have noticed something about you that made you perfect for this particular mission."

"I know what they saw in me," he bit out. "I was the only bloody person Schmidt would meet." He must have noted the confusion in her expression and continued. "I interviewed him several years ago when I was still at university."

"He must have liked your article."

His brow furrowed. "That's the thing. It was never published. Tensions were high between Great Britain and Germany even before they invaded Poland, so my editor scrapped the article." Elliott walked over and took her hands in his. Even through her gloves, warm tingles drifted up her arms. "I know this is asking a great deal, but would you reconsider helping me?"

She wanted to, though she wasn't certain it was the right thing to do. Tim Elliott could still be a German spy for all she knew. If this man was who he said, and the information this Rolf Schmidt could supply to the Allies would shorten the war, then shouldn't she take the risk? But if Mr. Elliott was lying, she could be arrested and thrown into federal prison for treason.

"I can get an identification, Miss Mathis. All I have to do is call my superiors in New York and they would have it to me in a few days. You could even talk to them yourself if that would ease your misgivings."

Ginny nodded, but she could tell that he was reluctant to take that plan of action. "Can you give me a moment to think about it?"

"Of course." He walked to the far corner of the room and stared out at the island.

Covering her face with her hands, she tried to quiet her jangled thoughts. *Lord, I need Your guidance on this. I think Mr. Elliott is being honest, but these are frightening times when I don't know who to trust. What do I do here, Lord?*

When she lifted her head, the answers were no clearer than when she'd bowed her head. Then she turned. Mr. Elliott's head was bowed, and his lips moved as if in prayer. Was this how God was giving her an answer? She still wasn't sure. Maybe she was supposed to step out on faith. Would God really want her to risk her freedom, possibly her life on this man?

When he rejoined her a few minutes later, he waited on her, then finally asked, "Have you made a decision?"

She studied the front of his coat and his scarf. Who had a scarf like this? Ginny picked up the tail end of it. "Where did you get this scarf? I know it from somewhere."

"I don't know." He glanced down at it. "Probably the same Girl Guide who put my shoulder back into place. Clementine is her name, but the rest of the girls call her Clem."

"You're talking about the Girl Scouts, as in my Girl Scout

troop." Shoving past him, she paced the room. "They found you on the beach the afternoon after the *Allan Jackson* was sunk. That's why they were at the lightkeeper's house. They put you up there." Ginny turned and glared at him. "Why didn't you stop them?"

"I was pretty banged up after having a boat sink from under me." His blue eyes glittered with anger. "Besides, do you think those girls would listen to me? No. You'd prepared them for this time, and they bloody well intended to follow through."

Another thought struck her. "You're the one who lit the lantern that night. Is that how you knew I was here? Have you been watching me?"

Guilt flittered in his eyes, then just as quickly dissipated. "I may have seen you once or twice."

"Then how did you know I'd be here tonight?"

"How do you think?" He pinned her with his gaze. "Belle."

Her shoulders slumped. Of course it was. That girl was always looking for some kind of adventure, the consequences be hanged. Was that why she had been so flighty the last few days—because she had a secret? Her nails bit into her palm. "She is going to be the death of me if I don't kill her first."

The man's warm chuckle filled the small space. "Don't be too hard on her. She means well."

"She may have good intentions, but this has got to stop. She could put herself in danger." She slammed her eyes closed. Just the thought of something happening to her sister made her stomach twist in knots. And she'd dragged the rest of the troop into this with her. Ginny's heart threatened to pound out of her chest.

"She's a good girl, Ginny. They all are. If you knew how they helped. . ."

But she didn't let him finish. "Just who do you think you are telling me how to handle my sister? You've known her, what—ten days now? You don't know anything about her."

"I know she admires you. Quite a bit, it seems."

That went to show how little Mr. Elliott knew Belle. Anyone who had spent even a minute in her sister's company would know she disliked Ginny intensely. "I'm sorry, but I don't think I can help you."

"Wait a minute. You're not going to help me?"

"No." She knew she was being peevish, but she had enough on her plate without him telling her how to deal with her sister.

"The information Schmidt could provide the Allies could possibly shorten the war from years to months." The tiny room shrank even more as he took a step toward her. "Don't you Yanks want this war over?"

Tim Elliott might be handsome and charming and have a lovely accent, but she would stand her ground. "I don't know you. For all I know, you could be an enemy spy pretending to be British. So no, Mr. Elliott, I'm not going to help you."

She turned to gather her equipment before realizing she'd never taken the map out of her coat pocket. There was no use staying tonight. Her nerves were strung too tight to sit around here waiting for something to happen. A warm cup of tea and a hot water bottle at the foot of her bed were the only things she needed after this episode tonight.

"It wouldn't be good if people around here discovered your troop was harboring a spy."

Ginny jerked around. "They're just kids."

"Boys the same age are serving in the military for the Allies and the enemy." Elliott crossed his arms, his gaze intent. "Some even serve in the resistance for the French and the Dutch."

He couldn't be serious. No one around Buxton would believe him. Folks around here had watched the girls grow from babies in their mothers' arms into girls on the brink of becoming young women.

Yet she couldn't dismiss what Elliott said. The war had brought out fear and distrust among people. Even folks who'd known each other for years looked at each other with a vague sense of suspicion. "You would ruin their lives?"

Taking her chin between his thumb and forefinger, he tipped her head back until their gazes clashed. "Are you willing to take that risk?"

"That's a stupid question," Ginny replied. Daddy would never forgive her if anything happened to Belle or Momma. The thought of her mother's response sent a shiver down her spine. "You don't seem the type to stoop to blackmail."

A flicker of something, maybe regret, shone in his eyes before the shadow fell, and he was once again the arrogant man demanding her help. "I'd do anything to stop this war, Miss Mathis. Blackmail will be one of my lesser stands."

Which could mean. . .anything. If Mr. Elliott was so determined to find this German officer, he would've found a way by now. That along with the fact that he'd spoken of the girls with such affection made her doubt his supposed threats.

But she couldn't risk it. She had to protect her girls at any cost. "All right, Mr. Elliott, I'll help you."

———————≈———————

When had he become a complete heel?

Tim looked out the lantern room's window, listening to the sound of the water, the steady ebb and flow small comfort to his battered soul. He was a jerk, as the Yanks would say. But what choice had he had? Without Schmidt and the information he had, this war would drag on for possibly years.

Movement on the ground caught his attention. Ginny Mathis walked slowly as if she carried the weight of the world on her slender shoulders. He'd done that to her. Shame washed over him. When he met her the next time, he would apologize and assure her he'd never do anything to hurt the girls.

He watched her walk up the path leading into town. Ginny Mathis was everything her sister said and more. Why had Belle never mentioned the way Ginny's eyes lit up with mischief or her deep devotion to her family? She'd stood up to him, just like her sister had. Those Mathis girls had backbones made of steel.

Tomorrow, he could come clean to Ginny about her troop and how they'd been a lifeline for him in the days since he'd been injured. To him, the girls reminded him of Iris and all the laughter and love they shared growing up. And Iris reminded him of Belle, always looking for adventure and completely loyal to those she loved.

He would make things right with Ginny. Right after she helped him get into the infirmary.

⌷ CHAPTER 8 ⌷

The back gate slamming shut sounded like a rifle shot, but Ginny was beyond caring. The deal she'd made with the devil to save her sister—no, the entire troop—burned through her veins like a fever. What was Belle thinking, harboring that man? Didn't she realize that by hiding him, she might have put the entire island in danger?

She grasped the screen door and pulled it open. The first thing she was going to do was march down the hall and yank her sister out of bed, and then. . .Ginny stilled. Tearing through the house and waking everyone up wasn't going to solve anything. And what about Momma? Her nerves were already on edge. Getting her all worried about Belle would just make more problems. She would have to wait until morning to confront her sister.

Or maybe not. Opening the kitchen door, she found Belle at the table, pouring herself a cup of milk. Ginny stepped inside, took off her coat, and hung it by the door. "What are you doing up this late?"

"I couldn't sleep. I have a lot on my mind." Belle stood and hurried to the cupboard for another glass. She filled it with milk, then set it down at the place setting across from her. "You're home early."

She really is a good kid. Mr. Elliott's words whispered through Ginny's thoughts. It wasn't that she disagreed with him as much as she worried about Belle's rash behavior. Still, it was difficult to stay angry when the girl looked so miserable. Joining Belle, she pulled out the chair and sat. "What's bothering you?"

Belle slumped back in her chair. "You don't want to know."

"I wouldn't have asked if I didn't." She sipped her milk and waited. Maybe her sister was ready to confide in her, which wouldn't correct the situation, but it would be far better than having to confront her.

Belle played with the end of her braid. "It's Ruthie. She won't talk to me."

This was unexpected. Ruthie and Belle had been thick as thieves since the day they were born. Oh, they had their scrapes, but it never went on for more than a day or two. "What happened?"

"She got mad about something I didn't do, and we got in an argument about it." She sniffed, her blue eyes wet with tears. "She's changed since her brothers joined up. It's like she's a different person."

Poor Ruthie. Her heart broke for the girl. She thought her brothers hung the moon and the stars, and now, to have them gone for months, even years, must feel unbearable to her. Ginny leaned against the table. "People do change, especially when they must make a big adjustment in their life. Just give her some time, and I'm sure Ruthie will come around."

Belle glanced up at her through wet lashes. "You really think so?"

Ginny nodded. "I don't see why not." A question nudged its way into her thoughts, and Ginny decided to ask. "What was it you didn't do for Ruthie?"

"It's nothing." She grabbed her glass and took several gulps of milk until she emptied it. Wiping her mouth with her sleeve, she pushed back from the table and stood. "Thanks, Gin. I think I can sleep now."

Ginny's temper rose. If Belle thought she was going to cut bait and run, she had another thing coming. "This wouldn't have to do with Mr. Elliott, would it?"

Belle gripped the back of the chair as if to keep from falling. "How did you. . .?"

But she interrupted. "He was at the lighthouse when I got there tonight."

"Oh." She glanced down as if to study the grain of the table. "He said he wanted to meet you, but he didn't mention anything about introducing himself."

Of course he didn't. Belle was a kid, and Tim Elliott was. . . His handsome face and the way he'd let her tease him flashed through her mind. She shook her head to dispel the memory. The truth was she didn't have a clue who the man was, and neither did Belle. "Why didn't you report him to the coast guard when you first found him?"

Belle stared at her, all wide-eyed innocence. "We were helping him just like it says in the Girl Scout pledge." She straightened and lifted her right hand, three fingers extended in the Girl Scout sign. "On my honor, I will try to do my duty to God and my country, to help other people every day, especially those at home."

Ginny inwardly groaned. As committed to the program as Belle and the other girls were, she could understand her actions, but that didn't make it the right thing to do. "Honey, I appreciate what you and the rest of the troop were trying to do, but this is different. We're at war, Belle. There's a battle going on right outside our front door." She stood and went around the table to where Belle stood. Putting her arm around her, Ginny tugged her close. "It's important for us to defend our home."

Belle glanced up at her. "But Tim is on our side. He's from England."

"He says that," Ginny corrected her, "but we have no way of knowing that for certain."

"I know he is." Her stubborn chin lifted a notch. "He tells us stories about growing up near someplace called Sheffield, and about his sister and her little boy, Will." Her expression softened. "Will lives with his grandparents right now because of the air attacks."

Whatever Tim Elliott was, he was imaginative. Or was he simply being truthful? Ginny could see how the girls would be sucked in by his story. Just the thought of a poor child having to live away from his parents was enough to make her reconsider her own feelings toward the man. "What does he say his sister does?"

"She works as a secretary. Her husband was a pilot in the Royal Air Force, but he died during one of the attacks over London."

"How horrible," Ginny whispered. Tim Elliott had certainly shared quite a bit of information about himself with the girls. But was it the truth? Even if it was, that didn't excuse the way he'd used the girls to get her to help him. "Belle, have you ever considered Mr. Elliott might be an enemy spy, pretending to be one of us?"

Her sister shook her head. "He's not one of them, Gin. Deep down in my heart, I know he's one of us."

Only the heart could lie. Belle hadn't learned that hard lesson yet. At thirteen, she still believed in a world where everyone told the truth about who they were. This would be a hard lesson for her and the others to learn. "Do you know why Mr. Elliott was at the lighthouse this evening?"

"To meet you."

Ginny nodded. "Because he is looking for someone and wants me to take him to the infirmary."

Belle bit her lip at the corner of her mouth. "I know he's been worried about finding that German officer."

Shock pulsed through Ginny. "He told you that?"

Belle nodded. "Not that he meant to. He ran a high fever for two days after we found him, and it kind of slipped out." She met Ginny's gaze. "But we haven't told a soul. I mean, besides you, but we'd already decided you needed to know."

It was small comfort to know Elliott hadn't told the girls about his mission intentionally. But why was he running a high fever? Had he been injured other than the dislocated shoulder she'd checked out? She shouldn't care. If he'd turned himself into the coast guard, he would've been treated at the infirmary while keeping them and the rest of the islanders safe. "When were you planning on telling me?"

"When you got home tonight," she replied sheepishly. "You probably don't believe me, but it's true."

Ginny wanted to believe her, she really did, but she just couldn't. Maybe if Belle had come clean before she confronted her, it would be different. But her sister, her entire troop, had kept a dangerous secret from her, one that could destroy their community. It would take time to rebuild her trust.

"Are you going to help Tim?"

Ginny studied Belle's worried expression. Her sister might not appreciate it, but she'd do anything to protect her, even from her own self. She drew a deep breath, then nodded. "I've agreed to help Mr. Elliott get into the infirmary so he can look for the German. But in return, I want you to do something for me."

Belle studied her warily. "What's that?"

"You and the rest of the girls are to stay away from him. Is that clear?"

Belle's expression grew indignant. "What did we do wrong? We were only trying to help Tim."

"There's nothing wrong with helping people, sis." Ginny hesitated, unsure how to proceed. "It's just for right now we must be careful whom we help. With all the submarine attacks going on offshore, we don't know who the tide might bring in."

"But Tim…"

"Tim," she interrupted. "Tim told me he would turn you and the other girls in to the coast guard if I didn't help him. Maybe he is who he says he is, but what if he's not? That kind of thing could ruin your lives."

"He said that?"

The hurt on Belle's young face broke her heart, but it was best she learned the truth. It would save her from more heartache later. "I'm sorry, but you need to know what kind of person he is."

"I'm so sorry, Gin." Belle turned, then threw her arms around her, burrowing her head into her neck. "I didn't think Tim was like that. He's so nice, and now I've got you in this mess. What are you going to do?"

If only she had a choice, Ginny thought, but she didn't. If Elliott was arrested, he could incriminate her troop. It would ruin families and destroy the girls' lives. No, there was no question she had to do this. Once they found this man, Tim wouldn't need her anymore, and her assignment from Officer Chapline would be finished. "I haven't seen anyone matching the description of the man. More than likely, he drowned."

"What if not? What will you do then?"

Ginny hadn't thought that far in advance. If Rolf was alive, and that was a big if, she would turn him in to the coast guard. How would Tim respond? Would he carry through with his threat to turn in the girls? Or had he been honest with her when he said Rolf Schmidt had information that might end this war sooner? All she could do was leave it to the Lord. "I've promised I would help him, so I will."

Belle tightened her arms around Ginny. "I'll be praying. I'll tell the other girls to pray about it too."

She smiled softly. Tim Elliott was right about one thing. Belle really was a good girl. Now if only they could get this adventurous nature of hers under control, things might settle down. At least now she knew what type of man Mr. Elliott was and would stay away from him. If not, who knew what kind of trouble her sister would find herself in?

———— ≈ ————

"Can't we go inside and have this meeting? It's cold out here," Lucy said, knotting her scarf under her chin.

Stomping around at the base of their concrete porch, Belle buried her hands deeper into her coat pockets for warmth. "Momma is inside, and I don't want her to hear about this."

"For Pete's sake, Belle. Why do you have to make everything sound so dramatic?" Clara huddled up close to the wall. "It can't be that bad."

"Oh yes, it is," Belle answered.

All eyes turned their attention on her. Since her late-night heart-to-heart with her sister, she'd been turning the conversation over in her head, trying to devise a plan that would help Ginny out of the mess they'd created. She'd called a meeting in hopes someone else might come up with a plan. "Ginny is in trouble, and it's all our fault."

"What do you mean it's our fault?" Clem asked, her legs tucked against her chest and covered with the coat. "What did we do now?"

"Does this have to do with her late nights at the lighthouse?" Lucy's eyes widened in delight. "I knew that was going to be a problem."

"Stop running your mouth, Lucy. It's because of us that Ginny is in trouble," Belle snapped, her spine stiffening in outrage.

"Mr. Elliott is using us to get Ginny to help him find that German guy."

It felt as if the world had gone still around them. "I don't understand," April said. "How is he using us?"

Belle swallowed. If she'd only done what Ruthie had asked and turned him in to the coast guard, none of this would be happening. "He's threatening to turn us in to the coast guard."

"So?" Clara replied. "It might do him good to get that shoulder checked out."

Belle closed her eyes. "You don't understand. We don't know who Mr. Elliott is or whether he's really on our side. We could get into serious trouble for helping him if he's not who he says he is."

April's face went pale. "Trouble?"

Clara patted her friend's back. "She's exaggerating. We're not in any trouble for helping someone who was hurt."

"But she's right. We don't know that much about Mr. Elliott. For all we know, he could be a German spy."

April dug into her pocket and retrieved a handkerchief. "That means we aided and abetted the enemy, which means treason."

"We can't commit treason," Clem barked with laughter. "We're only thirteen years old."

"Don't you listen to anything in Mrs. Wynn's class?" April bit out. "They had soldiers as young as eight fighting the Civil War. I'm sure that didn't stop the Yankees from shooting at them."

"I don't want to go to jail." Lucy's voice broke.

"Would you please be quiet?" Belle hated to raise her voice, but really, this nonsense had to stop. "We are not going to jail or anything, but we do need to help Gin out of this mess. Agreed?"

"Agreed."

"Good." Belle gave an affirmative nod. "Now all we have to do is figure out a way to do that."

"You don't have a plan already?" Clem asked.

Belle shook her head. "I had hoped you guys might have some ideas."

The girls fell silent, each one lost in her own thoughts. This was a huge mess, and most of it was her own doing. After Ginny had finally convinced her to go to bed, Belle had spent the rest of the night staring at the ceiling, confessing her part in this situation to the Lord and asking for a way out. Sunlight seeped through her curtains before she finally fell asleep, no closer to an answer.

"We should have taken him to the infirmary when we found him," Clara said. "That would have made the most sense."

"He asked us not to." Belle grimaced, looking back in hindsight. "That should have told me he was up to no good."

"We wanted to believe he was a nice person." Clara scrunched up her nose. "He does have that nice accent like Leslie Howard."

Belle smirked. "Just because he seems nice doesn't mean he is."

"True," Lucy agreed, then sat up. "Which means we don't have to be nice to him."

Clem stared at the girl and scoffed. "We've already been nice. That's how we got into this mess in the first place."

"No, we're in trouble because we didn't take him to the infirmary like we should have." Lucy smiled. "Don't you think it's time we changed that, particularly with that bad shoulder and the nasty cut in his side?"

"Why would he go with us?" Clara pulled her knit cap down around her ears. "He's already got Ginny helping him get inside."

"He doesn't know where the infirmary is, and Ginny goes straight from work to the infirmary in the afternoon." Lucy smiled. "We could graciously escort him to the infirmary, and if he were admitted before he met Ginny. . ."

It could work, but Belle needed to add one more detail. "I think we need to let Officer Chapline know that Tim is at the infirmary as well. I'll tell him that we tried to get him to go to the infirmary, but he refused. That way, if Tim decides to rat us out, we've beat him to the punch."

Lucy's eyes sparkled with humor. "We could even tell Chapline that Tim has a head injury. They'll keep him in the hospital for sure then."

Belle smiled. Lucy's idea wasn't bad. In fact, it was pure genius. Simple and straight to the point. And a concussion would explain Tim's wild ramblings about being fed and sheltered by the girls. "I think it's perfect, Lucy." She glanced at the other girls. "You guys can take him to the infirmary while I alert Chapline."

Clara glanced at her. "You're not going with us?"

She shook her head. "I promised Ginny I wouldn't have anything else to do with Tim. After everything I've put her through, I owe her that."

"I can understand that," April said.

"Of course you do, Miss Goody Two-shoes," Lucy teased as she gave her a smile. "But we love you anyway."

Belle closed her eyes. There was one more thing on the agenda. "If y'all don't mind, I think we should pray about this before we vote. I promised Ginny I would, but it would be nice if we all did it together."

Her friends nodded, then bowed their heads, and for the first time in days, Belle felt everything in her world was all right.

☰ CHAPTER 9 ☰

Tim threw another log into the fire, then settled the iron grate over the opening. Living in a flat, he was used to radiators and piped heating, but a fireplace took him back to cold mornings on his grandfather's farm. To the smell of fresh bacon sizzling in the frying pan, or the spats he and Iris would have over the last biscuit still warm from the stove. He'd been about his nephew's age when they'd gone to live with their grandparents. Will must be almost six now. He'd been barely three when his father's plane was shot down over the Channel. Did he look like his father or favor his mother? Did he even remember any of the adults in his young life at all?

Tim scrubbed his hands over his face. It was time he left this place. Once he apologized to Ginny and looked through the infirmary and morgue, he would call his office in New York and make the arrangements. Then he was never taking another Intelligence assignment again. He'd make himself a target in the army if he had to, anything but cause another woman to worry like Ginny Mathis was last night.

It would all be over this afternoon, then Ginny and her troop could move on to their next war project.

He glanced out the door. The girls were due here any

moment. Still, he could put himself to good use and make a pot of tea while he waited. He headed toward the kitchen, the air chilly with a hint of moisture. A front must be coming through. He'd have to search the closets for an old umbrella if he didn't want to meet Ginny wet to the bone. After lighting the stove, Tim grabbed the teapot and walked over to the sink.

A knock on the front door followed by a rush of cold air announced the girls' arrival. "Girls, I'm in the kitchen."

A thunder of boots hurried through the parlor and down the hall. He turned as they stumbled into the room, all cherry-cheeked and bright-eyed. Just the sight of them instantly lifted his spirits. "Good morning, ladies. How are you today?"

Clara shucked off her coat and tossed it over one of the kitchen chairs. "Good. At least it's not raining yet. There's nothing worse than having to walk in a cold, steady rain."

"I'd rather have rain than snow." Lucy plucked at her gloves then tugged them off. "It's pretty at first, but then it just gets dirty and mushy."

"I think snowflakes on the beach are pretty," April said, her expression pensive. "But then, nothing is pretty on the beach right now."

He'd never thought of snow falling on the seashore. "I bet it is pretty to watch, April."

"We brought you an apple ugly from the bakery." Clementine held up a paper bag. "Mom says they're going to have to stop making them." She glanced at the girls. "Sugar's being rationed now."

"I'd hoped that was a rumor," Lucy whined. "I do like a chocolate bar every now and then."

Tim went to the cupboard and came back with six cups, then looked around. "Where's Belle?"

"She was up all night." Lucy grabbed some plates and carried them back to the table. "Didn't she have a headache?"

"I'm not certain. Could be." Clementine grabbed a knife from the drawer, then rejoined them. "They wrapped it up, so it still should be good and warm."

The scent of cooked apples, cinnamon, and warm dough filled the kitchen as Clementine peeled back the wax paper. She cut a slice and placed it on a plate before handing it down the line.

Tim's mouth watered at the small flecks of sugar that coated the pastry. "I haven't had a sweet in almost three years."

"Then you're going to love this." April took her piece, then, setting it in front of her, bowed her head.

Ginny had done the same thing last night, only she'd stopped to pray about whether to help him. His own prayer life had suffered in recent months, but seeing Ginny and now April, he was encouraged to start again. As he had with Ginny last night, Tim followed April's example and closed his eyes. *Lord, forgive me for what I have put Ginny and these girls through. Help me to do Your will in my life. In Christ's name I humbly pray. Amen.*

When he lifted his head, four sets of eyes were trained on him. April reached out and touched his arm. "Are you a Christian, Mr. Elliott?"

No one had ever asked him such a pointed question regarding his faith. He nodded. "Yes, I am."

The girls glanced around at each other as if he'd just told them he was Merlin or something. They must have made some kind of decision, because they all went back to eating.

"You'd better eat up," Lucy cajoled, swiping some of the fruit mixture off her plate. "We have to get going soon if we're going to get you to the infirmary in time for your appointment with Ginny."

He sputtered and coughed as he choked on his tea. "You know about our meeting?"

"Of course we do." Lucy glanced around the table, then back at him. "Who do you think is going to take you there? I mean, you don't know where it is, now, do you?"

Tim hadn't thought about that. A rookie mistake, but he'd been so knocked off balance by Ginny Mathis last night, he'd barely been able to think straight. She was everything Belle had said and more. Under different circumstances, he would have liked to have known her better, but any possibility of that had flown out the window last night. The look on her face when he'd mentioned turning her troop into the coast guard haunted him. That was why he'd forgotten to ask for directions. He would make things right with her today, then leave town as soon as it could be arranged.

He quickly swallowed his pastry, savoring what he had tasted, and washed it down with the rest of his tea. Pushing back from the table, he stood. "Are we ready?"

The girls hurried to their feet and cleaned up the kitchen. Tim grabbed his coat as well as an umbrella and the scarf Clementine had loaned him, then met them at the front door.

"How far are we from the infirmary?" Tim asked as they left the house and started up the path that led away from his hideaway for the past week. Broken shells crunched beneath his feet as he glanced up at the gray sky.

"Just a few miles. It's on the main road the other side of Avon," Clara replied, tugging on her gloves. "We pass right by the coast guard station to get there."

The main road. The last thing he wanted was to reveal himself to anyone until he had some answers. Tim pulled up short. "Is there any way we can get there by way of the beach?"

"The Guard is patrolling the beach now," Lucy answered. "In fact, no one is allowed beyond the dunes until further notice."

"Then the main road it is," Tim said as he fell in behind them.

"You do intend to obey the order, don't you?"

"Why? Are you worried about us?" April laughed.

The truth is he was. He never could have made it without their help. Of course, they were Girl Scouts. Being helpful was second nature to them. But they had gone beyond the call of duty, feeding him and nursing him back to health. He had come to care for them.

Which was why he needed to find out what happened to Rolf Schmidt. Until he could confirm or deny the German officer's death, the girls were in danger.

Tim glanced around as they reached the main road, then veered right. Despite the cold and the thickening clouds, the island had a wild beauty about it. From here, he could see the whitecaps reaching their peak, then folding in on themselves, the foam a darker gray than the clouds. The sand had turned the color of coal dust, and jagged pieces of metal and wood dotted the shore. On his left, sparse groups of oak, pine, and other varieties of trees lined the calm waters of Pamlico Sound.

"Can you see the sunrise and sunset from here?" he asked.

Clementine laughed. "Of course we can. Can't you see both where you live?"

"Not like this place," Tim replied, watching a boat out on the sound. "New York reminds me more of London, but this place— you're blessed to live in this all year round."

April glanced around. "I can see why you say that. We take it for granted, but it really is a nice place to grow up. Everyone knows everyone else, and folks are so nice."

"If you haven't noticed, April is our troop's Little Mary Sunshine." Lucy grinned at the girl. "Doesn't she just make you sick?"

"Come on, Miss Grouchy Pants!" April teased her back. "Someone has to turn your frown around."

Tim caught himself laughing. These girls may bicker and

argue, but they were bound together like paper was to glue. It was refreshing to see, especially when everything else around felt like it was falling apart. Would these girls still be the sweet, refreshing innocent girls after the war, only more mature? Or would the war mold them into something they wouldn't recognize ten years from now?

"Hey, I forgot to mention," Clara started. "Officer Chapline asked if we could volunteer after school for a few hours. They've been releasing a lot of patients to mainland hospitals, and he thought we could help."

"Wait." Tim had to wrap his head around the news. "You mean, patients from the attacks are being released?"

Clara nodded. "That's why Ginny had to go in early today. They're trying to get the people who are mildly injured to the mainland where there are more beds. They've already had to shut down one wing of the infirmary to serve as a morgue."

"As long as I don't have to go to the morgue, I'll be happy to help," Lucy answered with a shiver.

"We're here." Lucy stopped in front of a large two-story building with a watchtower on the beach side. "This is the coast guard station, and across the street is the infirmary."

Tim studied the hospital. It was smaller than he'd expected, built more as an infirmary for the island's sparse population than as a hospital for battle victims. It was one story, made of brick and painted white to match the sandy parking lot. Only the black door and shutters, as well as what must be the coast guard insignia, differentiated it from all the surrounding buildings. In front of it, large tents were set up, probably to house the dozens of survivors who had been rescued offshore. A brutal way to care for patients, especially in the cold, but if it was all they could offer, it was better than nothing.

"You just go in that door to the left there, and the receptionist will get Ginny," Lucy instructed. "Anything else you want to ask?"

"You're not going in with me?" It sounded childish, but he would feel more at ease if the girls were with him.

Clementine glanced at her watch. "Geez Louise, we're going to be late for school if we don't get a move on."

"I can't be late again," Lucy called out as she started down the road. "Mrs. Thornburg will have my head on a platter if I'm not in my seat when the bell rings."

"I'm sorry, Mr. Elliott," April said as Clara dragged her away. "Truly, I am."

He grinned as the girls took off running. He could handle this. He only had to confirm Schmidt's death or begin to search the island for him. It was his mission after all. But it was also his chance to apologize to Ginny and make things right.

For some reason, getting into Ginny Mathis' good graces was the more important mission.

———— ≈ ————

"I need to speak to Officer Chapline," Belle said for what felt like the hundredth time. The problem was the boy behind the reception counter at the coast guard station. Billy Connor had dropped out of school last summer to enlist in the Guard when his teacher had threatened to hold him back again. "I have some information he'll want to know."

He leaned against the counter, a slight smirk on his face. "He has better things to do than talk to you, squirt. Besides, aren't you going to be late for school? You wouldn't want to have to do detention."

"This is more important." She glared at him. Billy had always antagonized the other kids at school, but he was sadly mistaken if he thought to bully her. "If Chapline isn't available, maybe I can talk to someone else. Is the second-in-command here?"

Billy snorted. "You're a stubborn little brat, so let's get this straight. There's no one here who wants to talk to a kid." He lifted the counter, then started toward her. "Now, get out of here before I call the police and have you hauled in for skipping school."

"Someone would have to dial the phone for you first," she snapped. She hated losing her temper, but she despised when people dismissed her because of her age. "In the time you've wasted arguing with me, he could get away."

"What's all this ruckus about?" A tall, middle-aged man in a starched uniform and spit-shined shoes thundered out from behind the counter and into the front room. "Who's going to get away?"

"Timothy Elliott." Belle ducked under Billy's meaty arm, then hurried toward the officer. "He's a British reporter. He was on the first boat the Germans sunk a little over a week ago. The *Allan Jackson*."

"Sir." Billy snapped to attention beside her. "This girl has a habit of sticking her nose in where it doesn't belong. If you like, I can drive her to school myself and report her to the principal for disciplinary action."

"No need for that. I'll tend to her."

"But, sir," Billy started.

"Go back to your filing, guardsman." The officer cut him off, then turned to Belle. "Would you follow me, please?"

"Yes, sir." Belle followed the officer, pausing once to give Billy a sweet smile. The military might be just what the boy needed to knock the meanness out of him.

For all the years she'd lived on the island, this was her first trip inside the coast guard station. The hallway was brightly lit, with photographs of previous guardsmen from the last century and the earlier part of this one. Offices sat on either side of the hall.

He led her into an office close to the front room, then

motioned her into a chair. "I'm Officer Darnell, one of Officer Chapline's aides, and you are?"

"Belle Mathis," she replied, sitting as though she were in church, hands on her lap and her legs crossed at the ankles. "You might know my sister, Ginny."

The man sat back in his leather chair. "Of course. I see the family resemblance. Ginny is a fine young woman, and her work for the coast guard has been exceptional."

So Ginny was secretly working for the coast guard. That was news to her. She made a note to grill her sister about it later. For now, there were more important things to deal with. "It's about a man that my friends and I found on the beach the afternoon after the first attack."

Mr. Darnell reached for a pad and paper. "And you said his name is Timothy Elliott?"

She nodded. "He's a British reporter working in New York. He was injured, but he didn't want to go to the infirmary, so we took him to the abandoned lighthouse keeper's house near Buxton."

"Who are we?"

"My Girl Scout troop." She named off everyone except for Ruthie. "We were afraid we could be in trouble because. . ." She hesitated. If Tim was on the wrong side of this war and they had helped him, they would be in serious trouble. Belle took a deep breath, then continued. "Tim is looking for a German officer who was traveling with him."

The man studied her from across his desk. "He told you this?"

"No. Well, yes, but he didn't mean to." She nervously fiddled with the end of her braid. "You see, he got a bad cut on his side during the attack, and I had to stitch him up, but for some reason he got a fever that afternoon, and it was so high and I was scared. . ."

"Belle." Officer Darnell gave her a comforting smile. "Slow

down. No one's in trouble. Just tell me when Mr. Elliott told you about the man."

"When he had a high fever."

"Good girl. Is Mr. Elliott still ill? Do we need to send an ambulance?"

She shook her head. "He's fine—at least he was yesterday when we took him dinner. Ginny didn't mention anything about him being sick last night when he showed up at the lighthouse, so I guess he's okay, though I don't know about this morning."

The officer's gaze sharpened. "What was he doing at the lighthouse with your sister?"

A knot lodged in Belle's throat. Had she said something wrong? The last thing she wanted was to get Ginny into hot water. "It wasn't a date or anything. Ginny didn't even know about him until he showed up at the lighthouse last night. I knew Tim wanted to see if she would help him get into the infirmary, but I wasn't sure how we were going to do that." She chuckled awkwardly. "You know Ginny. Such a stickler for rules."

The man scribbled on the pad. "I thought you said he didn't want to go to the infirmary."

"That's right, but then he changed his mind. He thinks the German might be there. Well, Ginny refused to do it, of course. She always knows the right thing to do." Belle leaned forward on the desk. "That's when he threatened to tell you the troop had been helping him. Ginny thought it might get us in trouble, and she didn't want our lives to be ruined."

"Is Mr. Elliott still at the house?"

She shook her head. "The girls took him to the infirmary this morning before school. They called Ginny into work early this morning, so he's supposed to meet her there."

Officer Darnell picked up his phone and dialed. "Yes, I need you two men over to the infirmary to pick up Ginny Mathis. If there's a man with her by the name of Timothy Elliott, bring him in too."

"Wait a minute." Belle flew to her feet, a little frantic. "Why are you bringing my sister in? She didn't do anything wrong."

Officer Darnell hung up the phone. "I just want to talk to her, Belle. I want to hear what exactly is going on. I'll take care of everything from here." He stood, walked over to the door, and opened it. "Guardsman Billingsly."

Belle froze. Why did he need a guardsman now? Was she in trouble after all? Was she about to be arrested? She hurried toward the door. "I've got to get going. I'm already late for school as it is."

A young guard joined them at the door. "Yes, sir?"

Belle slammed her eyes shut. She deserved whatever they were going to do with her. This would teach her to follow the rules rather than jump into any adventure that came along.

"Could you see Miss Mathis to school?" The man's voice was kind. "And let her principal know that she's been in a meeting with me."

Belle snuck a peek and found both men smiling at her. "You're not going to arrest me?"

"No." Officer Darnell placed a gentle hand on his shoulder. "But a piece of advice—always call us when you find an injured person on the beach. With this war, we must be cautious of anyone we're not familiar with. Is that understood?"

"Yes, sir." She turned to leave, then stopped. "And Ginny? She's not in trouble, right?"

"I'm just going to talk to her," he replied, then nodded to the guardsman. "Now, you need to get going."

"But. . ."

The officer gently nudged her into the hall, then closed the door. Belle stared at the wood grain. If she flung herself against it, would Officer Darnell come out and give her the answer she wanted?

"Miss? Are you ready?"

Belle turned, then nodded. She'd never planned to get Ginny in trouble, but things never went according to plan, at least not for her. Next time, she ought to follow Ginny's advice and pray before acting on her ideas.

She'd start now on her way to school.

⊨ CHAPTER 10 ⊨

Crossing the road, Tim pulled his coat around him, the wind off the ocean beginning to pick up. Reaching the door to the clinic, he opened it and walked inside. The reception area was well lit with chairs lined up in rows. A group of people, probably a patient's family, huddled in one corner, their eyes glassy from lack of sleep. He said a quick prayer for them, then approached an older lady sitting at a desk by the entrance to the patient area.

As he moved toward her, she glanced up at him over wire-rimmed glasses and smiled. "May I help you?"

"Yes, I have a bit of a problem." He glanced down at his arm. "I was on one of the boats that was attacked offshore. I've been staying in one of the houses down by the beach for the last few days, but my arm doesn't feel right, and I have a cut that needs looked at." After what had happened with Ginny, he'd promised himself he'd be truthful whether it put him in a bad way or not.

The woman studied him. "Why didn't you come to the infirmary before now? That cut could be infected."

"I know. I simply didn't think I was injured that severely, and so many men on the boat were burned. . ."

Her gray pin curls bounced as she nodded. "You must have been on the tanker."

"Yes, ma'am."

She glanced down at her appointment book. "A few days ago, we had patients in the tents out there, but with no attacks in the last few days, I believe we can fit you in."

"I'm supposed to meet with Nurse Mathis. She said to come by anytime."

The woman smiled up at him. "You know our Ginny? She's a lovely girl and an extremely good nurse, or she will be once she graduates. I've known her since she was just a baby." She tilted her head to one side. "Her mother and I quilt blankets for shut-ins at our church."

His inquisitive nature needed answers. "What was she like as a child?"

"Oh, she was sweet-natured, very much the apple of her father's eye. And such a tomboy! She'd rather be out fishing than learning how to sew or knit." She leaned closer. "Now, tell me, what part of Great Britain are you from?"

"Dungworth. It's about a stone's throw from Sheffield."

"A quaint little village, Sheffield." Her smile grew wider. "My husband surprised me with a trip for the coronation in thirty-seven. How long has it been since you were home?"

"A while, ma'am." Seven years to be precise. First, there'd been university, then the position in London with the *Times*. By the time the war started, there was no home to return to. His grandparents had passed, and the farm he'd grown up on had been auctioned off to pay off debts. He'd had nothing left but Iris and her boy. It had made it easy to take the job with British Intelligence, writing propaganda to sway the Americans' feelings toward the war. Never would he have thought he'd be pushed into the field.

Tim gave himself a mental shake. Time to focus on the mission. "Could you let Nurse Mathis know I'm here?"

"Of course." She picked up the phone and dialed. "Miss McCullough, this is Mrs. Pierce at the front desk. I have a young man here who has an appointment with Ginny Mathis. Could you let her know?" She nodded. "Thank you very much." Hanging up the phone, she waved him toward the seats. "She's finishing up with a patient at the moment, so it'll be a few minutes."

"Thank you."

After a quick survey of the area, he chose a seat near the door leading further into the infirmary. He felt on edge, as if waiting for something to happen, not quite sure what that something was. He scrubbed his hands across his face. This was not how he'd envisioned his life when he'd decided to become a reporter. A nine-to-five job was what he was after, with a flat large enough to suit the wife and maybe a kid or two. Like hundreds of thousands of other people, he hadn't planned on a war.

A discarded newspaper on the chair beside him caught his eye. Picking it up, he scanned the headlines. Ocean liner attack. Almost two hundred people feared dead. He tossed it down. Would Schmidt's information have saved those people? He didn't know. But there was the chance it could have made a difference, and that was enough for the moment. Tim bowed his head slightly. *Lord, I've made a lot of mistakes over the past few days. Please forgive me. Please help Ginny to forgive me, and help me find Rolf Schmidt, in Jesus' name. Amen.*

He lifted his head as the door opened and Ginny Mathis walked out. She looked professional and simply lovely in her white nurse's uniform. Her golden mop of hair had been pulled back into a white crocheted snood, a crime if he had anything to say about it. She glanced around, her eyes widening as he stood. She hurried over to him.

"Mr. Elliott," she whispered as she stole a glance at Mrs. Pierce and then stepped closer. "I was under the impression we would be meeting this afternoon."

He nodded. "We were, but when I heard many of the survivors were being released today, I thought it wise to move up our appointment."

She sighed, fidgeting with her hands as she thought. "I guess we can move your appointment up—but understand something. I have a lot of patients to tend to today, and I won't allow you to interfere with their care."

"I understand."

She gave him a slight nod. "Then come with me."

Tim hurried to the door, opening it for her. She gave him an uncomfortable look. "Thank you."

He followed her, the harsh smells of iodine, ammonia, and infection stinging his nose. Empty makeshift pallets lined the hallway while cards with the names of the patients were taped on the walls above. They went through another door that opened to a massive room. The patient areas were divided by thick curtains that stretched from floor to ceiling with beds in each one. In the center of the room, several desks had been pieced together to provide an area for the doctors and nurses to chart or store medication.

"If you'll follow me." Ginny walked to what looked like a small office, then closed the curtains around them as soon as he was inside. "I've checked all the patients who came in with broken arms, and none of them meets the description of your German."

"He's not my German." Stepping closer, he lowered his voice so only she could hear him. "How do you know he's not here? For all we know, Rolf speaks perfect English and could pass himself off as one of us. I'm the only one who has ever seen the man."

"Then how do you suggest we do this?" she asked in a no-nonsense tone.

This prickly Ginny wouldn't do at all. Reaching for her hand, he held it between his. "Listen, I'm sorry about the way I behaved last night. I wouldn't hurt your sister or her friends for anything in this world. I wouldn't want anyone to threaten my sister, and it was wrong for me to do that to you." He glanced down at her. "Can you forgive me?"

Her expression softened and he felt her fingers relax. "I appreciate that, Mr. Elliott. Belle can be a handful at times, which makes me worry."

"I know the feeling. My sister was three years behind me and was always in a tangle." He gave her what he hoped was an encouraging smile. "But she turned out fine, and it's my impression Belle will too." Tim wasn't sure how she would respond, but he felt he needed to offer. "If you don't feel comfortable doing this, I understand."

"No, it's all right. I thought about it this morning, and if this man has a way to help the Allies, then he needs to be found." She met his gaze. "Which is why I've decided to help you."

"Thank you." Tim squeezed her hand, then released it. Ginny Mathis truly was an extraordinary person. Under any other circumstances, he would've liked to have asked her for coffee or maybe dinner. But now? It just wasn't possible. "You know how the unit works. How would you suggest we do this?"

"It would probably be best if I looked at your wounds first." Ginny pointed to the examination table against the wall. "If you'll remove your shirt, I can recheck your shoulder. Are there any other injuries I should know about?"

"Well, I did get a small cut." He removed his shirt and hung it up before sitting on the table. "Belle stitched it up, but I'd feel more comfortable with someone who has a little bit more experience."

"Belle did what?"

The startled look she gave him made it hard for him to keep a straight face. "She did a good job on it, though I feared she might faint a couple of times."

"I'm surprised she didn't." She studied the wound. "She passes out at the sight of blood. I can't believe she did this." She glanced up at him. "She did a really good job."

"You seem surprised."

"Honestly, I am." Ginny walked over to the supply cart, found whatever it was she'd been looking for, and brought it back to the table. "The truth is, Belle and I haven't been on great terms since I came home from college. I don't know what to do to make things like they were."

"You can't turn back time, Ginny."

"What do you mean?" Her fingertips brushed his skin as she pressed a cotton square to his wound, and he hissed softly. Concerned eyes met his. "Does that still hurt?"

No way could he tell her the light touch had sent shock waves up his spine. "Maybe a little, but nothing to worry about." He cleared his throat. "Don't worry about Belle. You'll figure things out over time."

Ginny finished the exam, then turned to throw trash away while he redressed. When she returned, she slipped something from her pocket and unfolded it. "I've gone through our patient list for the last few days." She handed it to him. "I didn't see anyone named Schmidt on the list, but that doesn't mean anything. We have several patients who haven't been identified yet."

That was encouraging. Maybe Schmidt was among them. He buttoned the last button on his shirt and tucked in the tails. "Is there any way I could see them? Do you know what ship these people were on when they were attacked?"

She gave him a slight smile as she pointed to markings she'd made. "I thought you might need that information. The red dots are the ones who came off the *Allan Jackson*."

Tim studied her. She really was a gem. "What made you

change your mind about helping me?"

She stepped closer, her light scent of sea salt and lavender filling his lungs and invading his senses. "The night after the *Allan Jackson* sunk, an ocean liner full of people was attacked. There were over three hundred people on that boat. One of them was this sweet lady, probably about my age. She kept asking where her little girl was. She was five years old and asleep in their compartment when the boat was torpedoed. I went with her to the morgue to identify her daughter." She pressed her lips together to keep them from trembling. "If we can save one life by finding this man, then we should do everything we can to locate him."

A lump formed in his throat. Ginny wasn't being insincere. There was real concern and care for these victims in her voice. He admired that, admired her vulnerability and her care for these people. It was a trait lacking in the world today. "Thank you."

Her cheeks turned a delicate shade of pink, and Tim had to clasp his hands to keep from trailing his finger down the gentle curve. As if she could read his thoughts, her blush deepened. She stepped back and cleared her throat. "We should probably get started."

"Good idea. We should."

Tim followed her as they entered the ward. He'd not dated in the almost three years since his brother-in-law had died. The pain etched on Iris' face as she'd laid her love to rest had convinced Tim that he could never inflict that kind of pain on the woman he loved. He'd met women, had even shared a kiss or two, but he had never felt anything like this. He was attracted to Ginny, but it wasn't simply her looks or her figure. It was something else, something he couldn't quite name, an enigma of sorts, but it called to the deepest part of his soul.

Ginny turned him at the first curtain. "Let me see if my patient doesn't mind a visitor. It will only take a minute."

The curtains rustled around her as she disappeared. Tim listened to snippets of the conversation through the thick cloth, then heaved a disappointed sigh. The man's voice was too high and timid to speak with the authority of an officer in the Third Reich. When Ginny invited Tim inside a few moments later, his suspicions were confirmed.

Tim stepped to the foot of the bed. "I'm sorry to have disturbed you so. You're not the man I'm looking for, but you do look familiar." He turned to Ginny. "I think he worked in the boiler room."

She made a notation on her clipboard.

"Boiler room." The man in the bed didn't look surprised. "That sounds about right. I knew I wasn't from around here, and even if I was, I don't have much in the way of family."

Ginny gave her patient a sympathetic smile. "You'll start to remember more soon. It can take a while."

"Thank you, precious." He took Ginny's hand and squeezed it. "You just keep praying for me."

"Of course I will." Ginny returned the squeeze, then let go. "I've got to check on the rest of my patients, but I'll be back to see you."

"I'll be waiting."

Once she secured the man's privacy, she gave Tim a big smile. "Thank you. He's felt adrift wondering who he is. What you just did may be the catalyst that helps him regain his memories."

"Anything I can do to help." He preened as they walked to the next cubicle. "I was thinking. Rather than disturb your patients, maybe we should start in the morgue."

"That's a good idea. Maybe it would help if you gave me a description," she replied. "If we could weed out those who don't match Rolf's description, then we can focus on the ones who do." The smile she gave him made his heart hammer. "So?

What does he look like?"

Tim thought for a moment, trying to come up with the words to describe Rolf, and drew a blank. He chuckled. "I'm a reporter, but for the life of me, I'm drawing a blank."

"Okay, then. I'll play reporter." Ginny pulled a pencil and a small notebook from her pocket. "What color hair does he have?"

Hair? Tim shook his head. "He always wore a hat."

She touched the tip of the pencil to her lips. "Even with a hat on you can tell what color hair they have. Was it dark or light? Was he a blond like me?"

"Blond, but definitely not as pretty as you." Her slight smile felt like a blessing. "He was gray around the temples, and he had blue eyes. Aryan."

"Aryan? I never heard that used to describe someone."

"You'll be hearing that term used more in the coming months. Hitler favors these types." Tim scoffed, disgust roiling his stomach. "And has a deep hatred for others."

"I don't understand."

Word of Hitler's death camps had not reached the United States yet despite the fact they had been in existence for almost ten years. Maybe this was the story he should be writing instead of propaganda pieces the Intelligence department paid him to write. He spared a glance at the woman beside him. He would break the news to her later, once they found Rolf. Just not now.

Tim took her arm and led her back to the hallway. "Schmidt is about my height and build, and he has a habit of walking with his left hand in his pocket. Rumor is that he has arthritis and believes it's a sign of weakness."

"That's strange." Ginny crinkled her nose. "There are medications and exercises he can do to help with that."

Leave it to her to want to heal the man. "One last thing. He has a thick accent and speaks in a very commanding way. He's used to others taking orders from him, so it's his natural way of speaking."

"A no-nonsense type of man," she said. "I've known a few of those in my life."

The thought of Ginny having to deal with someone like Rolf gave him the urge to protect her. "Do they still bother you?"

Her throaty chuckle filled the air. "Only my dad, and deep down, he's a teddy bear."

"Good." He breathed a sigh of relief. "You don't seem like the type who likes being ordered around."

"Only when my sister has been up to no good."

"But I told you I was. . ." He caught the teasing glint in her eyes, then laughed. "You almost had me there for a second."

She gave him a smile, then glanced at her list. "I can tell you with absolute certainty that we haven't had anyone who matches this description brought to the infirmary."

Tim scrubbed his chin with his hand. "It's what I was afraid of. Without him, we don't know what the Germans are planning in the Atlantic."

"Don't give up. Just because he's not here doesn't mean he's dead." She glanced at her colleagues before turning back to him. "He could be at the infirmary in Ocracoke, or maybe he's holed up in a beach house just like you were. There are a hundred places he could be."

There was one possibility Ginny hadn't suggested. "Could someone on the island have taken him in?"

He could tell by her expression that the thought had never occurred to her. "Why would anyone here harbor a German, especially with everything going on off the coast?"

"There are Nazi sympathizers here in the United States, Ginny. Some are even sending their sons to Germany to fight for Hitler."

Her breath caught, and then she shook her head. "This is a small community, Tim. If someone was helping your German, everybody on this island would know about it. It's one of the few things about our island I dislike, everyone knowing everybody else's business."

"That's how it was in Dungworth, the little village where I grew up. I hated it at first, but after my grandparents passed, I missed the sense of community that had always been a part of my life." He paused. Was that why he liked this place so much? Because he could feel the sense of community and lifelong relationships he found himself missing at times? He glanced at Ginny. Or maybe he was ready for someone special.

If only the timing were right. Tim met her gaze. "Is the morgue nearby?"

"It's in the back of the building." She put her notebook away. "Let me tell the girls where I'm going, and then I'll walk you over."

After she told the other nurses she was on break, they walked down the hallway toward the back entrance. Before she opened the connecting door, she pulled her coat from a peg nearby, then handed him a men's jacket. "The coast guard brought in air conditioners and blocks of ice to keep the bodies until the next of kin could be located."

A blast of frigid air almost stole his breath when she opened the door. The harsh smell of formaldehyde hung like a heavy perfume in the air. There was a stillness here, almost a peacefulness, that stood in sharp contrast to the way they died. He moved down the aisle, the sound of his steps against the tile echoing throughout the room. Buckets of ice lined the room as did rows of sheet-covered bodies, the outlines of death stark beneath the cotton shrouds.

"I hate coming here." Ginny turned on the overhead light. "This place makes me feel like such a failure."

"Death comes for us all," Tim replied, trying to comfort her in any way he could. "What matters is that we're prepared to meet our God when it does."

"I know." She sighed. "I went to nursing school to help people, not sit around unable to do anything. We've had so many young people in here this week, and I just wish I could give it more time."

Tim nodded. The news of his father's death when he was in the newsroom last year made him feel the same way. All he'd wanted was more time. A chance to make things right with him. It was part of the reason he'd accepted the position in New York. He wanted to give someone else the chance he lost with his father.

He gently took Ginny's arms. "Perhaps we'd better get started."

"The sooner we've checked everyone here, the sooner we can leave this place," Ginny replied with a weak smile.

The next hour was a somber experience. With as much respect as the moment deserved, they uncovered each victim, each reflecting on the life that was lost. As Ginny secured the sheet over the last victim, Tim walked outside to the hallway. Why couldn't the Germans have waited to strike until he got Schmidt to New York? Then the Allies would have known how to stop the attacks.

The door opened behind him. She leaned on the wall beside him. "Those people in there, it's not your fault they died."

Maybe not, but it was Ginny's job to comfort. He pushed off the wall and turned to her. "If Rolf isn't here or in the infirmary, he's drowned, and his body hasn't washed up onshore yet."

"He could be in Ocracoke. We could call their infirmary right now and check. Don't give up hope," Ginny reassured him. "Sometimes, it just takes time."

"I'm out of time," Tim bit out as he started to pace. His superiors would have certainly heard about the attack as well as his and Schmidt's disappearance by now, which meant someone was on their way to take over. If they did find the officer, he would take the action as a breach to their agreement and disappear in the wind.

Still, he had no right to bark at Ginny that way. "It seems as if I've spent my day apologizing to you."

"Don't worry about it." She gave him a teasing smile as she started down the hallway. "I live with a teenage girl, remember?"

He grimaced. "I hope I'm better than that."

"Maybe a little."

He chuckled softly as he joined her. "I don't remember Iris being as outspoken as Belle, though I suppose she was at any given moment."

"Iris? Is that your sister?" Ginny flipped off the lights in one of the rooms, then rejoined him. "Belle said she lived in London."

"Yes. She was a handful like your sister, but she turned out okay. She moved to London when she and George were married. George died not long after the war started. Nearly broke Iris' heart. But she had Will to think of, so she stayed in London. Of course, that's different now. Will stays with his grandparents in Sheffield when his mother works at Bletchley Park."

Her eyes crinkled up at the corners when she smiled. "How old is your nephew?"

"Five going on twenty if the stories his grandparents tell have any truth to them. I'm afraid he's going to be a handful like his mother."

"It sounds like you adore him."

"Yes, I guess I do." Tim thought of the last picture of Will he'd received. The towheaded toddler had become a young boy. "I haven't seen him in over a year."

Warmth seeped through his sleeve and collected in the vicinity of his chest as she touched his arm. "Maybe this will be over soon, and you can go home."

It wasn't true of course, but it was a lovely idea to hold on to. He smiled at her. "That would be nice, wouldn't it?"

Ginny started to speak when the doors of the infirmary banged open. Two men wearing military uniforms burst through the doors with their pistols drawn. "Timothy Elliott?"

He shoved Ginny behind him. "Who's asking?"

The man took another step closer, and Tim caught sight of the emblem on the man's arm, the initials MP in large black letters. Military police. "We need you to come with us. Officer Chapline would like to talk to you."

Who had contacted the coast guard regarding him? He stiffened at the thought that it could be the woman he was protecting. Glancing over his shoulder, he caught her startled expression. "Did you do this?"

"No, of course not." Ginny pulled away from him, then walked over to where the soldiers stood. She nodded toward the weapons. "This is a hospital. We have enough on our plate without you shooting that thing off."

She was a gutsy little thing. He admired her for that, but he would do anything to keep her out of danger. He lifted his hands. "I'll answer a few questions if you'll holster your guns."

"All right." The men holstered their guns, then one grabbed a set of handcuffs off his belt. "Hands behind your back, sir."

Ginny pushed the cuffs away. "He said he'd go with you."

"Standard procedure, ma'am." The soldier stepped forward. "Mr. Elliott?"

Tim turned around, his hands at the base of his spine as the soldier placed the cuffs on him. "Don't worry, Ginny. I'll clear this up with their superior."

The other soldier turned to her. "Are you Miss Virginia Mathis?"

Tim tried to jerk around, but the man held him in place. "Why do you want to know who she is?"

"It's all right, Tim," she answered, but there was a slight tremor in her voice. "Would Officer Chapline like to speak with me too?"

"Yes, ma'am."

Tim heard her sharp intake of breath and felt like a heel. "She hasn't done anything wrong."

But the soldier ignored him. "Miss Mathis, Officer Chapline would like to see you in his office within the hour. He's anxious for your report."

Report? The pieces began to fall into place. Her nightly visits to the lighthouse. The map and pens she'd brought with her last night. He jerked around, pinning her with his gaze. "You work for the coast guard?"

"No, I just. . ." She glanced at the soldiers, then back at him. "I'm not at liberty to say anything."

"Don't worry. I have my answer." Disappointment lodged in his chest. He'd been skeptical as Belle went on about Ginny's qualities, but meeting her had confirmed everything she'd said and more. He'd thought her an open book with a ferocious loyalty to her family and friends. Yet even she had secrets.

"Come on, Elliott." The younger soldier took his arm and pulled him toward the door.

"Where are you taking him?" Ginny asked as the four of them walked through the ward and into the adjoining hallway.

"The coast guard station for now."

The faint scent of lavender he would always associate with her surrounded him as she came up beside him. "I will get this cleared up."

He didn't answer but simply walked away.

The oar cut through the shallow waters of Pamlico Sound, pushing the lifeboat toward its final destination. It had been a long journey, navigating the small vessel through Hatteras Inlet with many stops along the way to steal food and water. His brother had assured him the foliage in Buxton Woods would shroud their activities at the fishing camp that was set up according to his specifications. Then the second phase of his plan would commence.

The last week had been more difficult than he'd hoped, with one exception. Timothy Elliott had responded to the attack just as he'd expected. Elliott wasn't the type to leave a man on a sinking boat, and as expected, Tim had thrown him overboard in an effort to save him. The plan hinged on the man doing the right thing, and he had.

Now it was time to focus on the next phase of the mission. He studied the shoreline. Seagrass danced in the light wind against the land, the waterline a mixture of trees and small brush. Even in the cold, the air held an earthy quality, and he could almost taste the salt in the air.

The sea had been his home ever since he joined the navy some twelve years ago. No woman held his fascination like the waters of the Atlantic.

Now he must defend it for his country.

A fisherman casting his line caught his attention, and he steered his boat closer. Glancing up and down the shoreline, he called out, "Good fishing?"

"The best I've ever seen."

The wind swallowed up Rolf's laughter. The plan was a go. He jumped into the hip-deep water and grabbed a rope, dragging the lifeboat to shore. Once there, he overturned it and sank it deep into the water. He then turned to find the man standing at attention, the fishing pole on the ground.

Rolf raised his right hand. "Heil Hitler!"

"Heil Hitler!" the man repeated, then smiled. "Brother, it's good to see you."

The second phase of Rolf's plan was under way.

≡ CHAPTER 11 ≡

Ginny paced from one corner of the room to the other, fisting then stretching her hands as she tried to put the last few hours in focus. Belle must have alerted the coast guard that Tim was at the infirmary. It was the only way any of this made sense. No one else knew about their impromptu meeting at the lighthouse except for Belle, and knowing her, she figured reporting Tim to the authorities would keep her and the other girls out of trouble.

What really bothered her was the way Tim had looked at her as the military police had loaded him into the car. It was as if she had betrayed him somehow. How could that be? They had only met two days ago. He didn't even know her, though it felt easy to be around him, as if they'd known each other for months rather than minutes. She stopped to stare out the window. Why did it hurt that the man had such a low opinion of her?

The door to the office clicked open, then Officer Chapline stepped inside. "Good afternoon, Ginny."

She wasn't in the mood for pleasantries. Ginny turned to face him. "Why was I brought here? I had patients to attend to."

"Why don't you take a seat, and we'll get started."

His calmness irritated her. She marched over and took the chair directly in front of his desk. "You didn't answer my question."

"We'll get to that in a moment." He opened the folder, perused it, then turned his attention to her. "I want to know exactly when you found Mr. Elliott."

"I thought Belle would've told you." She sat at the edge of her chair, her nerves wound so tight, she was ready to spring like a jack-in-the-box.

"I'd like to hear it from you."

He seemed so calm, far cooler than what she felt at the moment. Maybe he was just looking for answers like she was. "He showed up at the lighthouse last night. That was the first I knew anything about him."

"You didn't know your troop of Girl Scouts had hidden him at the old lightkeeper's house?"

Ginny knew it looked bad, but they were thirteen, old enough to know better than to do something like that, particularly now. "I will keep a closer watch on them from now on."

He closed the file, then sat back in his chair. "What did Elliott want?"

"You know what he wanted," she answered, then scoffed when he just sat there. "He wanted access to the infirmary and the morgue so he could look for the same German we're looking for."

Chapline's expression turned interested. "Did he find him?"

She shook her head. "I knew Schmidt hadn't been in the infirmary. We haven't had anyone with any significant kind of accent, but the morgue was another story. Tim was able to confirm that Rolf Schmidt isn't among the dead."

The man drew in a deep breath and sighed, disappointed. "Which means he's either lost at sea or found a place along the beach like Elliott did and is holed up there."

"Maybe, but there is a third option."

His brow crinkled. "What would that be?"

As much as she dreaded the possibility, they had to consider it. "Someone on the island knows who he is and is helping him."

"That's a bit far-fetched."

"Maybe, but there's a big difference in Tim's situation and in Rolf's. Tim had help finding shelter and having his wounds tended to. I learned from Tim that Schmidt has a heavy German accent. That would have caught someone's attention if he came across anyone. That only leaves someone who knows him."

Chapline didn't look convinced. "I guess anything can happen."

Well, she had to bring up the possibility. No one thought the Japanese would bomb Pearl Harbor either. "Sir, with your permission, I'd like to contact the Ocracoke infirmary and see if they've seen anyone matching Schmidt's description."

He seemed surprised. "You have one? No one seems to know what the man looks like."

"Tim does. He interviewed Schmidt a few years ago for an article, but it was never published." She smiled at the memory of Tim's vague description. "I will say it's not very detailed."

"Better than the one we have now." He leaned back and studied her. "You managed to get more information out of Elliott than I have so far." He gave her a shy smile. "But then, I'm not as pretty as you are."

Ginny let the comment pass. She had heard the rumors that the liaison officer had shown some interest in her, but that was as far as things had gone. She liked William. He was a good man. He just wasn't the man for her.

He cleared his throat. "There's something else I need to discuss with you."

Oh no. She threw out a quick prayer. *Please, Lord, don't let him ask me for a date.* Ginny gave him a tight smile. "And that would be?"

He met her gaze. "I hate to do this, but I have to relieve you of your duties at the infirmary."

"What?" His statement sent tiny shockwaves through her. "Why?"

"Elliott blackmailed you to get him into the infirmary, and while I completely understand your concern for your sister, it's a dangerous situation to be placed in. Besides, the position was voluntary, so you won't lose any pay. Of course, the job at the ferry is still yours so you can continue to support your family."

Ginny blinked back tears. Nursing was more than a job to her. It was her mission in life, a way to help people during a difficult time while using the talents and skills God had given her. The thought of not seeing her patients tomorrow felt like a part of her soul had been ripped out and stomped on.

"There is something I'd like for you to do instead."

"What would that be?" she asked through trembling lips.

"I would like for you to pair up with Elliott and look for Schmidt."

Ginny wasn't sure she'd heard him right. "You want me and Tim to work together?"

He nodded. "Yes."

Of all the crazy. . .She straightened in her chair. "The man refuses to look me in the eye right now, so I don't think he's going to be happy to work with me."

"I think we can change his mind."

If the expression on Tim's face as he was being driven away was anything to go by, his mind was already made up. "Have you asked him about this yet?"

"No, but I'm certain when I point out the positives of such an arrangement, he'll agree to it."

"I wouldn't be too sure about that."

Officer Chapline reopened the file in front of him. "Do you know why Elliott did this assignment? He has a personal connection with Rolf Schmidt." He must have noticed she was about to respond because he continued. "Besides the article he wrote. Schmidt is credited with sinking a ship Elliott's father was commanding. All hands were lost."

Ginny's heart ached for Tim. To have lost his father and his brother-in-law. No wonder he'd been desperate to find Schmidt.

"If Schmidt is here on the island, then I believe you and Elliott are our best chance at finding him. He has personal knowledge of the German, and you know pretty much everyone on this island, which means you both can move around together without anyone questioning his presence."

She didn't want to admit it, but his idea had merit. Still, she couldn't give the man an answer until she talked to Tim and heard what he had to say. "Where's Tim now?"

"He's in a holding cell downstairs. We can't let him go until we get verification of his identity from New York."

So Tim was stuck here overnight. He must hate her. "Can I see him?"

"He's not exactly your biggest fan right now."

She shouldn't have expected anything less, yet she had. Maybe because she'd hoped for the same kind of forgiveness he'd asked for just this morning. "He thinks I betrayed him."

"Yes, I know. He thinks you should've told him about your work with us here."

"I only met the man two days ago." Yet it felt like she'd known him a lot longer, and she loved the way he let her tease him. The truth was, she liked the man.

Chapline rubbed the back of his head. "Your sister has been expounding on all of your good qualities, and I think that's influenced Elliott's feelings toward you."

"Belle talking good about me? That's a first." She chuckled. "Most of the time, she's too busy calling me a fuddy-duddy."

"Go talk to the man." He nodded toward the door before

135

grabbing another file. "One conversation might clear every-thing up."

It was the strangest assignment she'd ever received from Chapline, as if he almost cared whether she and Tim could get along. Of course he cared. He wanted Schmidt found and jailed. Ginny picked up her purse and knapsack and then stood.

"Remember, Ginny," the officer called out as she opened the door. "Work with Elliott, not against him."

Easier said than done. Tim may not want to work with her at all. After leaving the office, she took the stairs down to the first level, then was directed to the far corner of the building. As she walked down the hall to the holding cells, a young soldier came to attention as she neared.

Ginny stopped in front of him. "I'm Virginia Mathis, here to see Tim Elliott."

"Yes, ma'am." The man glanced over his clipboard, then gave a nod. "This way, miss."

The soldier walked her to a nearby room with a thick oak table and padded chairs. In the middle of the table, a coffee ser-vice with hot coffee and butter cookies had been prepared.

"I'll be right back with the prisoner," the guard said.

"He's not a prisoner," Ginny corrected him. "We're just wait-ing for verification of his identity."

"Yes, ma'am." The guard excused himself, then left.

Ginny went over to the table and sat down. Now, how was she going to convince him to work with her? She could remind him of all the positives of working with her, but was that enough to persuade him? Of course she'd tell him about her work as a coastal watcher and apologize for the situation at the infirmary.

She reached for two cups. Maybe she was looking at this all wrong. Tim's father must have meant the world to him for him to go to such lengths to bring Schmidt to justice. If she could make him see they stood a better chance of finding him working together instead of apart, Chapline's plan might stand a chance.

The door opened. Ginny glanced up as Tim walked in. He stopped, staring at her as if he'd never seen her before. There was no hint of forgiveness in his handsome dark eyes, and it struck her how badly she wanted it.

Maybe all she had to do was ask like he had this morning. Ginny swallowed. "Hi."

He didn't answer. Instead he walked around the table and sat down across from her. "Miss Mathis, are you here to gloat? Or did you just want to see what I looked like behind bars?"

For Pete's sake! Ginny picked up the coffeepot, poured some into a cup, then handed it to Tim. "I wasn't the one who told the coast guard about you."

"I find that hard to believe."

"Well, I didn't." Taking a napkin, Ginny took two sugar cookies from the plate and offered them to him. "Eat these. Maybe they'll sweeten up your disposition."

"I don't want biscuits, and my disposition is the way it is because you double-crossed me."

His accusation felt like a knife in the chest. She shook her head. "I'm sorry for whatever part I played in you being detained, but I'm telling you the truth. I didn't turn you in."

"Then who did?"

She leaned against the table. "I'm pretty sure it was Belle, and to a lesser degree, the girls. I made the mistake of telling Belle about our meeting the other night, and I think she wanted to protect me." She shrugged slightly. "They didn't know you never intended to turn them in."

"That does sound like something the girls would do." The hardness in his eyes began to soften. "And you work for the coast guard?"

"I'm a coastal watcher. I watch for attacks at the lighthouse and keep an eye out for anyone on the island who seems out of place. For my pay, I'm given volunteer hours at the infirmary." Ginny took a cookie from the tray and broke it in two. "At least I was."

Tim stared at her from across the table. "They took away your privileges."

"It's probably for the best," she replied, but really she didn't see how relieving her of her duties was in anyone's best inter-est. The staff was already stretched to the limit. Why wouldn't Chapline let her use her time and talents to help?

"I'm sorry. Anyone who has seen you with your patients would know you were born to it."

"Thank you." It was the kindest thing he could have said to her. "I'm sorry about all this. I should've known Belle was up to something." Ginny gave him a shy smile. "We seem to be apolo-gizing to each other a lot."

"Would you like to begin again?"

His offer eased the nervous tension inside her chest. She nod-ded. "That would be lovely."

The easy smile he gave her as he reached for the sugar made her stomach do a pleasant little flip. "I guess Chapline has talked to you about the two of us working together."

"I wasn't sure how you would feel about it after this morning," she replied, then popped a piece of cookie into her mouth.

"It does make sense. It would give me a chance to openly look around without sending everyone on the island into an uproar."

She chuckled. "No one would have made a peep about you, what with that delicious accent of yours. People would be coming up and introducing themselves just to hear you speak."

"You like my accent, huh?" His voice took on a gravelly tone, low and terribly attractive.

Oh goodness, if he kept talking like that to her. . .Ginny cleared her throat. "You get to go around unheeded. So what's in this deal for me?"

His eyes danced with mischief. "You get the pleasure of my company."

For some reason, the thought thrilled her, but it wouldn't do for him to know that. So she rolled her eyes. "Is that all?"

He laughed, a wonderfully deep sound that made her toes curl. She was going to have to guard her heart with this man. Tim held up his cup to her. "Partners?"

Ginny clinked her cup with his. "Partners."

☰ CHAPTER 12 ☰

Ginny turned her car into the driveway, then put it into park. Shutting the motor off, she leaned back into her seat and closed her eyes. This had been a bear of a day. Truly horrible in ways. First, the fiasco with Tim this morning and being relieved of her duties, then having to go to the infirmary to pick up her things and say goodbye to the staff and her patients. Worse still, her patient in bed two took a sudden turn and died before anything could be done to help him. Poor man. He had been a real sweetheart too. This was his last voyage before retiring to be with his wife, children, and grandchildren. Now he'd be buried thousands of miles away.

Her sigh echoed through the small confines of the car. She hated this part of the job, especially when it made no sense. This man had only done his job, delivering bananas and pineapples to New York City, and he was killed for it.

Finding Rolf Schmidt might put an end to these attacks.

Ginny stretched her neck. The only good thing about the day was she was back on good terms with Tim. After they'd worked through the situation this morning, they spent the next hour hammering out a plan to locate Rolf or confirm his demise. Tomorrow, she would contact the Ocracoke infirmary with a description of

Schmidt. Then she would pick Tim up after he was discharged, and they would go over what she'd learned at a local coffee shop. They would figure out where to go from there.

A knock on the glass caused Ginny to jump. She jerked her head around to find her sister making a silly face, the muted sound of girlish giggles seeping into the car.

Belle curved up her hand and held it to her mouth. "Well, are you going to roll down the window, or will I have to shout myself hoarse?"

Ginny struggled with the window but finally got it down. "I was taking a moment."

"Rough day?" Belle's voice softened. As much as she could be a pest, there was a tender side to her too. "I could send the girls home if you want."

She shook her head. It was their usual meeting today, which wouldn't take long. Besides, she wanted to talk to them about Tim and their activities since the first attack ten days ago. "I'll want to freshen up first."

"I'll get the girls some refreshments. We'll be in the kitchen waiting."

"Thank you. I won't need long."

Ginny watched as Belle rounded up the girls and corralled them inside. She had some ideas of how they could help in the search, but she would have to talk it over with Tim first. After what the girls had put him through, he might not want their help. Maybe she shouldn't involve the girls at all. They had enough on their plate with the ongoing fat and tin collection drives and cookie sale coming up. Those activities should keep them busy for the near future.

Decision made, Ginny grabbed her purse, knapsack, and lunch pail, then exited the car. A bracing northerly wind blew all thoughts of the day from her mind. By the time she'd freshened up and walked into the kitchen, her spirits had lifted.

Glancing around, she noticed the vanilla and chocolate cookies on the table. "I take it the Girl Scout cookies arrived."

"I tried to stop them," Belle said as she dunked a chocolate one in her milk. "But that was like stopping a horde of feral cats."

Ginny glanced at the open cardboard box beside the refrigerator. "Am I going to have to hide them like last year?"

"Maybe." Clem stacked a vanilla and chocolate one together, then took a bite. "It's just they're so good."

"You know you're going to have to pay for these," Ginny reminded them as she picked up the unopened boxes to carry to her room. How was she going to supervise cookie season on top of everything else? Selling the treats was almost a full-time job itself. With her job at the ferry and helping Tim with his search, it was almost a good thing she wouldn't be going to the infirmary anymore.

When Ginny returned from her room, the girls were cleaning up. "Belle, where's Momma? I thought she had the kids today."

"Mrs. Jones picked them up early. Momma must have got a check from Daddy, because she said she was going to the bank and then shopping," Belle replied, drying a plate.

"Good," Ginny answered. Then she could speak freely about the girls' dealings with Tim without her mother overhearing and getting worried. "If you're ready, let's get started."

Belle grabbed the small American flag from its place in the window, then turned to face the girls. "Attention. Salute. Pledge."

With their hands over their hearts, they solemnly faced the flag.

I pledge allegiance to the flag of the United States of America, and to the republic for which it stands, one nation, indivisible, with liberty and justice for all.

Pride for her country swelled inside Ginny as the words

flowed over her. People took their freedoms for granted sometimes. But despite their differences, they'd stood as one since the
attack on Pearl Harbor and would stand together until the boys
were safely home.

The girls recited the Girl Scout Promise, then returned to
their places at the table. Ginny stood at the head of the table,
looking down at their eager faces. They were the future of this
great nation, and she was humbled to play a small part in it.

"Have I told you how proud of you I am?"

The girls glanced at each other, then to Belle. Her sister looked
up at her. "Are you okay, sis?"

"I'm fine, and no, you're not in trouble," she teased and was
rewarded with a few nervous giggles. "So what's on the agenda
today?"

Clementine looked at her notes from the last meeting. "We're
supposed to organize our first fat drive for the war effort."

"You mean like bacon fat?" Lucy screwed up her nose. "What
are they going to use that for?"

"If you hadn't missed that meeting, you would know." Clem
gave the girl a quelling glance before continuing. "The military
needs fat, oil, and lard to make bombs and grease the guns on the
larger boats."

"Oh." Lucy grimaced. "It's still disgusting."

It was time to take over the meeting. "We need to set up a
schedule so folks will know when we'll be by to pick up their
donation. We don't know how long this war is going to last, so
until it's over, our boys need bombs."

"Should we combine the metal drive with this one? It might
make it easier on people if we only show up one day a month,"
Clara suggested.

"We may need to stretch that to every six weeks," Ginny
replied as she reached over and took the last vanilla cookie in the

package. "We'll have enough fat by then to turn in rather than have to find a place to store it."

"That works for me," Lucy whispered, looking slightly pale.

Ginny glanced around. "Where's April?"

"I went by her house so that we could walk here together, but she's helping out her dad today." Clara started to reach for a cookie then thought better of it. "Something about his ham radio."

Ginny nodded. Frank Smith was an enigma of sorts. He wasn't well known in their community, and she couldn't remember ever seeing him in church. In fact, she wasn't even sure she could pick him out of a crowd. April was a good girl and a good friend, and Ginny didn't want her to miss out on what her friends were doing.

Belle lifted her hand. "I'd like to make a suggestion. Something I think we should have been doing since the war started."

Ginny glanced at her sister. She couldn't remember Belle ever looking this serious. "What would that be?"

"I think that for the duration of the war we should pray for our country." Belle bit her lower lip as if she were unsure of herself. "Before this thing is over, a lot of the people we know will be sending people they love off to fight. We should ask the Lord to watch over our boys and to protect them and protect us too."

Ginny could barely swallow past the knot in her throat. Tim had been right. Belle was a good girl. She looked around. "What do you ladies think about that suggestion?"

"It's always good to pray." Clementine glanced around, her expression uncomfortable. "But I never seem to really know what to say."

"I felt the same way, but then my momma told me something that helped," Clara replied, tenderly resting her hand on Clem's forearm. "She said that when we can't find the words, Jesus is there praying right along beside us."

"That's lovely." Ginny would have to tuck that piece of advice away for those moments she didn't know what to pray. Her own relationship with God had been a bumpy one over the last few years, but since the bombing at Pearl Harbor, she had found herself turning to Him more and more. "Do you girls want to give this a try?"

Three of the girls nodded, but Lucy remained silent. "Lucy, why don't you want to pray?"

She shrugged. "I don't know. It just seems pointless at times."

Ginny knew exactly what the girl meant. "It can feel that way, but we have to just keep praying and watching for an answer from the Lord."

"But he never answers my prayers." There was something in Lucy's voice, almost like disappointment.

Ginny wasn't sure what to say. She'd felt the same way at times, but then she only had to look back at her life to see God's hand at work. Lucy was so new in her belief she might not have much to refer to.

Ginny reached out and took the girl's hand. "Lucy, do you remember the moment you asked Jesus to come into your heart?"

She nodded. "It was the Fourth of July, and it was so hot, everybody had their fans out, trying to get cool. I didn't ask Momma or Daddy if I could go—I just stepped out in the aisle and almost ran to the altar. I couldn't wait to be saved."

Ginny blinked back tears. "That was an answer to prayer. Yours and your parents."

"I never thought about it that way."

Ginny continued, "We have to hold on to these kinds of moments when our faith is weak and remember that God answers prayers."

Lucy nodded. "I'm not sure about it, but praying won't hurt."

This was something she would have to work out for herself.

Ginny straightened. "Since the majority voted to pray, I think we should start today." She nodded at Belle. "Since it was your idea, would you do the honors?"

Eyes closed, each girl bowed her head, and Ginny followed suit. Belle began, "Lord, we come to You today to ask for protection over our boys and to comfort their families during this separation. Bring peace to our nation. Help us to defend against our enemy. In Jesus' holy name I pray. Amen."

"Amen."

Silence fell over the room, each girl lost in her own thoughts. So much sacrifice already, Ginny thought, and the worst could be yet to come. She drew in a deep breath, then forced a smile. "Clementine, what's next on our list?"

The girl flipped over the paper. "We need to discuss how we can help the animals who are being affected by the attacks." She glanced up. "I was thinking that we could also collect lobster traps from folks all over the island and convert them into birdcages so we have a safe way to bring them home."

The girls discussed the issue and a few other projects. By the time they settled on a plan of action, two hours had passed. Ginny stood at the corner of the table. "All right, girls. We need to wind things up. But before we do, we need to talk about Mr. Elliott."

"Oh no. We're in trouble," Belle said under her breath.

"You're not in trouble. I know what you did for Tim Elliott, seeing to his wounds and taking care of him like you did. I only wish you would have talked to me about it."

"I'm sorry, Ginny," Belle replied. "We were just trying to help."

She gently touched her sister's shoulder. "I know. But as we discussed before, we're living in a dangerous time. There's a war going on right off our shores." She could see she was losing them, so she tried a different approach. "Anyway, what I wanted to say was that Tim will be staying on the island for now, and as long as your parents are all right with it, you can go see him."

Clementine had stopped writing and focused her attention on the discussion. "Are you sure he wants to see us?"

Belle stared up at the ceiling. "She's not going to like this."

"You mean the fact that you tricked him into going to the infirmary this morning, then had him arrested? Then you're right." Ginny studied each one of them. Guilt haunted their expressions. "I didn't like it. I lost my position at the infirmary because of it."

"Oh no," Lucy gasped.

"Is that why you were upset when you got home?" Belle stood and wrapped her arms around Ginny. "I told them you hadn't done anything wrong. Why would they do that?"

Ginny dropped a kiss on her sister's head. "It's all right. We worked everything out. Tim will be released as soon as his office sends him a new identification card. He'll stay at the lightkeeper's house until his new passport arrives. Until then, I'll be helping him find the German man he's been searching for."

"Wait a minute," Belle exclaimed, pulling away from her. "What about all that stuff you said about how we didn't know him and couldn't trust him? And now you're going to help him?"

"I did say that, didn't I?" Ginny swallowed. "I was wrong. I made a decision about Tim before I got to know him. Now I know that he's trying to stop the submarine attacks."

Clara eyed her. "So he's everything he said he was?"

"Yes." And more. Tim was funny and charming, not to mention attractive. But his stay here wouldn't last forever, and he'd sail home, leaving her with a broken heart. Well, she'd have to stay on guard.

"Is he mad at us?" Clem's question broke through her thoughts. "I mean, we did turn him in to the coast guard."

"Maybe we should apologize," Lucy suggested.

"That's a good idea. Maybe we could collect some firewood and have the house ready when he comes home," Belle said, her enthusiasm contagious. "Maybe we could bake him some brownies."

"You need to talk to Momma about that. She'll know what's being rationed." Ginny held out her hands for the girls to join her. "Now, let's dismiss."

Ginny watched as they gathered in a circle and sang. In this moment, everything felt right as rain.

▰ CHAPTER 13 ▰

Tim laid on the lumpy mattress, a sorry excuse for a pillow under his head. This was better than some jails he'd seen in his years reporting for the *Times*. His accommodations felt like Buckingham palace compared with Wormwood or Wakefield. Still, the warm comfort of the lightkeeper's house was more to his taste.

He sat up, stretched his back, and then stood. After days of being cared for by a bunch of Girl Scouts, he felt restless to get started. Sitting still had never been his strong suit. Even as a young boy, he'd spent hours walking Pop's farm, sometimes herding sheep, most of the time making trouble. But even that became boring after a time. It was probably why he decided to be a reporter, this need to be on the move.

For the moment, he needed to focus, but his mind kept drifting back to Ginny. She'd been so sweet with her apology yesterday, but he was coming to realize that was her character. He should have figured Belle would want to protect her sister. The girl idolized Ginny—the entire troop did. Without Belle's interference, he wouldn't be working alongside Ginny now. One day, he'd have to thank Belle.

Tim paced. He needed to think about their next move. It depended on what Ginny found out from her call to the Ocracoke infirmary. If Rolf wasn't in there or in their morgue, there were two possible options. Either he was dead and lost at sea, or more worrisome, he had made it to shore and someone had taken him in. But who? According to Ginny, no one on the island was German, but people could hide behind a new name. In fact, it was a common occurrence after the Great War. A thought struck him. Was it possible someone Rolf knew had been on the island since then? But that was over twenty years ago. Still, it was worth looking into.

A metal door clanged open, followed by footsteps and the melodious jingle of keys. "Mr. Elliott?"

Tim turned to find a boy not much older than Belle wrestling with the lock on the door. Once he opened it, the guard stood to one side. "Officer Chapline would like to speak to you, sir."

He ran his hand across his day-old beard. "I guess there's no time for a shave."

His humor was lost on the boy. Kid probably didn't shave yet. "My instructions were to bring you to my superior officer as soon as possible, sir."

"Of course." Tim grabbed his coat from the back of the chair and hurried to the door. What had taken Chapline so long to confirm his identity? A five-minute phone call to New York would've cleared the whole matter up. Instead, the officer had left him to sit in a cell overnight.

It was a short walk and a flight of stairs up to the liaison officer's office. Tim studied the room as the door clicked closed behind him. It was large with a comfortable-looking couch and chairs. Behind the couch was a large window that looked out over the ocean. As offices go, it was nice, but the view was what made it breathtaking.

The door opened again, and Chapline walked in. "I'm sorry to keep you waiting, Tim. The wire was down for most of the night. We just got it back up an hour ago. Your office sent us your information a few minutes ago."

"Good to know you weren't keeping me locked up for laughs," Tim replied, taking a seat across from him. "When are you going to release me?"

"You're free to go now if you wish."

Something told him that the meeting wasn't over, despite the fact he'd been freed. Tim leaned back in his chair. "What's on your mind, Chapline?"

He sat up, his arms resting on his desk. "Look, we're going to be working together, so you can call me Will."

"That will be easy to remember. I have a nephew named Will," Tim replied. "So what is it, Will?"

"Something Ginny said yesterday. I thought we were only looking at two options concerning Schmidt. Either he's dead or he's holed up somewhere on the island like you were." He massaged his forehead. "Then Ginny brought up the possibility that the whole thing could have been planned. That Schmidt knew the *Allan Jackson* would be attacked and saw it as a way to get on the island."

"And someone here, probably of German descent, was waiting for him." Tim glanced at him. "Do you have a census of the island? If we could go through it and find someone who might have moved here after the Great War, we might find Rolf."

"I can get one, but it's going to take some time." Will reached for his pen and made a note. "You think we have a German sympathizer in Buxton?"

"Maybe, but I think the more likely answer is someone who fought for Germany in the Great War." Tim thought for a moment. "I'd also like to take a look at the ledgers from Oregon Inlet. It's just a hunch I have, but I'd like to rule it out."

"Certainly. I'll have them delivered to you this afternoon." He made another notation. "Are you sure you want to stay at that old house? I could get you a nice motel right on the beach."

"Thanks, but I'm settled in there. Plus, it's close to the lighthouse." Tim had decided it was a good place to meet Ginny where they could go over their findings each day. It was also secluded, a good place to kiss a woman without the prying eyes of her Girl Scout troop watching.

"All right then. I'll have the last month of ledgers delivered there as well as some supplies this afternoon. I'll also see what I can do about getting the electricity turned on."

"Good." Tim rose. He was ready to get cleaned up and get some sleep. "I appreciate your help, Will."

The man stood and extended his hand. "If you need anything else, please let me know. We want to find this man and get the information he has."

"That's the goal." Tim took his hand and shook it. Now that they were all on the same page, they needed to find Rolf.

"Thank you. You've been a big help." Ginny hung up the phone and marked a check by the two remaining names on her list. There was no denying the truth. Everyone on the *Allan Jackson* had been accounted for except for Rolf Schmidt. But it was the other news that stole her breath. A report of stolen canned goods out of someone's pantry in Hatteras was filed around the same time as a report filed by two fishermen about a man oaring what looked to be a lifeboat through Hatteras Inlet a week ago. Could the two be connected? If they were, could Schmidt be the man who was seen?

There were only two choices. He'd holed up like Tim had, or someone was willingly helping him. But who in their tight-knit community would harbor the enemy?

"You're thinking mighty hard about something."

Folding the piece of paper she'd been working on, she glanced up as her friend Mary Frances joined her at the ticket desk. "The girls want to do a cleanup project at the beach, but with the coast guard patrols, I think we're going to have to put that on the back burner for now."

"That's too bad." She glanced at the inky black water beneath the ferry. "It still smells like a gas station around here, and we haven't had an attack in a while."

"Just the lull before another storm," Ginny replied. Tim had told her the reason for the pause in the nightly attacks was that the subs could only carry twelve torpedoes and had to reload along the coast in occupied France.

"Well, I'll take the lull." Taking out her compact, she reapplied her lipstick, then blotted it. "Those bombs ruined my beauty sleep."

"I don't sleep well, so it didn't bother me."

"You don't sleep? Then how in the world do you find the energy to keep up with those girls?" Stretching her legs, Mary Frances slumped back into the chair. "By the end of the day, all I want to do is take a bath and go to sleep."

"That would be lovely." The thought of a nice hot bath scented with lavender oil sounded wonderful right now. The temperature had dropped ten degrees in the last hour, and she'd lost the feeling in her fingers.

Mary Frances eyed her. "Why do you think you can't sleep?"

"I don't know. Maybe I have a lot on my mind."

Or maybe she just had Tim on her mind. He was supposed to call her when he was released, but it was almost the end of her shift and she'd heard nothing from him. Had there been a problem with his paperwork? Was the coast guard keeping him another night? No, Chapline would have called her if there was.

Maybe she should go by there after her shift. At least then she could tell him what she learned from her phone call to Ocracoke. Where was Tim, and why hadn't he called her?

Mary Frances snapped her fingers, startling Ginny. "Were you listening?"

Ginny drew in a deep breath, trying to push her thoughts of Tim to the background. "I'm sorry. I just have a lot on my mind between work and my troop and now cookie sales."

"Girl, you need a night out." Mary Frances' ruby red lips stretched in a wide smile. "And I've got just the guy for you. He's a naval officer, kind of cute but a really sweet guy. We could drive over to Kitty Hawk. I heard they opened a USO there. We could go dancing. Anything to let off a little steam."

Just listening to her talk made Ginny exhausted. She wasn't a great dancer, and large crowds only made her feel boxed in. Her idea of a night out was having a crab bake by the shore.

"Saturday is the only day I have to help Mom around the house, and Sunday is church, then dinner with my family. So you see, I don't really have time to go dancing."

"Come on, Ginny. We work like a pair of dogs around here." Mary Frances waved at two sailors boarding the ferry, then turned back to her. "We deserve to have some fun."

Only, what her friend was suggesting didn't sound like fun to her. Besides, she had too much to do. "I'm sorry. I just can't right now."

"I understand." She gave Ginny a sympathetic smile. "But I'll keep asking you. Just because we're in a war doesn't mean we can't enjoy ourselves every now and then."

"I know, and I do appreciate you asking." Ginny glanced down at her watch. "I'd better get out there. The ferry is set to arrive in a few minutes."

"I'd better get back at it too." Her expression turned solemn. "I heard the infirmary was shipping a bunch of patients inland this afternoon. I'm glad to see them leaving rather than coming in."

"Me too." Ginny sighed. The plans to transfer patients had been in the works for a few days now, and she should have been on the team that would transport them to Chapel Hill, then return. But the decision to release her from her volunteer position had changed all that. Had they had enough trained professionals to transfer patients while nurses watched those who were left behind? They were running low on nurses, and her swift departure had put more stress on them.

"If we keep having these attacks, we may have to consider building a hospital. I heard you can't even get into the infirmary unless you have an appointment now." Mary Frances pointed out the window. "You'd better get out there. I see the ferry, hon."

Folding the paper, Ginny stuffed it in her pocket and rose. While the infirmary was fine for sunburnt vacationers and the occasional tropical storm, it couldn't hold the numbers it had in recent days. They were running out of real estate for patients quickly. If the attacks continued, and there was every indication they would, a plan for additional beds would need to be thought out soon.

The horn from the ferry chased her to the door. "See you later."

Eyes closed, Mary Frances gave her jaunty little wave. "Have a good one."

The rest of the day flew by. The number of patients transferred was twice the number Ginny remembered from their meetings. Over the next few hours, hundreds of people from both the Hatteras and Ocracoke infirmaries walked or were carried onto multiple ferries. Things finally settled down by the time Ginny was ready to go home. Reaching for her keys, her fingers skimmed the folded paper in her pocket. She needed to find Tim and tell him what she had discovered.

As she walked down the sidewalk to the parking lot, she saw him leaning against her car. Wearing a trench coat with gray pants, Tim looked like William Powell from the Thin Man films. Mysterious but approachable. She sighed. Too bad she didn't look anything like Myrna Loy.

He straightened as she came nearer. "There you are. I was wondering how long before you would get off."

"The ferry was running late this afternoon." She stepped around him and put the key in the lock. "You were supposed to call me when you got out."

"I didn't want to bother you at work. I know you're saving money to go back to school."

She straightened. "How did you know that?"

His crooked smile did funny things to her heart. "How do you think?"

"Belle strikes again." She unlocked and opened the door.

His soft chuckle brought a soft smile to her face. "She can't help it. She thinks you hung the moon."

"You keep saying that, but I've never heard her say anything nice about me." Ginny glanced at him. "Well, are you going to get in?"

"I was hoping you might say that." He hurried around to the passenger side and got in. When they were comfortably inside, Tim turned to face her. "Really, how was your day?"

Ginny wasn't sure how to respond. No one ever asked about her day at home. "It was busy as usual." She told him about the patients being transported and her desire to be with them. "I did get invited to go dancing with a coworker at the new USO in Kitty Hawk."

"You did?"

Was that a hint of. . .maybe jealousy in those two little words? Would she like there to be?

"What did you say?"

She put the key in the ignition and started the car. "I said no."

"Really." He sat back in his seat. "He probably wasn't too happy with that answer."

"Who said it was a man?" Ginny put her hand over her mouth. It really was rude to laugh. "I do have friends who like to dance."

He chuckled. "Maybe the question I should ask you is if there's a boyfriend?"

"Who has time for a boyfriend?" She snuck a peek at him. He was seriously interested in her answer. "No, I don't have a boyfriend."

"Good." His lips spread into a smile. "Wouldn't want him getting in the way of our work."

Good grief, she couldn't tell if he was teasing her or not. She backed out of her parking spot, then eased onto the road. Once on the highway, she slipped her hand into her pocket and removed the paper she'd been working on. "Speaking of work, I had a chance to call the Ocracoke infirmary today. Nobody in the clinic or the morgue matches Schmidt's appearance, but I realized something. Everyone on the boat has been accounted for but him."

"Don't you think that's strange?"

"Oh, it gets stranger." She stopped at a stop sign. "When I was talking to the nurse in Ocracoke, she told me about the weird things that had been going on, like food going missing and medical supplies taken from a doctor who lives on the island. Then she told me that two guys out fishing reported seeing a man oaring a wooden boat through the Hatteras Inlet late last week. They thought it was odd because of the ocean currents."

"You think it was Rolf?"

She shrugged as she eased the car forward. "I don't know, but it does seem strange that all this was happening just as he went missing."

"I've been doing a little digging myself today." He told her about his idea of connecting someone on the island to the Germans' loss in the Great War. "If someone changed their last name to sound more Americanized, none of you would ever know that they were from Germany or that they fought in the war. I'm also checking the ferry ledgers to see if any known suspects pop out at me."

"How long will it take to get the census?"

"A week."

"Oh." As much as they needed to find Rolf, she already dreaded the day when Tim would leave.

"You sound disappointed."

She shook her head. "I thought of something, but I don't know if you'll think it's a good idea."

He shot her an encouraging smile. "Out with it, love."

The endearment curled its way around her heart. "Well, if the reports of a boater entering Hatteras Inlet are true, then that means this person would end up somewhere along the sound. There's a lot of places a person could hide in that area."

"Could we hike it?"

"That's how the girls do it. It usually takes a couple of hours to go from Buxton Woods to Hatteras Inlet, but we always stop along the way to catch crabs and have a crab bake."

"That sounds rather nice." He leaned back. "Do you think the girls would like to go with us?"

She glanced at him. "Are you crazy? I won't put the girls in danger like that."

"It's just a walk. We're not storming the castle." Tim leaned toward her. "We can't go wandering off into the woods. Your reputation would be ruined."

"I'm almost a nurse. I've seen my fair share of. . ." Ginny felt herself blush. "Anatomy. Besides, anyone who knows me knows

I'm not that kind of woman."

"True, but there's no sense in giving people a reason to talk." He took her right hand from the steering wheel and held it to his chest. "I would never put you or the girls in any danger. I promise."

She almost skidded off the road, her heart was pounding so loud. Deciding she'd rather live, Ginny turned off down a dirt road, then parked.

Tim glanced around. "Why did we stop?"

She couldn't tell him the truth—that his touch did crazy things to her—but she could come close. "I can't concentrate and drive at the same time."

"You want me to drive."

"No." Then she'd be on the passenger side, and it would feel too much like a date. "Let's just sit here and talk."

"All right." He turned slightly toward her. "When would you like to plan our hike? I figure both you and the girls are free on Saturday."

Curling her legs under her, she faced him. "You're not worried about the girls?"

"No. From what I've seen, they can take good care of themselves." He took her hand in his. "I don't anticipate seeing Rolf, but if we do, we'll simply turn around and alert Will."

She grinned. "Will? Are the two of you friends now?"

"To a degree. I was being honest when I said I don't want your reputation ruined. If you ever decided to come back here after school, I don't want anyone holding this over your head."

That he was considering her future made her like him more. Still, she'd promised herself that she'd keep the girls out of this, but what if there was another way? "I have another idea."

"Well, the first one was good. Let's hear this one."

Ginny was relatively certain he was going to hate this one. "Why don't just the girls and I hike the area? If Rolf sees us, he won't know we're looking for him and will leave us alone."

"No."

There was an edge to his answer that irritated her. "No? Just no? We can't even talk about it?"

"What's there to talk about?" He let go of her hand, robbing her of his wonderful warmth. "You hiking with a group of Girl Guides through the woods is asking for problems."

"We've been doing it since *I* was a Brownie. My girls know this island like the back of their hand." She noticed the confusion in his eyes. "It means they're familiar with the sound."

"And if Rolf takes you and the girls hostage?"

"Then the man is crazier than we thought," she teased, but he wasn't having any of it. "Do you know why I became a Girl Scout leader?" A glance at Tim answered her question. "It was the stories my mom told me about the Girl Guides during the Great War. Girls as young as seven or eight set traps and hunted for meat to provide food for their villages. They learned first aid and worked in hospitals to free up nurses needed elsewhere. The elder guides even served overseas setting up hospital tents and driving ambulances."

"I didn't know that."

"It's not surprising. As girls, we're told the best we can hope for is a good husband and a home. But those stories gave me hope that we could be more. That I could be more. I wanted to make a difference in this world. And that's why you have to let us do this. If we find any sign of a boat and anything leads us to believe someone has recently come ashore, we'll turn around and come straight to the lighthouse."

"No," he said more emphatically. "This is my mission, and I'm not going to foist it off on you."

So much for new beginnings. Maybe she should come at him

from a different angle. Ginny laid her hand on his arm. "Officer Chapline said you have a personal stake in delivering Schmidt to your superiors."

"Chapline should mind his own business," he bit out.

"Probably, but he thought I should know before I agreed to partner with you on this." She slid her hand down to hold his. "Tell me about your father."

Tim took a shuttered breath. "There's not much to tell. My father left us with my maternal grandparents after our mother died."

"When's the last time you saw him?"

He hesitated for so long, she thought he wouldn't answer the question. "It was the summer before I left for university. He thought my going to school was a waste of time and money, and thought I'd be better off in the navy."

Oh dear. She might have her battles with her father, but he'd always believed she could do anything she wanted. "What did he say when you told him you were going to school?"

"You mean besides cutting me off?" His mouth thinned into a tight line. "He told me I was a disgrace. Thankfully, I'd saved enough money to pay for my first year, and worked to pay my way the rest of the way through. My grandparents even sent him an invitation to my graduation, but he couldn't be bothered."

The pain this man had inflicted on Tim broke her heart. All he wanted was to make a life for himself doing what he loved most. Why couldn't his father understand that? His job was to nurture his children, give them the confidence to believe in themselves, not break their spirits with cruel words. "What happened to your father?"

Tim stared out the windshield. "He went down with his ship, along with five hundred other men, after Rolf Schmidt attacked off the coast of Gibraltar." He hesitated. "There were no survivors."

Ginny sniffled, swiping at the tears on her cheeks. "I'm so sorry, Tim. I truly am."

He glanced at her, clasping her hand so tight, it hurt. But she wouldn't let go. "I don't know why it bothered me so much. I really didn't know the man."

"He was your father, no matter how rotten he was at it. Of course it hurt."

He reached in his coat and pulled out a handkerchief. "You look as though you could use this."

"Thank you." She mopped her face, then blew her nose. "I'll wash it and return it to you."

He chuckled softly. "You're such a Girl Scout."

"Are you okay with the girls and I helping you find Schmidt? It's as important to us as it is to you."

"No, Gin." He cupped her cheek in his hand, and with the pad of his thumb wiped the last of her tears. "If something happened to you or the girls and I wasn't there. . ."

He didn't say anything else. He didn't have to.

They drove the rest of the way to Buxton in a companionable silence, only the muffled sound of the waves at high tide filling the air. As they came to the path that led to the lighthouse, Ginny slowed down and pulled to a stop. "I guess this is your stop."

"I guess." He glanced at the lighthouse and then back at her. "You want to meet at the lighthouse later? Maybe we can go over the ferry's ledgers together."

"I can't tonight. The last couple of days have taken it out of me." She smiled softly. "I may even be able to sleep tonight."

"Then maybe tomorrow."

She nodded in agreement. "Tomorrow then."

He opened the door, then before she could respond, he

brushed a kiss against her cheek and got out of the car.

Ginny watched him for a moment before pulling out onto the road again. Yes, she was in trouble, even more so when Tim discovered her plans.

Because she was on a mission.

⊒ CHAPTER 14 ⊑

He'd almost kissed her.

Tim walked up the path leading to the lighthouse, a smile on his lips. Ginny understood the complicated feelings he had concerning his father. Even more so, she grieved for what he'd lost. For what Rolf Schmidt had stolen from him, the chance to prove his father wrong. That one goal had pushed Tim through university. It had led him to his position with British Intelligence, and his mission here.

In a way, it had led him to Ginny.

She was quite something, this island girl. Tenderhearted yet determined, kind but honest to the point of bluntness. Sitting close to her in her automobile and not being able to hold her, kiss her, had been almost unbearable. But staying in Buxton wasn't the plan. For both their sakes, he needed to guard her heart as well as his.

The door was unlocked when Tim let himself into the house. He expected the house to be cold, but the blazing fire in the fireplace gave the place a homey feel. Shucking off his coat and tossing it on the couch, he glanced around. The cushions had been fluffed and the blanket neatly folded over the back of the couch. The layer of dust had been removed, leaving the wood furniture with a glossy shine. A peek in the front bedroom revealed that the bed had been made as well as the bathroom supplied with towels and new toiletries.

He gave a low whistle. Will had managed to fix things up nice.

As he came out in the hallway, he heard voices coming from the kitchen. Quietly, he opened the kitchen door. At the sink, Belle washed dishes. Clara lifted the lid of a pot on the stove, releasing the scent of tomatoes, green beans, and other vegetables into the air. Clementine peeled potatoes at the table while Lucy stocked the refrigerator with whatever was in the grocery sack.

Tim watched for a moment longer. He couldn't stay mad at them. They were simply protecting Ginny when they turned him in to the coast guard. They had drive and didn't fear working for what they wanted. He liked them in a kid-sister kind of way.

He stepped into the kitchen. "Should I have laid out a bowl of milk or some cookies for the Brownies to clean my house?"

Belle jerked around, her hands covered in soapsuds. "You weren't supposed to be here yet."

Tim stepped further inside and turned on the light switch, instantly brightening the room. "Where else was I supposed to be while a bunch of hooligans cleaned this place to within an inch of its life?"

"We'd thought you'd be with Ginny, looking for that man," Lucy replied. "Not that we're not glad to see you."

"How did you know the tales about the Brownies?" Belle asked as she placed the last dish in the strainer and drained the sink.

Clementine looked at Lucy, puzzled. "What is she talking about?"

"The Brownies, silly!" Belle grabbed a dish towel and wiped her hands. "They're fairies that come and do things around the house to make it more cheerful. People rewarded them by giving them milk and sweets, but you don't want to upset them, because they can be very naughty too."

"I used to read Iris stories about the Brownies when she was young." He leaned back against the wall. "She wasn't a Girl Guide, but she enjoyed the stories just the same."

"Ginny used to do the same thing with me. They were the only books Momma brought with her when she came from London."

Tim smiled. Something else he had in common with Ginny. "How long has your mother been here in the States?"

"A couple of years after the Great War. Momma nursed Daddy back to health after his ship was attacked just before the war ended." Belle wiped down the countertop. "They married in London, then Daddy brought her back here. Ginny was born the year after that."

"Kind of romantic, don't you think?" Lucy asked.

"Yes, it is," Tim replied, then glanced around. "You ladies have been busy. This place looks lovely."

"We didn't want you to come home to a cold house and no food in the kitchen." Clara filled a teapot and placed it on the stove. "We felt bad about getting you arrested and thought we'd apologize."

"That's sweet, but you didn't have to do that."

"Yes, we should have. I'm sorry. I was the one who came up with the whole idea." Belle took his arm and led him to the table. "I should have let Ginny handle things. She's smart about things like that."

Yes, Ginny was smart. And stubborn with an adventurous streak that matched Belle's.

"So tell me." Belle sat down beside him. "What was it like being in jail?"

Clementine leaned on the edge of the table. "Did you bang

your tin cup against the bars?"

"Was it as cold and dark as it is in the movies?" Clara asked.

"What are you girls watching at the cinema?" He thought Ginny was forthright and to the point, but he didn't realize it was ingrained in American girls from birth. Tim crossed his arms. "To answer your questions—it wasn't bad, simply a bit uncomfortable. I didn't have a tin cup. I was warm and could even see the ocean from a window across from my cell."

"Well, that's disappointing," Lucy said, resting her chin in her hand.

"Did you have any visitors? Clementine popped another potato into the small pot in front of her. "I think jail would be lonely."

"Yes, I did." He wasn't certain how much Ginny had told the girls, but he would be truthful with them from this moment on. "Ginny and I had a long visit yesterday."

"She told us, though why she's helping the coast guard after what they did to you, I don't know," Belle said just as the teakettle whistled. "Let me get that."

Tim figured Ginny would be as honest with the girls as she could, but he didn't want to get into the discussion they'd had about using the girls as extra sets of eyes. Even now, to think of Ginny and the girls walking the sound alone tied his stomach in knots.

Belle set a mug of water with a tea bag in front of him. "I brought you some tea from Momma's stash. She said she knows what it's like to need a good cup of tea."

"Tell your mother thank you." He wrapped his fingers around the warm pottery. "Besides school and cleaning up this place, what have you been doing today?"

"Well," Clementine started, "we came down to the beach to see if we could find any birds that might need cleaned, but the coast guard wouldn't let us walk the shore."

"That's too bad." Relief flowed through him. Patrolling the beach meant the coast guard was aware of the rather large holes in their defense and doing what they could to repair it. "Why were you looking for birds?"

For the next thirty minutes, they discussed how the animals were affected by the nightly attacks. As Tim listened to them talk about their desire to help the wildlife that called the beach home, he began to understand how much this place meant to these girls. It was home, but it was more than that. The island gave them a sense of comfort and stability, a community of friends and neighbors that went back for generations in some cases. They recognized the wildlife had been affected, but what about themselves?

Tim pushed away his teacup. "How are you dealing with all the attacks?"

"It gets scary sometimes." Clara took a cube of sugar and stuck it in her mouth. "The bombs seem like they're going off in the living room sometimes."

Clementine cleared her throat. "I figure as long as those Germans are not coming onshore, I'm not gonna worry about it." She picked up Tim's cup and saucer, then carried them to the sink. She turned toward them. "If they do land here, I'll be ready."

"They wouldn't be stupid enough to land here," Lucy said. "They'd really be in for a fight then."

Listening to them, Tim realized Ginny was right. These girls would do whatever it took to protect their community, even become an extra set of eyes and ears for him. It was like this back home, where everyone was pulling together, fighting for their way of life. Even their majesties stayed in the bombed-out capital rather than retreat to safer ground.

Yet he had a difficult time agreeing to let them hike along the sound alone, knowing the possibility existed that Rolf was there. There was too much of a risk, and he refused to take that chance on the girls or Ginny. He had to come up with another way to smoke Rolf out of hiding.

———————≈———————

"What do you think that was all about?" Belle asked her friends as they walked down the dusty path toward the village. "Why was he so interested in how we felt about the attacks?"

Clementine ran a little way ahead, then kicked a tin can back to them, shifting it from one foot to the other. "Maybe he's worried about us."

"I know my mom is." Clara pulled a scarf from her coat pocket and wrapped it over her head. "I can't even leave the house without her giving me the third degree."

Belle clasped Clara's arm and pulled her close. "Your momma is worried because your brothers shipped out last week, and she's nervous something could happen to you or Ruthie."

Belle leaned in closer and whispered, "How is Ruthie?"

"She's having a hard time with the boys gone." Clara met her gaze. "I told her you suggested we pray for the boys around Buxton who are leaving to join up. I could tell it meant a lot to her."

Belle struggled to swallow the large lump in her throat. "But she's still not going to hang out with us."

Clara patted Belle's hand. "Not right now, but she'll come around. You'll see."

Belle wasn't so sure. Since the day they'd argued, Ruthie had avoided her. She didn't come to troop meetings anymore or hang out at her house in the afternoons so they could dish on everyone. She'd even avoided Belle at school. Belle sniffed, forcing back the tears. It felt as if she'd not only lost her friend but a sister whom she loved very much.

"Who knows why adults ask the questions they do?" Lucy stole the can from Clem and kicked it down the road. "Unless Tim's up to something."

"I swear, Luc, you are the most suspicious person I know." Clem retrieved the can and kicked it back to them.

Clara pulled her knit cap down. "He was at the coast guard station overnight. Maybe it was to wait on new orders."

"He's looking for one guy," Clem exclaimed. "Not the entire Nazi party."

"Well, we already know he and Ginny are working together to find this man." Belle glanced up the road to find someone hurrying toward them. As the girl drew closer, Belle called out to her. "April, we were expecting you at Tim's. Where have you been?"

Their friend looked pale and was shaking. "I couldn't go to Tim's. I just couldn't."

"It's okay. We had everything cleaned up and ready for him when he got home." Clem rubbed April's back. "We were just throwing around the idea that Tim was hiding something and wondering what it could be."

April stopped in the middle of the trail and stared at them. "Do you think he knows something he's not telling us?"

"Of course he does. He's working with British Intelligence." Lucy gawked at her friend, then shook her head. "Sometimes I worry about you."

April rolled her eyes. "I know he works for them. What I'm saying is maybe he's come across something that would hurt one of us, so he doesn't want any of us to know about it."

Belle studied her friend. April had always been more cautious, even bowing out of some of their riskier adventures rather than get into trouble. But something bothered her, and Belle was determined to figure out what it was. "What's going on, April? What could he know that we don't?"

She half expected it to be something silly, but the stark expression in her friend's eyes told her whatever it was, it was serious. April glanced around, then back at the group. "You can't tell anyone what I'm about to tell you."

The girls gathered into a tight circle, each raising the right hand in the Girl Scout salute, then nodded. Well, everyone but Lucy.

She shrugged. "How do I know if I can keep it a secret if I don't know what it is?"

"Lucille Owensby, if we told your momma some of the things you've sworn us to keep secret, she wouldn't let you out of your room until you were married." Clara pointed an accusing finger at her.

"All right. You don't have to be so nasty about it." Lucy lifted her hand. "I promise."

All eyes shifted to April. Poor girl was wringing her hands, her gaze focused on the sandy path. Belle put her arm around her waist, praying it would give her the support she needed. "Remember how I told you I have an uncle from Michigan visiting us? Daddy says he's been here before, but I don't remember it. I must have been very small when he came the first few times. Anyway, he's younger than my father, but my father treats him . . .differently, as if he's someone important."

Lucy eyed the girls. "I had to make a Girl Scout promise for that?"

"Be quiet, Luc." Clem nodded to April. "Go on."

April drew in a long breath. "The other night when Daddy thought I was asleep, I overheard them talking." She hesitated. "They were speaking in German."

"Are you sure?" Belle asked, rubbing her friend's back. "I mean, how do you know? It's not like any of us have ever heard German before."

"My mom taught me a few songs in German before she left. I never thought much of it. She taught me French songs too." She gave them a weak smile. "Momma knew several languages."

"Do you think you're German?" Lucy asked.

April shrugged. "I don't know. My parents came to this country sometime during the Great War. Daddy has always had a love of the water, so he decided that he wanted to come to the Outer Banks and make boats. So they settled here."

"Then why wasn't your father asked to make boats for the military like my dad was?" Belle asked.

"I don't know. It didn't make sense to me either." She swallowed. "But if my father's German, it would explain a lot."

"Who would've thunk that our April was honest-to-goodness German?" Lucy stared at her.

"Stop it, Lucy, or I'll tell everyone at school your granddaddy fought for the Yankees." Letting go of April's waist, Belle stood in front of her. "You know this doesn't change anything? It doesn't matter where you came from but who you are right now."

"Honey, is there anything else you need to tell us?" Clara asked.

Large tears dripped down April's cheeks. "Last night, they were on Daddy's ham radio. I didn't understand why he decided to take up the radio as a hobby, but when I heard them last night, I wondered if he had an ulterior motive." Her face convulsed in a sob. "Daddy was talking to someone in German over the radio. I understood a few of the words, and I think I know who they were talking to." Her grief-stricken expression tore at Belle's heart. "They were talking to someone on the submarines."

Oh, dear Lord, please help her. No wonder April was scared to death. Her father was the only person she had left in this world, and he was colluding with the Germans. Belle didn't know what to do.

Clara handed April a clean handkerchief. "Are you sure about this, April? Because if you are, we can't keep this a secret."

Fresh tears wet her face. "But he's all I have. If he's arrested for treason. . ." She crumpled to the ground.

April was right. Frank Smith wouldn't go to prison. People convicted of treason were executed. Another helpful lesson from Miss Wynn's history class. Fear knotted Belle's stomach, but she refused to give in to it. April needed her friends. If Frank Smith and his brother wanted their island, she would defend it or die trying. "We need to tell Ginny."

"But she's working with the coast guard. She'll tell Chapline," April whined. "I know what he's doing is wrong, but what will happen to me? I have nowhere else to go."

"You'll come and stay with us," Belle answered, tugging her into a hug. "We have plenty of room, and we'll be like sisters. But we must tell Gin. She'll know what to do."

"When?" Clem asked. "We can't sit on this kind of information for too long."

"All right." Belle needed to think. Momma had the Jones kids until late this evening. If she could corner Gin before she left to meet Tim, this just might work. "Can everyone have dinner at our house tonight?" Everyone nodded. Belle turned back to April. "Tell your dad we're having a sleepover and bring everything you need to stay. If he's talking to the submarine commanders, then they might be ready to start the attacks again."

"When are we going to tell Ginny?" Clem asked.

"Tonight at dinner."

"If she believes us," Lucy scoffed.

"Oh, she'll believe us," Belle said with more confidence than she felt. After everything they had done—hiding Tim, then turning him in to the coast guard when it suited their purpose, getting Ginny involved—her sister was over their shenanigans.

But this time was different. Their homes were in the Germans' crosshairs.

⧚ CHAPTER 15 ⧚

"You look very at home with a baby in your arms." Momma smiled as she gazed at Ginny rocking the youngest Jones in her arms.

Ginny inwardly grimaced. It wasn't that she didn't want a husband and a family someday, but the timing had to be right. She still had a semester of nursing school, and then she wanted to work for a year before she got married. That is, if she found the right man.

Her thoughts strayed to Tim and the kiss on her cheek he'd given her. She could tell by the way his eyes had darkened and the slight catch in his breath that he wanted more than a chaste kiss. She had wanted more too, but she barely knew him, only that he made her laugh and could curl her toes with one look. He wouldn't mind if she worked, wouldn't expect her to give up her passion. If fact, he seemed to admire it, which was unusual in most men.

But it wouldn't work. Once they found Schmidt, Tim would be off to New York on his next mission and she'd be stuck here, waiting for the war to end so that she could get on with her life.

At least, that was the plan. Then why did the thought of Tim leaving make her feel so blue?

"I think he needs to be burped."

"Oh, you're right." Ginny gently tugged the nipple out of the infant's mouth, the bottle making a tiny popping noise. She put the bottle on the coffee table and then placed the baby over her diaper-clad shoulder and tenderly patted his back. "Just a burp, little bug, and you can have some more."

"Maybe you should care for babies when you get out of school. Once the war's over and the men come home, everybody will be having babies. You mark my words."

She glanced at her mother playing with Sally, the baby's two-year-old sister. "Is that what happened after the Great War, Momma?"

She nodded. "Don't you remember all the children on your first day of school? Why, you had three Virginias in your first-grade class. That's when we started calling you Ginny."

"You've always liked being around children. Did you and Daddy ever think of having more than just me and Belle?"

"If you don't mind, I'd rather not talk about it." Momma went back to the puzzle she was working on with Sally, but her shoulders sagged a bit and the smile she'd worn had disappeared. "This week is the last week I'll be keeping the children full-time."

"Why's that?" Ginny tucked the little boy into her arms and offered him the bottle again.

"The coast guard came around and warned everyone to stay off the water, even the sound." Momma lowered her voice. "But I heard from Maybelle Sellers that those Clark boys were out fishing a few days ago and ran into a U-boat that had surfaced. The boys said the Germans told them to leave before they got hurt."

Sounded like something those Clark boys would do. Always taking a risk. "What's Mrs. Jones going to do? She makes her living off of fishing the sound."

Momma put a piece of the puzzle in place and smiled at the

little girl. "She said something about moving back in with her mother in Wilmington and working at the factory there. Said it's less hours and more pay."

"Her mother would probably watch the children while she works." Ginny nodded. "That makes sense. It's got to be tough on her with two babies under three and Tom away in the navy."

"Maybe." Momma shrugged. "I can't imagine leaving our home for who knows how long. It's one of the reasons your daddy and I decided I would stay here, and you would come back home. This war is bad enough as it is. No sense taking Belle out of school and dragging her away from all her friends."

"What about me, Momma?" Ginny spouted out before she knew it. "I had built a life with friends and a career in Chapel Hill. Why did Daddy force me to come back home? It wasn't to take care of you and Belle. The two of you manage everything perfectly well on your own."

Momma met her gaze. "I needed you here."

"I don't understand."

"You haven't been sleeping since you came home, have you?"

"What has that—"

She continued, "You go out walking or whatever it is you do to get tired so you can sleep. I have problems like that sometimes, where I can't sleep. Usually, it's a bad thunderstorm or a gale." She mashed her lips together. "Or the explosions offshore that keep me up. It's the reason we wanted you to come home. So Belle wouldn't have to deal with it all by herself."

This sounded much worse than simple insomnia, almost as if her sleeplessness was triggered by something. Had her mother suffered from some form of trauma that interfered with her sleep?

Cradling the baby, Ginny stood and quietly moved to the playpen where she laid the sleeping boy down. She turned to her mother. "How about soup and sandwiches for supper?"

"That works for me." Momma gave her a soft smile. "And could you do me a favor and not mention what I just told you to anyone? You know how funny people get when they don't understand something."

Why was her momma talking as if this was some kind of mental illness? "Of course. I won't tell a soul."

"Good." She visibly relaxed. "If there's any soup left over, put it in that thermos on top of the refrigerator. I know Ida would appreciate it after a long day fishing."

"Sure." Ginny walked out of the living room, down the hall, and through the kitchen before stopping just inside the kitchen door. Was that why Daddy had asked her to come home? Because he and Momma feared she had a mental illness? Daddy could have told her, could have explained what treatments she was using. Or maybe he was afraid to tell her. Doctors still prescribed institutions to those who stuttered or acted differently from others. Maybe it was time Ginny wrote him and found out what was going on.

Turning her thoughts to dinner, she headed for the pantry and grabbed two quart jars of homemade vegetable soup as well as a pint of Momma's grape jelly. She glanced along the full shelves. She hadn't thought much about the yearly canning her parents always did, but if the rumors about food rations were true, they would have enough vegetables and preserves and jellies to last them well into next year.

She had just pulled the soup pot from under the counter when the back door opened. Belle, followed by Clara, Clementine, and Lucy, walked in, and they all hung up their coats. Instead of their usual chatter, they were strangely quiet.

Ginny's concern grew as she studied the somber faces. "What's happened?"

Belle walked over and shut the door leading to the living

room, then turned and met her gaze. "We have something we need to talk to you about, but we can't start until April gets here."

Alarm bells clattered through her. "Is she okay?"

"No, but she does need to stay here for a little while." She glanced at the jars of soup. "Can they stay for supper?"

"It must be serious if you're asking." She handed Clara and Lucy bread, homemade jelly, and peanut butter. "Make nine sandwiches. We're sending supper home for Sally and her mother too."

The girls worked quietly, which was enough to worry Ginny. What had happened since they'd left for school this morning, full of excitement at helping Tim settle into his temporary home? He wouldn't have told them about their drive home or the disagreement they'd had about the girls' hike around the sound. They had agreed that anything dealing with the girls would be done together.

The scent of fresh vegetables and tomatoes filled the kitchen. Ginny was filling the bowls as the back door opened. April stood in the doorway, a large bag in one hand and her pillow under her arm. She didn't say a word, just dropped everything to the ground and fell to her knees. A gut-wrenching wail tore through her small body as she crumpled to a heap on the floor.

Setting down the bowl and ladle, Ginny ran to her, falling on the floor in front of her. "April, darling, what is it? You can tell me anything."

The girl bent forward as if someone had ripped out her very soul and sobbed. For the next few minutes, all Ginny could do was comfort her. When the crying finally subsided, Belle and Clem helped April up and walked with her over to the table.

"Let's eat first, then we can talk."

Several minutes later, they'd gathered around the table. Taking her seat at the head of the table, Ginny set her napkin on her lap, then gave the group an encouraging smile. "Who would like to say grace?"

"I will," Belle offered quietly, but instead of her usual short prayer, she seemed to struggle with the words. "Lord, we know our world is at war. We see it every day on the beach and hear it every night off our coast. Please protect us from our enemies. And please be with April. She's so scared. Help her to know You're always with her. Bless this food, Lord. Amen."

"Amen."

Belle glanced at April. "You ready?"

The girl nodded, her cheeks already wet from tears. Her skin was pale beneath her faded tan. Clementine and Lucy sat close by, ready to give her a shoulder to lean on if necessary. Ginny's heart broke. She wished she could wrap the girl up in her arms and make it all better. But that wasn't the way the world worked.

Ginny locked gazes with April. "You can tell me anything, honey. What is it?"

As if the dam burst, the story poured from her. Her father speaking German. The mysterious appearance of an uncle she'd never met. The German communication she had overheard. No wonder the girl had been scared out of her wits. Ginny would be too if she weren't so angry. Was this how they were to live until the Allies won the war? Always peeking over their shoulders, wondering if the butcher or mechanic or a neighbor was an ally or an enemy? Her mind rushed to Tim. How had Tim and all those other people withstood the constant bombardments and threats of invasion?

Be strong and courageous. Don't be frightened or dismayed, for the Lord your God is with you wherever you go. A Bible lesson she had learned in her childhood came roaring to life. God was here, even in this moment of fear and distrust. They must hold on to that.

Ginny glanced around the room. The concern that they felt for April had stooped the girl's shoulders. Fear dulled their eyes.

But there was also a sense of determination, a strength that was the lifeblood of these islands.

"Do you believe us?" Belle asked.

Was that what they were afraid of, that she would think their overactive imaginations had cooked this up? She pulled her sister into a hug. "Of course I believe you." She glanced around the room. "We need to talk about a few things."

"You mean like who we're going to give this information to?" Lucy cut her sandwich in half, then cut off the crust. "I vote for Officer Chapline."

"No!" April cried out. "They might arrest him."

Ginny nodded. It was more a certainty he'd be arrested if everything April said was true. The man was a danger to their community, their country. They had to report him to the authorities.

"You could tell Tim," April said quietly. "He'll know what to do with this information."

Ginny thought so too. Tim would let Chapline know about April's discovery about her father. But she wanted April to come to this decision for herself. It would be her putting her father behind bars, and possibly worse. She had to be at peace with her decision. "Why do you say that?"

"Because I think the man Tim is looking for is my uncle."

She had come to the same conclusion. "Probably. What is he like?"

"Hateful. He was always barking at me like I have nothing better to do than to wait on him. And he always walks around with his hands in his pockets as if he's hiding something." April covered her face with her hands.

It sounded like the man Tim described, but it would be better if he could get a good look at him. "What did he look like?"

April gave her the same description Tim had. Blond hair. Blue eyes. Just a little bit younger than her father who was in his fifties. When she finished, she spat out, "I hate him."

Ginny understood. In April's eyes, her entire life had been a lie. Everything she'd believed in, the man who was supposed to protect her—all that had destroyed as much as any of those boats that had been sunk. It would take time, but they would help her move past this moment and maybe, even one day soon, they could show her a way to forgive this man of his many transgressions.

While Belle and the other girls helped April with her things, Ginny went into the living room and called the operator. "Florence? Hi, this is Ginny. Has the phone to the lightkeeper's house been connected? Could you connect me? Thanks." The phone rang a couple of times before Tim picked up.

"Hello?"

"Hi, it's me. Ginny." She rolled her eyes. Of course the man knew it was her. He'd spent enough time with her to know her voice.

"Is everything okay?"

"No, not really. I know I said I couldn't meet you tonight, but this is urgent. Can I meet you around eleven?"

"Of course." He hesitated. "Are you sure you're all right? You don't sound like yourself."

"I'll be fine once I talk to you."

"Glad to know I can be of assistance." She could hear the teasing smile in his voice. "Eleven tonight. I'll be there."

Ginny put the receiver back in its cradle, then leaned back against the wall. Maybe they had finally found Schmidt and all this cloak-and-dagger stuff was over. Tim would find the closure he needed regarding his father, and she would have an interesting story to tell her children one day about the British reporter who'd been washed up on the shore.

She stepped down the hall and back into the kitchen. The girls were quiet as Ginny came to the table. "I'm going to talk to

Tim tonight." She glanced at April. "You can stay with us for as long as you like. I don't want you going back to your house. It's too dangerous there."

"They're not there."

Ginny was confused. "I thought they were using the ham radio at your house."

She nodded. "They were, but when I went back to get my stuff, I noticed my dad's things were missing."

"Where would he go in the middle of the winter?" Belle asked.

"He goes to his fishing shack." April gave them a weak smile. "He goes there sometimes to get away from everything."

Or to get away from watchful eyes. Mr. Smith must suspect April had heard him and Rolf talking on the radio. "Do you know where this fishing shack is?"

April shook her head. "He bought it about a year ago, but he's never taken me there."

A year. They'd been planning this even before Pearl Harbor had drawn America into war. But Schmidt had been on a ship that was attacked. Why, if the Germans knew he was there? Had he been so prideful, he never thought he'd die himself? Of course, the man was full of pride and selfishness and hate.

If he wanted a fight, he would get one.

"I think we should find the dirty Germans ourselves," Lucy said, tossing her napkin on the table. "I don't know about the rest of you, but I don't want any of them near my family."

"Me neither," Clem agreed. "Just the thought of them in Buxton makes me sick."

"I've done my part," April whispered as a fresh batch of tears began to fall. "I'm just a kid, anyway. What could I do?"

"You need to listen in Mrs. Wynn's class more." Belle patted April's hand. "She told us last week that there have been child soldiers since the beginning of time. They fought in both the

Revolutionary and the Civil Wars. Why should we expect to be any different?"

"What has this got to do with the price of tea in China, Belle?" Clem exclaimed. "Are you saying we should enlist?"

"No, but you can make a difference despite your age."

Ginny turned around to find Momma standing at the kitchen door. "I'm sorry, Momma. The girls were excited about some of the things we're doing for the war effort and got a bit loud."

"I heard what you were talking about, and you can make a difference in the war." She hesitated, then walked over to an empty chair and sat down. "I don't talk about it a lot, but I was a Girl Guide during the Great War."

"You were, Momma?" Ginny slid back into her chair. "You never told us that."

She picked up a crumb, and then another. "It's hard to talk about at times."

"What did you do, Mrs. Mathis?" Lucy asked.

"I was a Senior Guide, about your age when the war started. We learned first aid so that we could help in the hospitals to relieve nurses." She dusted the crumbs onto a dirty plate. "I was about thirteen then."

"That's a lot of responsibility for a kid," Clara said, resting her cheek in her hand.

"We had to grow up fast back then. If we didn't, others would suffer." She continued picking up crumbs. "When I was fifteen, I was elevated to ambulance driver and sent to the Western Front."

Ginny closed her eyes, trying to remember her high school history and failing miserably. One thing she did remember was that the battles on the Western Front had been particularly brutal.

"Momma," Belle said, "you saw some terrible things."

She nodded. "But we did a lot of good there too. Saved a lot of lives." She glanced around the room at each girl. "That's why

I know you can make a difference in this war. Because I made a difference in that one."

"Thank you, Momma." Ginny reached across the table and took her hand. All these years and she was still discovering facets of her mother. She'd always admired her mother, but this made her respect her so much more.

It also gave Ginny an idea. The girls should have a choice in how they helped. Of course, their parents would have to give the okay, but each girl should decide for herself what part she'd play in the war effort.

One thing she knew they all could do was hike. She explained her idea—that they would hike from Buxton Woods to Hatteras, looking for clues of where Schmidt might have come onshore. If they came across anything suspicious, they would return and contact Officer Chapline immediately.

"That's perfect, Ginny." Her sister grinned at her. "We'll not only walk the sound. We'll be helping Tim out too."

"I would like to help Tim find him," April said.

The other girls agreed and then started cleaning up. Soon the room was filled with laughter and girlish chatter. This was what she always thought of when her troop came to mind. Always there for each other, through good and bad.

Ginny reached down and squeezed her mother's shoulder. "Those weren't stories about other Girl Guides you told us when we were little girls, were they?"

Momma gave her a sweet smile. "You never would have believed me if I said they were about myself."

≡ CHAPTER 16 ≡

A familiar shadow moved across the small dunes that led up to the lighthouse, then into the door below. Tim pulled away from the window and waited for the *clicky-click* of her boot heel against the cast-iron stairs below. He'd been on pins and needles since her phone call earlier this evening. What was so urgent that couldn't wait until the morning?

The light sound of her steps announced her arrival to the rest area that had been built into the lighthouse when it was first constructed. He'd thought it silly at first—it was only two hundred and fifty-seven steps to the top. But then he'd met Ginny, and he realized he loved every part of the lighthouse because she did.

As she rose above the floor, she gawked at him in surprise, then slowed her pace. "I thought we were supposed to meet in the lantern room."

"I'll admit it." He shrugged. "I wanted to see you."

"I wished this was a social call, but it isn't."

Taking her gloved hand, he led her over to a small table and chairs. Helping her get comfortable, he took the chair next to her. "All right. What is so urgent?"

When she looked up at him, her eyes were wide with worry. "April is staying with us for a while."

Tim didn't understand. What was so urgent about April staying with the Mathis family? "I thought she had an uncle visiting from. . .um. . .someplace up north."

"Michigan," she affirmed.

"I'm surprised she would leave like that. Wouldn't her father make her stay?"

"He and this uncle of hers are who made her leave."

"Did they. . ." His fists clenched at his sides. April was just a kid, and her father was supposed to be the one person who should protect her.

"No, it's not like that." She covered his fist with her hand. "April overheard her father and uncle speaking in German when they thought she was asleep. She heard them again one afternoon after school, and from what she could understand, they were talking to the subs along the coast. Here's the part you'll be interested in. Her uncle matches your description of Rolf Schmidt."

"You're kidding me." He stood, then grabbed her hand and pulled her toward the stairwell. He hadn't felt this giddy since the first time he'd seen Ginny. "We've got to notify Will, then set up surveillance around her house."

"We can do that, but they're not there. April went home to pack her bags and her father's things were gone. She thinks they went to a fishing shack her father bought last year, but she's never been there."

"So she doesn't know where it is?"

"No, but we know Schmidt's here and he's communicating with the submarines."

He raked a hand through his hair. "How exactly is he doing that?"

"Ham radio," she answered reluctantly. "Frank Smith bought one last year."

"Why does that name sound familiar?"

"Because there are dozens of Frank Smiths running around the United States," Ginny offered.

Ignoring her comment, Tim pressed on. "Schmidt is commonly changed to Smith when a German family migrates. It was particularly common after the Great War. I know the department has been trying to find a Frank Schmidt for years." He noted her expression. "He served as a naval commandant for Germany during the Great War who fell out of favor with his commanding officer when they lost the war in the Atlantic. The department lost track of him soon after the war ended."

"So the intelligence community had no idea he was here?"

"Not until now. There'd been rumors, of course, and there was some talk he was working with a German organization trying to incorporate Hitler's philosophies with American beliefs."

The stricken expression on Ginny's lovely face tore through him. "There are people here who want to destroy our way of life?"

Tim wanted so much to console her, to tell her it wasn't true, but he couldn't. She needed to know what they were up against. "There are many Germans who are displeased with how they were treated after the Great War and landed here looking for a better life. Most of them have grown to love their adopted country, but there's a small percentage who view Hitler's rise to power as their fatherland taking its rightful place in the world."

Ginny shook her head as if to put this new thought into its place. "I can't imagine anyone thinking this war is a good thing."

"I think of it like that Bible verse about the blind not being able to see. If these people would open their eyes, they could see the goodness of what our freedoms give us. Instead, they would rather fall in line behind the dictator whose only purpose in this world is evil."

"And I thought Belle was the naive one."

Tim walked over to the window. "Something this precise and well-thought-out had to be in the works for over a year." He glanced back at Ginny. Even in the moonlight, he could see the pity in her eyes. "How did the intelligence department miss this so badly?"

"They miss things. It happens." She lifted her hand to his cheek and smiled up at him. "But we have the advantage now."

He met her gaze. "Because we have a general idea where he's at."

"You've got to admit, it's better than having to look in an entire ocean."

Tim laughed as he pulled her into his arms. The faint scent of lavender that clung to her like a second skin wrapped around his senses like a delicate clasp. Ginny truly was the loveliest girl, yet that wasn't what attracted him. She had substance, a fierce loyalty to her family and friends, and a heart to serve others that touched a part deep inside he thought long dead.

"Gin." Without thinking, he raised his hand to her face, his fingers caressing the softness of her cheek. She leaned into his caress, and he considered it a small victory.

"We're going to get this guy, Tim," she whispered. "I promise you that."

He tilted her head back slightly until her lips were just a breath beneath his. "Would you like to seal that promise with a kiss?"

Her light nod vibrated through his fingers. It was all the permission he needed. He took her mouth with his, savoring the softness, the curve of her lips, the way her arms fit perfectly around his neck. When he reluctantly lifted his head, she pulled him back into her arms. He surrendered again, deepening the kiss until she clung to him.

Tim lifted his head and looked at Ginny. Her lips were slightly swollen, her cheeks flushed to a delicate pink, but it was her eyes, so silvery blue in the bright moonlight, that held him spellbound.

"That was. . ." She sighed, and it took every ounce of willpower not to pull her into another kiss. Instead, he enjoyed her head against his shoulder, their heartbeats in rhythm with each other. He was still enjoying the feel of her head beneath his cheek when she broke away from him. "What do you think we ought to do?"

"I was quite happy to stand here and hold you all night."

She blushed again, then shooed him away as he tried to pull her against him again. "We need a plan."

"All right." He stepped back and leaned against the wall. "I still think searching the sound's shoreline might give us some clues, but if we do it, we do it together."

"Now that April's father suspects her our cover is blown, so I agree to your terms."

He crossed his arms over his chest and smiled. "I've never had that happen before. Did a woman actually agree with me?"

"Watch it, buddy, or that first kiss might just be your last." She yanked a scarf out of her pocket and tossed it at him.

"Our next kiss will be our third. I kissed you the first time, then you kissed me."

She glared at him. "Are you keeping score?"

"With you, always."

Ginny looked around as if confused. "Did we decide what time we'll leave Saturday morning?"

"I was thinking nine."

"Good, that will give me time to collect the horses. You can ride, can't you?"

He chuckled. "I grew up in the country. Yes, I ride."

"Now that that's settled"—she turned and headed for the stairs—"I want to check out something April said."

"And it's in the lantern room?" Tim followed behind her.

"No, but the maps I need to look at are."

When they reached the lantern room, Ginny headed straight for the maps under a makeshift table. Spreading them out, Tim was impressed with the details she'd noted in the margins. "I hope Will appreciates all you're doing for him."

"I highly doubt it." She chuckled softly. "He thinks the girls stick their noses in coast guard business too much. For instance, I taught the girls how to read maritime and suggested that they be given a section of the beach to monitor, but he wouldn't even hear me out about it." She studied the map, then pointed to an area almost in front of the lighthouse. "April said that a ham radio will only reach so far and that when she heard it, she heard the sound of waves crashing and a bell. That would mean the subs were above water."

"That makes sense. U-boats must resurface every twenty-four hours to replenish their air supply."

She pressed her fingers over her mouth. "They must be coming up in the afternoon then. The waves crashing could be high tide, and the school rings a bell when it lets out. The army only flies over in the morning and that's just to spot the wreckage."

"Hmmm." The Yanks weren't ready for the destruction the Germans had in mind. With little to no air coverage and civilians watching the beach, this island could easily fall into Hitler's hands. Did Rolf understand that? If April's father was Captain Frank Schmidt, he probably patrolled the East Coast during the Great War. Rolf said he had a new battle plan for the Atlantic. Was he a key part of Germany taking the Eastern Seaboard? The thought infuriated Tim.

"Are you all right? You got very quiet."

Tim pinched the bridge of his nose. "Can I see your maps of the attacks?"

"Of course." Ginny pulled a rolled map out and handed it to him. "What are you looking for?"

"I'll know it when I see it." He unfurled the paper and studied her markings. "This." He pointed to a grouping of red marks. "The greatest proportion of sinkings have happened between Buxton and Hatteras, with most happening directly in front of the lighthouse."

Ginny studied her work. "I should have noticed that."

Tim rubbed her back. The last thing he wanted was for Ginny to beat herself up over this. "The U-boats aren't venturing very far, as there have only been one or two attacks to the north and to the south. My best guess is the subs are hiding in this area." He circled a large area just off the coast.

"That's not possible. Those sandbars are always shifting, so you never know how deep the water is from one minute to the next."

"It's brilliant. It's the last place anyone would look." Tim caught the disbelief in her expression and smiled. "It's the perfect place for them to surface and refill their oxygen tanks, and there's deep water nearby in case they need to dive. Rolf and Frank are watching the shore like you are and giving the captains information about what the military is doing."

A loud explosion jerked their attention toward the ocean. The night had turned blood red as a fire tore through a vessel not far from the shore. The boat had righted itself in the water when the second torpedo tore through the hull, sending sparks so high they looked like stars.

"When did April hear them talking to the submarines?"

"Yesterday afternoon," she whispered.

Rolf's plan was under way.

≣ CHAPTER 17 ≣

Ginny poured the small pan of warm milk into the mug and stirred. After hours of tossing and turning, a nice cup of cocoa might help her sleep. It had as a child, especially on stormy mornings when the wind would rattle the windows and rain would clatter like penny nails on the roof, startling her out of her sleep. Papa always greeted her in the kitchen, the milk already warming on the stove. It had been one of her loveliest memories of childhood.

She blew on the steaming liquid, then took a warm, sweet sip. It was a small miracle she wasn't as big as a barn, with as much cocoa as she had put away over the years. It was one of the reasons she had visited the lighthouse every night instead. But even that had done nothing to calm her worries tonight.

Ginny pulled out a chair and sat down at the kitchen table. At least they had a plan. They would take the girls horseback riding along the sound Saturday morning, with crabbing and a crab bake along the way. After Tim had walked her home, he'd taken her car to the coast guard station to update Will on the developments and see that April was protected.

Sitting back, she cupped her mug in her hands. It was all too much for her right now. She'd rather think about those moments when Tim pulled her into his arms and kissed her like she was the only woman in the world. She closed her eyes, the warm chocolate on her lips not nearly as sweet as his kisses. She had even pulled him back for a second one! She'd never done that.

A muffled explosion tore through the quiet, and Ginny glanced up at the clock. Four o'clock. The Germans were working late tonight, and not far offshore. Another explosion went off and shook the house. A faint cloud of dust formed around her as bits of Sheetrock and loose tiles fell from the ceiling. Ginny had just settled in again when a scream pierced through the walls.

She scrambled to her feet, then dashed through the house to the bedrooms. When she opened the door to Belle's room, the bed was turned down, but Belle was missing. Maybe she'd gone to the restroom, but Ginny would have seen her as she walked through the kitchen. If she snuck out. . .

Another loud groan twirled Ginny around. Her mother's room? She hurried down the hall to the bedroom her parents shared and pushed the door open. That's when she saw them. Belle held their mother, rubbing her back and whispering softly to her as her mother rocked back and forth.

"What. . . ," Ginny started, but the pleading glance Belle gave her quieted her questions for the moment.

Momma whimpered softly. "They're all gone. All of them."

"Who is she talking about?" Belle glanced up at Ginny. "She keeps talking about people being gone?"

"I don't know." Ginny walked the short distance to where they sat, then crouched down beside them. "Who's gone, Momma?"

"All of them." Tears wet her mother's face. "I was only gone for four days, and now they're all gone."

Ginny sat down and pulled Momma close. "Where did you go?"

She laid her head on Belle's shoulder. "The doctors said I worked too hard. So they sent me away to Paris to rest. When I came back, they were all gone."

After their conversation this evening, things were beginning to make sense. Momma had worked the Western Front. Tears welled in Ginny's eyes. "A lot of people died in the war, Momma. You were blessed to make it back home alive."

"I don't feel blessed. I should have been with them."

She heard a sniffle, and Ginny turned to find her sister in tears. "It's okay, sis. She's just reliving her time in France."

"But why? She usually doesn't do this unless there's a bad storm."

The explosions from the German attacks. Was that what had triggered her mother's insomnia? How often did she wake up, storms raging inside her, her memories from Verdun or the Somme playing out before her? There were treatments, of course, but nothing that could be done now except keep her calm and eventually get her to bed.

Finally, the memory released its grip on her mother, and she slumped against Ginny. Belle crawled over to the bed and stripped a quilt from it, then returned, covering them. When Momma's breathing slowed into an easy rhythm, Ginny turned to her sister. "Has Momma ever talked to you about being in the Great War?"

Belle shook her head. "No. I mean, I knew she met Daddy while he was in a hospital outside of London, but I didn't know until this evening that she was a Girl Guide. All those stories she told us when we were kids, do you think she was talking about herself?"

Ginny pushed the silvery blond hair away from her mother's face and kissed her brow. "She basically told me they were when you girls were cleaning the dinner dishes tonight. No wonder she knew so much about the Guides. She lived those stories."

The bombing stopped, lulling them into a sense of peace. A few minutes later, they bundled their mother in a quilt and put her to bed. Momma curled up on her side and almost instantly fell asleep as if the entire episode had never happened.

Ginny clicked the door shut, then turned to Belle and whispered, "You look like you could use some hot chocolate."

"I could use something."

Ginny wrapped her arm across her sister's shoulders. "Come on, squirt. Let's go downstairs and make us some."

Once they got downstairs, they worked together as a team. Belle rinsed out the pan Ginny used, and Ginny got the milk and the cocoa. As they waited for the milk to warm, Belle leaned against the kitchen counter. "Why do you think she still does this? I mean, it's been forever since the Great War."

"It's not been that long. What Momma went through was a major event in her life. It traumatized her. There's a diagnosis for it. It's called shell shock."

"I never heard of that." Belle stirred the milk. "What is it?"

Ginny pressed her lips together. "It's hard to explain, but what happens is when a person goes through a traumatic experience, their senses are so overwhelmed, they don't how to respond. Things can remind them of that traumatic experience, and it's like they're living it all over again."

Belle took the pot from the stove and poured the milk into two cups. "So every time there's a bad storm or there's an attack, Momma relives what happened to her in France?"

Ginny nodded as she stirred the chocolate. "It looks that way. I never even knew she'd been to Paris."

"You think Momma met Daddy in London or at this hospital she worked at in France?"

"I don't know." There seemed to be a lot of things she didn't know about their mother. Was this the reason Daddy had wanted her to come home? Having a nurse in the house who understood something about shell shock made sense. She just wished he had trusted her enough to tell her. Ginny took a cup and handed it to her sister. "Why didn't Daddy tell me about Momma?"

"I don't think he knew how." Belle took her cup and walked over to the table. "You know how folks are about someone who has spells."

Yes, Ginny knew how people responded to psychiatric issues. People thought it was contagious like a cold and shunned the sick person when they needed help the most. People with mental conditions were treated badly both in the state institution and by people out in the general public. They were ostracized and talked about, considered "less than" and generationally flawed. Ginny would not allow anyone to treat her mother like that. "I wish Daddy would've told me."

"Daddy never would've told me if Momma hadn't woke me up screaming one night." Belle took a sip. "He said that the place Momma was at was constantly getting shelled. She had a hard time with storms or loud noises ever since. Since the bombing started, this has been a nightly thing."

"Why didn't you tell me this was going on?"

Belle leaned back in her chair, looking more like a woman than a girl. "You had so much going on between your work at the ferry and volunteering at the infirmary. Now this thing with Tim. I know you don't sleep well. That's why you go to the lighthouse every night. I guess I just didn't want to burden you with this."

Belle had considered her feelings? Her sister had grown up since Ginny had been home. "You've put some thought into this, haven't you?"

"Well." She shrugged. "Me and the girls have. You've got enough on your plate. Besides, I look at this as my contribution to the war effort. I may be cleaning birds and collecting fat and tin, but this is something too, I guess."

Ginny reached for her hand. "It's more than something. If it ever gets to be too much for you, you tell me."

Belle entwined her fingers with her sister's. "It's not too much, sis. I love her. I can handle it."

Ginny had underestimated her sister. What else was Belle capable of doing? "I'll stay up. You've got school in the morning. If Momma needs me, I'll be there to take care of her."

"Are you sure, Gin? You've got work and then you have to meet Tim."

A muffled explosion echoed softly in the room. They fell quiet, waiting for their mother to call out. When several moments passed peacefully, they relaxed.

"The Germans are going to keep them busy at the infirmary in the morning," Ginny said wistfully.

"You miss it, don't you? Working at the infirmary, I mean." Belle shook her head. "Why did old Officer Chapline have to take that away from you? It's not fair."

"A lot of things in life aren't fair." She cupped Belle's chin in her hand. "Go to bed. I'll survive without a little sleep, but you can't. Now, scoot. Take your hot chocolate to your bedroom. I'll come by as soon as I clean up to tuck you in."

Belle nodded. She picked up her cup and headed across the room. When she reached the door, she turned. "I can't believe April slept through this. It must take a stick of dynamite to wake her up in the morning."

"She's dealing with a lot right now. She's probably worn out."

"If only her mother were here."

Ginny stared into her cup. She'd never been a Nosy Nellie, but the more information they had about April, the more they could help her. "Does she ever talk about her mother?"

Belle shook her head. "It's almost like she's been forbidden to talk about her, like she'll be in trouble if she mentions her. That's no way to live."

"No, it isn't. We need to find her, so any information you can get from April would be helpful."

Belle nodded. "Did you talk to Tim tonight and tell him what was going on?"

Ginny took a sip of her drink to cover the heat in her cheeks. "Yes. The navy has surrounded their house in case either Mr. Smith or his brother shows up."

"What are you two going to do next?"

"You mean me and Tim?"

Belle gave her a strange look. "The two of you are working together?"

"Yes." Why was her heart in her throat at just the mention of Tim? "He's going with us on Saturday. We thought maybe riding would be nicer than hiking the sound."

"Oh, good. I love to ride." She yawned. "Tim's a good man. He even knew the story about the Brownies Momma used to read us."

Ginny wasn't surprised. He probably read them to his sister while their father was away.

She glanced at her sister. Despite the normal teenage silliness, Belle was growing up to be a wonderful young woman. "Go to bed and don't worry about anything. I'll take care of it."

Belle nodded. "I love you, sis."

Warmth flooded Ginny at the sweet words. "I love you too."

———— ≈ ————

The horses pawed at the ground, as anxious to get started as Ginny was. Tim had taken it upon himself to check the saddles, adjusting and tying down their gear. Off to one side, the girls fidgeted with excitement, decked out in blue jeans and straw hats. There had been no attacks near them the night before, so everyone was rested and ready to go.

Ginny walked over to where the girls stood. "Ladies, Mr. Drummond only had five horses available, so someone will have to pair up. We'll change positions at the halfway point."

"Who are you going to pair up with, Ginny?" The question was followed by a torrent of giggles.

Ginny felt her cheeks grow hot. The girls were just teasing her. They couldn't know that she'd had the same thoughts of pairing up with Tim, holding tight to his waist, her ear pressed against his back, listening to his heart.

"Are you blushing?" Belle teased.

Probably, but she didn't need to confirm the fact. "You can draw straws to figure out the girls who will partner up, or you can volunteer. With only five of you. . ."

"Six, Ginny."

She turned to see Ruthie come through the padlock toward them. Belle broke from the group, meeting the girl halfway, then throwing her arms around her in a big hug. Ginny felt a sigh of relief go through her. Her sister had missed Ruthie sorely since their argument. It was good to see the girls make up and be friends again.

When they joined the group, Ginny smiled at the girl. "Glad to have you back, Ruthie."

Tim joined them, wiping his hands on his handkerchief. "I think we're ready."

A few minutes later, Ginny led the group out of the corral and to the path that would take them into Buxton Woods. It was a rare warm day, a nice reprieve in the middle of a cold winter. A perfect day for a ride. She glanced over her shoulder to catch Tim watching her, and she blushed again.

A minute later, he caught up with her. "Every time I look at you, you're blushing, Miss Mathis. What is that all about?"

"Nothing. I just naturally blush a lot."

"Really? I was hoping I might be the source of those blushes. Because it would mean you were thinking about me, just as I've thought about you for the last few weeks."

She chuckled. "You haven't even known me that long."

"Ah, yes, but your sister paints a very lovely picture of you, Ginny." His gaze grew tender. "I liked you before I ever met you."

Her breath caught in her throat. "Oh."

"All right, you two. Stop flirting up there," Belle called out. "We're trying to earn a badge here."

Ginny felt herself go red, which drew a sharp bark of laughter from Tim. "Yes, we must be good examples to these young girls, Miss Mathis."

She rolled her eyes. "I'm going to get you for this."

"I certainly hope so," he replied with a wicked smile. He sat up. "Ladies, anyone been to the matinee lately?"

"We saw another Thin Man movie last night," Belle called out. "Those are Ginny's favorites. She thinks William Powell is a dream."

"William Powell, huh?" Tim asked, glancing at her.

"Clara and I saw *The Philadelphia Story* last week," Ruthie said. "I've liked Jimmy Stewart since we saw him in *Shop around the Corner.* He just seems like he'd be a nice person. So kind and everything."

"I love Clark Gable." Ginny could hear Lucy's sigh from here. "He's just so handsome and romantic."

"You didn't like him in *Gone with the Wind*," Clara reminded her.

"That's because she read the book first," Belle replied. "Books always ruin the movie."

"I think it's the other way," Lucy answered. "And that Vivien Leigh didn't deserve Clark. He was much too good for her."

Tim leaned slightly toward her. "You have a group of theater critics in the making."

Ginny grinned. It was good to hear the girls talk about normal things like movies and all the other things teenage girls talked about. Maybe this would be a recess from the realities of war.

As the trees thickened, the path thinned, forcing them to ride single file. Ginny relaxed in her saddle, enjoying a rare moment of peace and quiet. She had spent time in these woods as a girl, fishing from the sound, weaving daydreams about the life she'd have when she grew up. Never had she thought a war would turn her dreams upside down. But then, who ever dreams of war?

"It never ceases to amaze me how different the sound side is compared to the ocean side," Clementine said, a hint of wonder in her voice.

"I think it's neat that you can see the sunrise over the ocean, then watch it set over the sound." April patted her horse. "There can't be too many places in the world you can do that."

"That's because we live on a barrier island. What that means is it's a narrow island close to the mainland that protects it from storms." Ginny nudged her horse forward. "Things like dunes and woods slow down hurricane-force winds so that the mainland doesn't get the brunt of the storm."

"I've only lived through one of those, but that was enough," Lucy called out. "I thought the house was gonna blow in around us."

"I agree." A shiver raced down Ginny's spine as she remembered the storm from six years ago. The high-pitched wail of the wind and the torrential rain had interrupted her many nights in the months afterward. But Daddy was determined to stick it out, and Momma...

Ginny focused on that moment. Had Momma had one of her episodes then? She didn't remember, only knew that Daddy had told her to sit in the hallway with little Belle. Maybe he thought she knew about Momma because of that night? Maybe that's why he hadn't told her when he'd made her come home.

"Woolgathering?" Tim asked softly.

She shook her head. "Just thinking about something. I'll tell you later."

"Are we almost at the sound? These trees are in the way of my view," Lucy called out.

Ginny and Tim exchanged a look before she replied. "It's up ahead. We'll stop there to let everyone stretch their legs."

"Maybe it would be a good idea if you told us what we're looking for," Clara said. "So we can be looking for it."

"You don't have to tell the whole island for something, ninny," Ruthie whispered at her sister. "It's secret."

"I'm not a ninny," Clara protested.

"A loudmouth then," Belle hissed.

Ginny glanced at Tim. "I'd better settle this before another war breaks out here."

Ginny fell back, then moved her horse between the two girls. "No fighting or we will turn around and go home. Is that understood?"

"Yes, ma'am."

"Good." Ginny settled in behind the group, letting Tim lead. It had been a few years since she had walked these woods, and then only in the summer. Being winter, only a single pine offered any color, its clumps of needles holding steadfast to the branches. Dead leaves carpeted the ground, some blown into small piles along the walking path. A boat would stand out like a beacon in this stark landscape.

"Can we ride ahead?" April asked.

Ginny nodded. The three horses took off at a gallop, but she wasn't worried. The kids on the island learned early to ride. It was the only way to get around sometimes.

When Ginny reached them, the girls had hitched their horses

to a tree and were tossing rocks into the water. Ahead, Tim canvassed the area. Ginny leaned up in her saddle. "Anyone beat my record yet?"

"I didn't see you do it, so it didn't happen." Belle dug at a rock in the ground until she pried it loose. Holding up her prize, she grinned. "This one here is a beauty."

Ginny watched as her sister walked to the water's edge and, with a practiced throw, skipped the rock over the water five times. This was how it should be for them, without the threat of war dangling over their heads like an ax. Belle, April, all of them deserved the kind of childhood she had. Things were hard, and they might not have had much in the way of material things, but they had enough.

"Ginny!"

Ginny jumped down from her mount, then hurried to where the girls had gathered at the waterline. Clementine walked along an outcropping of rock in front of them.

"What are you doing, Clementine?" Ginny asked.

"There was a loud thud right there when I threw my last rock," Ruthie answered, pointing to a place to the right of the rocks. "Clem went out to investigate."

She could see that. "Clementine, you need to get back here this instant. Those rocks could be slippery, and I don't want you falling in."

Instead, the girl took a long stick she carried and poked it into the water. "There's something down there."

"I don't care what it is." Ginny cupped her hands around her mouth. "Back here. Now."

"Yes, ma'am." She gave it one hard push. The wooden bottom of a boat rose to the surface, then sank just under the surface. Clem looked back at Ginny. "Do you still want me to stop?"

Ginny thought, then turned to the other girls. "Let's make a chain out to her. Stay on the rocks and hold hands. I'll put one arm around Clem's waist." She hurried ahead of them. At least the water was calm, and the rock outcropping appeared dry. She reached Clementine, then waited as the other girls fell into place. Once everyone was secure, she nodded to Clementine.

The next push moved the boat forward, but even from an angle, Ginny could see the name stamped in ominous black lettering.

The *Allan Jackson.*

Was this where Rolf had made shore? Was this his attempt to hide his whereabouts? Ginny inched closer to Clementine. "Do you think we can turn it over and get it to shore?"

The girl nodded, then turned and hit it again, this time on the side of the vessel. The other side rose, then fell. Large drops of water soaked through Ginny's jacket as the boat settled back. But Clementine wasn't ready to give up yet. Lifting the pole over her head, she struck the boat with the full weight of her upper body. The boat arched and teetered a moment before flipping to rest upright.

"That's what we're looking for," April said, her gaze trained on the lettering.

"Good grief, this Schmidt character isn't too bright to leave it here right near the trailhead." Belle shook her head.

Clementine discarded the pole into the water, then bent at the waist, drawing in a deep breath. "It wasn't that easy."

Ginny rubbed the girl's back. "Let's get back to shore and sit down. Get one of the girls to get your canteen and drink some water, all right?"

"Yes, ma'am." She gave Ginny a weak smile. "I can't wait to tell Tim we found it."

"Found what?"

The familiar male voice sent a tingle of awareness up Ginny's spine. Jerking around, she felt her feet slip. She tried to keep her balance, but the world felt as if it were leaning at a different angle. The next second, she was suspended in midair, almost floating. The first wave crashed over her, stealing her breath. She bopped upward and had just enough time to gasp before the next wave hit her. Ginny stretched her legs out. The water couldn't be that deep, but there was nothing beneath her. If the girls would throw her a rope, she could tread water until one was found.

Before she broke the surface, a masculine arm wrapped around her and pulled her up against him. "Bloody cold!"

"It's winter. It's supposed to be cold." She mashed her lips together to keep her teeth from chattering, then grimaced.

"Your face might freeze like that." Tiny droplets fell as he shook his head. "You wouldn't want that."

"Why not?" At least when he teased her, she forgot about the cold.

"You're too beautiful for that." Releasing her waist, he slid his arm beneath her knees and lifted her. "This is the rescuing part, so if you'll slide your arms around my neck. That's a good girl. Almost there."

Water sloughed off them as he walked them into the brush. It was warmer here onshore, but with these wet clothes, they still risked getting sick. If they didn't get dry and warmed up, hypothermia would set in.

Ginny turned and found four of the horses gone. "Where are the girls?"

"I sent them back to Mr. Drummond's. Then they're going to head to your house and get the fire going."

She nodded. "I really do need to go home and get out of these wet things."

Tim's breath felt warm against her cheek. "There might even be some hot cocoa involved. I hear that's your favorite."

"You know that too?" Belle had shared a lot with Tim. She

only wished she knew as much about him.

"I've got to get you warmed up. Your lips are turning blue."

"You could kiss me." Had she said that out loud? No, it wasn't like her at all. It also wasn't a bad idea.

"You always have the best ideas." His lips captured hers, shooting blissful warmth throughout her body. Her hands curled around his neck, her fingers tangling with the wet strands of his hair. He angled his head slightly, then teased her lips into deepening the kiss. She felt heated from the inside out and couldn't seem to get close enough to him.

Too soon, he lifted his head. "I'm going to have to rescue you more often."

The low rumble of his voice told her he had been as affected as she was by the kiss. Ginny opened her eyes to find Tim watching her, his eyes a darkened shade of blue. "Only if I can rescue you too."

He gave her a roguish grin. "Deal." For one brief moment, she thought he might kiss her again, then he drew back. "A warm fire and a hot drink will have you back to normal before you know it. You think you can stand?"

"Yes."

He held her steady as her feet touched the ground. Taking her hands, he watched her. "Are you sure?"

Ginny nodded. "I'm fine, though I'm not usually that clumsy."

"I startled you. I shouldn't have walked up on you like that." Tim picked up his coat and dropped it over her shoulders.

Ginny knew the real reason for her clumsiness. Seeing him approach earlier, watching her as if she were the only person there, had made her realize that she was falling for him in a big way, and that wouldn't do. There was school to finish and a nursing career to embark on. She didn't have time for love. . .only her heart didn't seem to be listening. "I'm glad you were there. Did you see the boat?"

Tim took her hand and threaded it through his arm, causing a pleasant sensation of warmth to flood her insides. "Rolf must have landed here."

"It looks that way." They walked slowly toward the horse, as if he were enjoying these few moments alone as much as she was. She needed to keep her mind on the mission at hand, so she filled him in on their discovery. "With it being turned upside down like that, I think Rolf used it as a cover then tried to sink it when he was finished with it."

"That makes sense." Letting go of her hand, Tim took the horse's reins and led him over to a felled log. Using Tim's shoulder as balance, Ginny mounted, then scooted forward to give Tim room behind her. When he was settled in the saddle, he wrapped one arm around her waist and pulled her close. His heart thundered against her back, and she smiled. Did he feel the same way she did, that the feelings they shared weren't just a wartime romance, but something more? Part of her thrilled at the notion, while the other, more sensible part thought it was a mistake to get involved. As soon as the German was found, Tim would head back to New York, and where would that leave her? With a broken heart.

Tim nudged the horse back up the trail. "Rolf picked a good place to come ashore. There's not a soul around."

"No one except for Mr. Murphy." She nodded toward a wooded trail in the opposite direction. "He's the unofficial historian of Buxton Woods. His family has lived here since before the Civil War. If anyone is hiding out in these woods, he knows about it."

"Do you think we could come back after we get changed and talk to him? I'd like to know what he saw."

Ginny understood Tim's desire to locate Rolf and his brother, but it would have to wait. "By the time we get back and get cleaned up, it will be too late. It's a long walk to his house, and no one wants to be out here after dark."

His arms tightened around her, but he finally agreed. "Then tomorrow. I know it's Sunday, but could we leave early in the morning? It'll give us time to look around."

She was going to suggest the same thing. "The girls are probably disappointed. I know they were looking forward to today."

"I'm sure they'll find something else to keep them occupied." Tim lowered his voice to a whisper. "I thought for a moment they were going to practice their first aid skills on you."

"Then I'll count it a blessing to have avoided that." She chuckled. "Just send them over to our house. I bought some yarn and six sets of knitting needles for them to make socks and gloves for our boys."

His breath was warm against her ear. "You're truly remarkable. The way you've taken those girls under your wing and taught them skills they can use every day. They're blessed to have you." He hesitated. "I'm blessed to have you."

Ginny didn't know what to say. A thank-you felt so wrong, not when her heart longed to share all that she felt for him. The truth was, she was blessed to know him, to spend this time with him, so why not tell him? "I cherish the time we've spent together, Tim. I truly do." The silence stretched out, and she felt the impulse to fill it. "That, and the fact that you're a good kisser."

Tim let out a bark of laughter. "Just good. I guess I'll have to practice more." He kissed the shell of her ear, his voice a growl. "You know the old saying, practice makes perfect."

Practice? With whom? She jerked around and glared at him. "Who are you thinking of practicing with?"

He kissed the tip of her nose. "Do you know of anyone? You could give me a referral."

Ginny knew a dozen or so girls who'd jump at the chance, not that she had any notion to tell them. "I can't think of one right off the top of my head. Maybe you should practice on a pillow. Girls do it all the time."

His dark brows arched up. "Did you practice kissing on your pillow? What a waste."

Of course she had, but he didn't need to know that. She might die of embarrassment if he did. Ginny shook her head. "I've heard other girls talk about it."

"Other girls, huh?" He met her gaze. "You know what I think?"

She didn't have a clue. She shook her head.

His eyes darkened as they drifted to her mouth. "That if we keep up this conversation, I'm going to drag you off this horse and show you just how good a kisser I am."

Heat flooded her cheeks as she imagined the scene and realized she wouldn't protest. In fact, she'd jump off the beast herself if it meant he'd give her another one of those scorching kisses. As much as she'd like to explore these new feelings she had for him, they had a mission to accomplish. Ginny faced forward.

His laughter rumbled against her back. "Scaredy-cat."

She supposed she was, but he'd be going back to New York once they located Schmidt. She'd be left here on the island, nursing her broken heart.

"I still can't believe they found the boat and managed to get it topside," Tim said a few minutes later.

Thank heavens, he'd changed the topic. She could talk about her troop all day long. Ginny grinned. "You can thank Clemmie for that. They're a very resourceful group of young ladies when they put their minds to it."

She nestled against him, enjoying the warmth and the feel of his body against hers. Would he still think she was a scaredy-cat if she told him that this was what had made her blush earlier? That being held by him was so much better than she ever could have imagined?

"You know," he whispered softly, "when you said we'd have to partner up to ride, this was what I thought of, holding you like this. When you blushed, I'd hoped the same thought had crossed your mind."

They truly were of one mind. "Maybe."

He dropped a kiss on her head in response. Time passed too quickly, and before she knew it, Tim was leading the horse into the corral. Dismounting, he placed his hands on her waist and helped her down, holding her a moment longer than necessary.

Taking the reins, he held out his other hand to her. "I'll take care of the horses. You go home and get warmed up."

Ginny didn't dare tell him she was perfectly warm. Riding in his arms had done that to her. "I can help."

"Go on. It won't take me long."

"All right. But wear some heavy boots tomorrow if you have them. If you don't, I can dig up a pair of Daddy's." She took off his coat and handed it to him. Their fingers tangled before finally entwining. "Thank you for saving me. I'm not sure how I'll ever repay you."

Tim leaned over and brushed a soft kiss to her lips. "And thank you."

"For what?"

He smiled as he let go of her hand. "For just being you."

———— ≈ ————

Ginny should have known the girls would be waiting on her when she got home. She had barely turned the lock on the kitchen door when she smelled the delectable combination of cinnamon and cooked apples. With Mother visiting family in Ocracoke, there was only one possible culprit cooking. Ginny pulled off her coat and gloves and hung them up before going to the kitchen.

April and Ruthie sat at the table with a large sack of flour and several mixing bowls. Like mad scientists in a picture show, they mixed ingredients, one turning a large serving spoon while the other poured in flour, baking soda, and sugar. At the stove, Belle supervised Clara and Lucy as they poured canned apples into a large soup pot. Clem stood off in one corner, a ribbon of apple peel dangling from her pocketknife.

She should be mad. After all, they had made a huge mess that she'd more than likely have to clean up. But she couldn't muster up even one angry thought. It was like Tim had said—they were good girls, and if they made a mess every now and then, there was no reason to make a federal case of it.

"Ginny." Six pairs of eyes stared at her, and Belle came toward her. "I know we've wrecked the kitchen, and we have every intention of cleaning it up." She glanced back at the girls. "We just thought it would be nice to have an apple pie while we listen to the radio this evening."

She could go for a piece of pie. Ginny smiled at her sister. "That's a great idea. Anything I can do to help?"

Belle blinked, then shook her head. "Why don't you get out of those wet clothes and take a bath? We've got everything under control."

"Are you sure? I'm pretty good in the pie-making department."

Ruthie eyed her suspiciously. "Are you sure you're okay, Ginny? You're acting strange."

Ginny couldn't help herself. She laughed. "Why? Because I offered to help?"

"Well, there's that. And the fact you didn't pitch a fit when you saw the mess we made." Belle laid her hand across Ginny's forehead, then shook her head.

"Then I'm really going to scare you." Ginny glanced around the room. She wasn't sure what had gotten into her, but she liked it. "How about we have a slumber party? That way, no one has to go home tonight. We can bunk down here tonight, then you girls can go to church in the morning."

Belle's eyes widened. "Are you serious? You know how much I've wanted to have one." She grimaced. "But what about the lighthouse? Don't you have to go tonight?"

Ginny shook her head. She'd need a good night of sleep if they intended to hike to Murph's tomorrow. She wished she could call him, but he didn't have a phone. The man didn't like any of the modern conveniences. "Once we put the pie on, we'll make pallets in the living room so that you can listen to the radio. Just remember that there's church tomorrow. All right?"

The girls nodded their agreement. Good, now that that was settled, she could take a relaxing soak. Maybe she should use some of that honeysuckle bubble bath Momma had bought her for Christmas. She had just grabbed the latest issue of the *Ladies' Home Journal* off the counter and crossed the room when Belle's question stopped her.

"How was Tim when you left him?"

Ginny buried her face in the magazine, her cheeks aflame from the memory of Tim's kiss. "He was cold and wet, but he seemed fine."

"I bet he was better than fine," Ruthie said, fanning herself with her hand. "It was so romantic, the way he rescued you."

"She was only in six feet of water." Clem snorted, dropping the apple peel into the trash can. "She could have made it back to shore without any problems."

"But it wouldn't have been nearly as romantic." Ruthie sighed. "And the way he swept her in his arms and kissed her. Oh my!"

Ginny twisted around, her heart beating wildly in her chest. "You were spying on us?"

Wiping her hands on a towel, Belle rushed to her, shaking her head. "It wasn't like that, Gin. Clem dropped her pocketknife and went back for it."

Ginny crossed her arms. "And the rest of you?"

"We couldn't let her go back there alone," Belle pleaded with her. "There's a German spy on the loose."

Ginny stormed down the hall. Belle was right, of course. In her embarrassment, Ginny had forgotten the whole reason they'd ridden out to the sound in the first place. Still, those moments with Tim had been personal. Private.

A touch at her sleeve jerked Ginny around. Belle stared up at her, her eyes brimming with tears. "I'm sorry, sis. We should have waited for Clem, then come home."

Ginny shook her head. "I'm the one who should be sorry. It's just that. . ."

"That we were spying on you just for the sake of it?" Her little sister shrugged. "I can see why you'd think that. I haven't made it easy on you since you came back. It's just you put up such a fuss about coming home, and I thought it had something to do with me." The hurt in her expression put a knife in Ginny's heart. "We haven't been as close as we were before you left to go to college."

"Oh, Belle." Taking her sister's hand, she tugged her into her arms. "It didn't have anything to do with you. I simply wanted to finish school."

"So you could enlist. I know." Belle glanced up at her, her pale blue eyes bright with tears. "It's why I told Daddy I couldn't handle things with Momma. I begged him to bring you home."

"You?"

Belle nodded. "I was so scared something would happen to you, and with Momma the way she is, Daddy thought it was a good idea."

Ginny considered it. If she were honest with herself, her time at home had been far better than she'd expected. Her experience at the infirmary had proved invaluable and would serve her well in the years to come. Since she'd discovered the truth behind

Momma's night terrors, Momma had been able to talk about her time in France, which seemed to help her sleep.

Then there was Belle and Clem and Ruthie, Clara, Lucy, and April. How blessed she'd been by their curiosity and their willingness to help in any way they could, and their adventuresome spirit! She'd grown to love them, odd since she'd only taken on the troop because Belle had nagged her.

And there was Tim.

She leaned down and kissed her sister's head. "Go finish the pie. I'm going to go take a nice long bath, and then I'll be down to share a piece."

"You're not mad at me?"

Ginny shook her head. "You were right. It was best for everyone that I come home, even if I couldn't see it at the time."

Belle's face lit up as she squeezed her tight. "Really, sis? 'Cause I think so too."

She tweaked the girl's pigtail. "Now, finish up that pie, and we'll make breakfast for dinner tonight. Oh, look out in the freezer. There's a gallon of vanilla ice cream we haven't eaten yet."

"Really?" Belle turned and hurried back into the kitchen. "Girls, we've got ice cream for the pie!"

If the hooting and hollering from the girls was anything to go by, she wouldn't get a minute of sleep tonight, but she found she didn't mind. Ginny climbed the stairs to the second floor, with a hot bath and thoughts of a certain handsome Englishman to keep her occupied.

≡ CHAPTER 18 ≡

Tim pulled up the collar of his coat as he walked up the path to Ginny's house, the crushed oyster shells under his feet a new experience for him. If there was one thing he could say about the islanders, it was that they were resourceful. Well, most of the Americans he knew were, come to think of it. They would need that resourcefulness in the weeks and months to come.

Taking the steps up to the front porch, Tim hurried to the front door and knocked. A peal of girlish squeals rose behind the door, startling him until he realized it was Belle and the other girls. He glanced down at his watch. Eight o'clock. Too early for church yet. More than likely, it was a hen party. Iris had loved having her friends over for a night of gossip and goodies that lasted well into the next morning. Poor Ginny. She probably had another sleepless night.

He was about to knock again when Belle opened the door, wearing a bathrobe and her brightest smile. "Good morning, Tim. Kind of early to be calling, don't ya think?"

"Good morning to you." He smiled back at her. "And your sister is expecting me."

Suddenly, the doorway was crowded by the rest of Ginny's troop. "She didn't mention meeting you this morning."

"That's because you'd want to go with us, and you can't," Ginny replied as she came down the stairs. She turned to him, her smile shy, a memory he would hold close for the rest of his days. "Good morning, Tim."

"Good morning." He wanted to give her a not-so-proper morning kiss, but with six impressionable girls watching them, he settled for a long look. Her hair was pulled back, revealing her long neck and rosy cheeks. The boy's flannel shirt and blue jeans did nothing to hide her soft curves and long legs. The faint scent of honeysuckle as she grabbed her coat and gloves from a nearby chair drew him like bees to honey.

Taking her coat from her, he held it for her as she slipped into it. As she slid her hands into her gloves, he whispered so that only she could hear, "I want to kiss you so much right now, I can barely think straight."

Her cheeks turned a delightful shade of pink as she turned back to the girls. "You've got almost two hours before Sunday school starts. There's toast and fried ham in the kitchen. Clara and Ruthie's parents are coming by to drive you to church. Belle and April, they've invited you to lunch as well. I shouldn't be too late. We're just going to see Mr. Murphy."

"Tell Murph I said hello. . .and be careful. Those woods out near his shack are dangerous," Belle called out as she scurried toward the kitchen. She turned in the doorway. "Come on, you guys. I'm starving."

Once the girls had left the room, Ginny turned to face him. "Ready?"

"Not yet." Drawing her into his arms, he bent his head and pressed his lips to hers. She pressed herself closer, her hands sliding over his shoulders before settling at the nape of his neck, her fingers curling into his hair. He deepened the kiss, sensation threatening to spiral out of control. To love Ginny was an adventure he wanted for the rest of his life.

But what of her? She'd never spoken of love, and with her, he didn't want anything less. Lifting his head, Tim studied her for a long moment. Though her eyes were still closed, her expression held a dreamlike quality, her lips with a just-kissed look that called him back for more.

Instead, Tim gently untangled her arms from around his neck and stepped back. "I'm sorry, Ginny. I shouldn't have. . ."

She shook her head as if shaking off the memories of the last few minutes. "It's fine. I just hope the girls didn't snoop on us like they did yesterday. I mean, they weren't really snooping. Clem lost her pocketknife, and with Schmidt on the loose, the rest of them couldn't exactly let her go back alone. So. . ." She stopped and met his gaze. "I'm babbling, aren't I?"

Tim smiled at her. "Just a little."

"I'm sorry, it's just that I've never felt this way about someone before, and I don't know the rules. I mean, I've dated before and even had a few crushes, but never anything like this. But then, I've never had these feelings for. . ." She blinked. "I'm doing it again, and I've never been much of a talker."

Tim took her hand in his. "I know what you mean. I've never had these kinds of feelings for anyone else before either. It's the reason I stopped kissing you. I care for you too much to fall into the same old patterns I had before I committed myself to Christ. Those kinds of relationships simply lead to heartache."

"Did you love them?" Her question held a note of uncertainty. "These women in your past?"

"I thought I did, but none of that compares to what I feel for you. That's why I want to go slow, take some time to see where this relationship is going." Rubbing her delicate knuckles with the pad of his thumb, he stole a glance at her. "What do you think?"

"You're right. I don't want to regret anything that happens between us, Tim."

He lifted her hand and brushed a kiss against her fingers. "That doesn't mean I'm going to stop kissing you at times."

Her light chuckle soothed him. "I hope not! If you did, I'd just kiss you."

He barked with laughter. "Feel free to kiss me anytime you please." Opening the door, he stood to the side. "Ready to go?"

Ginny nodded as she grabbed her scarf and wrapped it over her head. "Ready as I'll ever be."

The walk to Buxton Village, then to Buxton Woods, took longer than Tim expected, but he enjoyed every second talking with Ginny. They covered a wide array of topics, from music—both enjoyed Glenn Miller and Bing Crosby—to movies to books. Ginny told him of her desire to serve as an army nurse overseas, while he shared his desire to one day write a book. The war was forgotten for those few moments they spoke of their hopes and dreams for the future, a future Tim saw Ginny playing a starring role in.

"Why do you like Jimmy Stewart so much? I mean, he's a good enough actor and everything, but nothing special." Tim pushed back a bare limb, then took Ginny's hand to help her step over the fallen tree.

"He gained weight just so he could join the army last year, and I've read he intends to fly bombers for the new air force." She tightened her grip as she jumped from the log. "That makes him kind of special in my book."

"So you like real-life heroes?"

Looking up into his eyes, she pressed her lips together, then spoke. "Not so much heroes as people who live out their principles. Most people say one thing, then do something else, but those people who stand up for what they believe, those are the folks I admire the most." She squeezed his hand. "Like you."

Tim snorted. "Me? I don't think so."

"Of course you do. You could have refused to bring Captain Schmidt to New York. You could have stayed at your office and written articles instead of almost drowning off the coast when your ship was sunk." She entwined her fingers with his. "That makes you a hero in my book."

Guilt settled over him. He hadn't taken the assignment for the greater good, but for more personal reasons. If he was going to have any kind of relationship with Ginny, he had to be honest. "I had my own reasons for wanting the assignment."

"What were they?" Sunlight turned her blond hair into shards of light. "You don't have to tell me."

Tim turned and took her by the shoulders. "But I need to tell you so you know the kind of person I am."

"All right then. I'm listening." Ginny sat down on a thick tree limb sitting close to the ground.

Where did he start? He paced the small clearing. "I've told you about growing up on a farm alongside my sister when we were kids. It was my grandparents' place not that far from Sheffield. My mother died giving birth to my sister, and Papa decided that going to sea was preferable over staying home and raising us. He'd visit, of course. Sometimes, he'd even stay the week, but most of the time he'd flitter in and out of our lives whenever he could afford time away from his ship. But when he went down with his ship, it almost killed Iris. She was always closer to him than I was, and after losing her husband. . .It was almost too much for her to bear." Tim met her gaze. "I wanted to kill Schmidt for what he'd done to Iris and Will. I thought if he was dead, we could move on with our lives." Slamming his eyes shut, he dug his fingers into his hair. "But I couldn't do it."

"You saved him that night on the boat."

How well Ginny knew him. He drew in a shaky breath, then nodded. "I couldn't do it. No matter what horrible things he's done or how many people he's killed, I couldn't kill him."

Shock ran through him as she took his hand in hers. "Of course you couldn't. That's not who you are."

"But he killed my father and thousands of innocent men."

"That is the burden Schmidt will have to bear."

Tim glanced down at their joined hands. "So you're not disappointed in me?"

Her answer was to rise on tiptoe and kiss his cheek. "Are you kidding? I admire you more. We're not judged by what we think about doing but by the things we do. I think we're going to learn a lot about people, some good and some not so good, during this war. I only pray we come out the better from it."

If he doubted his feelings for this woman, this moment confirmed his suspicions. He was in love with her, and if she gave him a chance, he would happily spend the rest of his life proving it to her.

Wrapping his arm around her waist, he pulled her against his body. "I'm about to kiss you again."

"Is that my warning?" She snaked her arms around his neck and pulled him close.

"The only one you'll get," he whispered against her lips, then pressed forward.

Several moments later, she pressed her hand against his chest and gave him a little push. Tim held her for a moment longer, then stepped out of her embrace. Her voice was low and husky when she spoke. "We'd better get a move on if we want to get out of here before dusk."

Tim held out his hand to her. "How large are these woods?"

Her soft chuckle warmed him as she took his hand. "It seems funny to have a forest here at all, it being so close to the ocean. Yet it's been here since before history was ever recorded about these islands. Some folks think it should be a national park, but that would mean more visitors, and the same folks who want the park don't like the idea of being overrun by out-of-town guests."

"I can understand that." Privacy was very important to him. Tim pushed back a low-hanging branch, then waited for Ginny to safely walk through. He let the branch go behind him. "You said Murphy's family has been here since the Civil War."

She led him around a grove of trees. "His grandfather fought for the Union Army. When he was discharged, he was given land here on the island for his service. His family has fished these waters ever since."

"It sounds like a bit of paradise."

"Paradise can get boring at times," she replied pensively. "It's one of the reasons I went to the mainland for college. On the island, I felt so cut off at times from the rest of the world."

"It felt that way during the Blitz. Cut off from the world, that is. Great Britain is just a small island like yours. Except it's warmer here, and the beaches offer a better view than ours," he quipped.

"Yet it holds such history and majesty, it's hard to think of it as an island at all." She smiled up at him. "Thank you. Sometimes, I forget how blessed I am to live here."

"It happens to everyone. We want what we don't have," he said. "I'm the same way. I came to New York wanting to make a difference in this war, but I've realized the articles I've been writing aren't what the world needs. It needs the truth about what Hitler is doing and stories about good people fighting the fight."

"You sound as if you've made some decisions about your future."

Tim had—the first being he couldn't imagine a life without Ginny. That settled, everything else fell into place. Once this episode with Rolf was behind him, he would return to New York and offer his services to the AP wire. It could mean a more dangerous assignment in Europe, but they would cross that road when they came to it.

For the moment, his focus was on Rolf and keeping Ginny safe. "Have you known Mr. Murphy for a long time?"

"Since I was seven. Murph is a hermit in ways." She turned and pressed her gloved hand to his chest. Warmth pooled beneath her fingers. "That's not to say he's unkind or anything. He's a very nice man. He only lets a few people into his inner circle."

Tim covered her hand with his. "I take it you're one of those chosen few."

The rosy color that infused her cheeks answered his question. "If Murph saw anything suspicious, he'll tell us."

They talked about everyday topics as they walked through dense underbrush and patches of trees. The scent of decaying leaves hung in the cold air. In the distance, a lone bird cooed softly, as if calling out for a feathered friend to join him and getting no answer. They zigzagged their way through a marsh that emptied into a small clearing carpeted with ivy.

"We're here."

Tim glanced around. Unless Mr. Murphy was coming out of thin air, he didn't see anything. As he turned, a glimmer of light flashed in the corner of his eye. Turning in the direction of the light, he saw it, a tiny shack with walls held up by overgrowths of ivy and some other vines. The gray timbers that made up the sides looked weather-worn and ready to tumble to the ground in a pile of sticks. The roof was rusted white in places, the tin probably placed there by the old Union soldier himself. As they drew closer, the nauseous smell of dead animals grew stronger. A quick glance around revealed the source. Flies swarmed around a rusted metal barrel in the side yard.

The front stairs creaked beneath their weight as Ginny knocked on the front door. A thunder of footsteps sounded from inside, beating a path to the front of the house. The door swung open, and a huge mountain of a man glared down at them. His skin was dark as strong coffee, his arms straining against the bindings of his cotton shirt.

Eyeing Tim, the man barked, "Whatcha want?"

"Hi, Murph," Ginny answered instead. "It's been a long time."

The man's gaze fell on Ginny, and his expression softened. "Ginny girl, what are you doing out here? You know these woods ain't safe."

"Don't worry. I've got Daddy's pistol in my coat pocket just in case." She smiled up at the big man. "How have you been? I haven't seen you in town in a while."

"No complaints. Long as I have food in my belly and a roof over my head, I'm fine." His gaze sharpened as he glanced over her shoulder to Tim. "Who's he?"

"Oh, I'm sorry." Ginny moved slightly so she could make the introduction. "This is Tim Elliott. He's a friend of mine."

A friend? Tim bristled at the word. What they had was so much more than friendship. At least, he felt that way. But how did Ginny feel about him? He'd need to know before he made any more plans. He stepped around her and offered the man his hand. "Timothy Elliott, sir. Ginny has told me so much about you."

"She has?" He eyeballed him, then turned to Ginny.

She nodded. "He's a good guy, Murph. You can trust him."

"Can't be too certain these days what with the ocean on fire and everything." He clamped Tim's hand in his meaty hand. "You must be here about the man that came onshore the other day. I knew he was trouble the minute I saw him."

Tim glanced at Ginny, his gut telling him Murph would finally have the answers they'd been searching for about Rolf. "Can you tell us what happened?"

"Nothing much to tell. I was working on my nets down by

the sound a couple of weeks ago when I heard some men yelling something about that crazy man over in Germany. It was too late for decent people to be out in those woods, so I knew they were trouble. I followed them for a bit until I saw who they were." He glanced at Ginny. "One of them was that sweet little Smith girl's daddy, but the man who come up out of the water, I ain't never seen him before."

"What did he look like?" Tim asked.

Murph turned to him. "It was too far away to know exactly what he looked like, but he did have almost white hair and looked like he'd seen a ghost."

"Seen a ghost?" Tim glanced back at Ginny.

She touched his sleeve. "The man was pale skinned."

"Oh." If he intended to build a life with Ginny, he'd need a dictionary of southern sayings simply to manage a conversation with her friends. "It sounds like the man we're looking for. Do you happen to know where they went?"

"I know exactly where they are. I sold Mr. Smith an old shack I owned close to the edge of the woods about a year ago. The only reason I did it was because he said it was for his little girl, and I figured a man wouldn't lie about his kin like that." Murph crossed his arms over his chest. "If I'd known he wanted to hide some German fella there, I wouldn't have done business with him."

Ginny laid her hand on the man's forearm. "I know you wouldn't have. You've always thought the best of folks."

Tim watched as Ginny comforted her friend. She had a way about her, the ability to put someone at ease no matter the circumstances. It was a unique quality that few people had, and another trait he loved about her.

Tim rubbed his temples. This was their chance to catch Rolf and his brother. Excitement built inside him. Maybe then Tim could lay his father to rest. Coming back to stand beside Ginny, he asked the man, "Could you show us this shack? We'll need to contact Officer Chapline and get some reinforcements before we can go, but we'd appreciate it if you'd show us how to get there."

The man turned to Ginny. "Are you coming too?"

She nodded. "I'll be there."

Tim tensed beside her. Now that they knew where Schmidt and his brother were, there was no reason for Ginny to be put in further danger. He hoped he could make her see reason once they returned to town later tonight.

"Anything else you can think of?" Ginny asked. "Every little bit helps."

The big man thought for a moment. "He sank a perfectly good boat. Not sure why, but he was in no hurry to drag it back to shore. Which tells me he has no intention of getting off the island, at least not that way."

Tim hadn't thought of that. There was only one reason he could think of for Schmidt to stay. A full-scale invasion with Schmidt at the controls. Tim's gut twisted at the thought.

"We found it today. It's floating at the trail's head if you want it."

"Why, thank you. You've always been a sweet one," Murphy said, then leaned toward her, his eyes fixed on her. "How are you doing, baby girl? I heard your daddy forced you to come home."

Tim's ears perked up. Ginny wasn't the kind of woman to be forced into anything. "What is he talking about?"

Ginny leaned in, the scent of honeysuckle clouding his thoughts. "Daddy was asked by the military to go to Virginia Beach to lead a team in building a new fleet. Momma doesn't like being alone at night, so he asked me to come home."

"Belle's home." Tim was prying, but he couldn't help it. Ginny mattered to him. He wanted her to be happy. "Your mother wouldn't have been alone."

"Can we talk about this later?"

So there was more to the story. Why couldn't her mother and Belle move in with Ginny rather than the other way around? Inland, they would be safe, and Ginny could finish her nursing degree with her class. Why did she have to be the one to make a sacrifice? One glance at her told him she wasn't in the mood to answer any more of his questions, at least not now.

"Is there anything you need?" Ginny asked the older man.

"Maybe some of your momma's homemade vegetable soup next time you're out this way. His white teeth shone bright. "I've been hankering for some soup and cornbread."

"I'll bring you some when we come back. Does tomorrow sound good to you?"

"It sounds wonderful. I can almost taste that soup now."

Placing her hands on his crossed forearms, she brushed a kiss on his plump cheek. "Thank you for your help. We appreciate it."

"I know you do, hon." Murphy shooed them off the porch. "You'd best be going home. The winds are picking up, and these old bones are telling me we're in for a storm."

"I'll bring you a couple of jars of Momma's soup as soon as I can. Bye now." The wood creaked as she stepped back, then waited until the door closed. Once Murph was inside, she turned to Tim. "Ready?"

"Are you going to tell me why your father forced you to come home?" he asked as he took her hand and helped her down the untrustworthy stairs.

"I knew you were going to ask me about that. The truth is, it's not important anymore."

But the reporter in him wouldn't let it die. "Why did your father force you to come home?"

"Because Belle was afraid to be left alone with my mother." She pulled her hand from his, and he mourned the loss. "She was on the Western Front during the Great War, and the ship attacks are too much for her to bear." Her eyes looked tired as she stared out over the sound. "She has shell shock."

He'd written an article on the subject. It had been difficult to listen to what those men and women suffered on the battlefield and heartbreaking to consider the stigma they carried with them every day. He slid his hands down her arms. "What was your mother doing there?"

"Those stories she told me about the Girl Guides—it turns out they were about her. She served as an ambulance driver during the war. From what I've gathered, the hospital where she worked was bombed while she was on leave in Paris. She lost many of her friends."

"I'm so sorry, Ginny." He truly was. Having interviewed patients with shell shock, he knew how traumatic it could be for the person as well as their family. "Is she seeking treatment?"

"Not yet, but once I talk to my father, we're going to look into it." She smiled, but it didn't reach her eyes.

"We'd better get back." Tim caught her hand and threaded his fingers with hers. He'd never been the type of man who liked holding hands, but with Ginny, it felt natural. "You and Murph seem to be close friends."

"We are." She squeezed his hand almost as if she enjoyed it as well. "It's kind of an odd friendship. He's very old-fashioned and happy to live in his little island shack for the rest of his days, while I couldn't wait to leave this place once I graduated high school. Strange that we get along so well."

"How did you become friends?"

She relaxed beside him. "He saved my life when I was a couple of years younger than Belle, and I'll be forever grateful he did."

The thought of Ginny dying stole his breath. "What happened?"

Ginny hesitated as if unsure how to start. "My sister isn't the

227

only one who can be adventurous."

That was a surprise coming from a woman as cautious as her. "Just how adventuresome were you?"

"When I was ten, I talked my parents into letting me go on a camping trip with some older girls from my school. Momma wasn't too happy about it, but I thought it would be fun to go camping and have a crab bake on the beach. I'd never been to one, and I just wanted to go."

That sounded like something a young Ginny would do. "That doesn't sound too adventurous. How did you get in trouble?"

"I thought I'd impress my new friends by finding some huge crabs for the bake. The crabs weren't big enough near the shore, so I went out deeper." Ginny shivered against him as if reliving the moment. "I got caught in a riptide, and none of the other kids noticed. I didn't know what to do. Every time I tried to get back to shore, it felt like I was drifting farther out."

He could have lost her before he ever met her. Riptides were deadly. He brought her hand to his chest. "How did Mr. Murphy save you?"

"I was so tired, and the fire on the beach seemed farther and farther away. Murph had been out fishing for tuna when he saw that I was in trouble." Ginny looked up at him, her blue eyes moist with unshed tears. "He dragged me into his boat and wrapped me up in a blanket before he headed to shore. He gave those kids what for when we got to the beach. I don't think I would've made it much longer if he hadn't shown up like that. We've been friends ever since."

"Did he tell your parents?"

"No. I went to his place to thank him for saving my life, and he gave me a swimming lesson in the sound. He taught me how to react if I ever got caught in a riptide again." Her brow furrowed. "It took me two years before I went back into the water, but Murph was there, pretending to fish as he watched me from his boat. I haven't been afraid to go back into the water ever since."

"I understand. There were times after the boat sank that I thought I wasn't going to make it. I love swimming, but I don't want to go back in anytime soon."

She glanced up at him, mischief in her eyes. "Scaredy-cat."

He chuckled. "At the moment, it's too cold for a dip, but maybe this summer. . ." The word trailed off. After Rolf and Frank's capture, he'd be heading back to New York, then who knew where. He didn't want to leave her, but he had an obligation to crown and country just as she had obligations to her family and friends here.

"It's all right, Tim. We'll figure this whole long-distance thing out."

He glanced down at her. Her cheeks and lips were cherry pink from the cold, but it was her eyes that drew his attention. Clear blue with a certainty he wished he felt. "What if I'm sent over to cover the fighting in Italy or Africa? There's a real possibility of that happening."

"I would write you every day, letters and letters about all the boring stuff happening here at home." She gave him a gentle bump to the shoulder. "With you being a writer and all, I would expect a letter or two in my mailbox every week, and two on Christmas."

"I guess this kind of courtship will be happening ten thousand times over with the war going on." He gave her a swift kiss on the lips. "I just like to do my romancing in person."

"I'd love that too, but this way we'll probably get to know each other better without the attraction between us getting in the way."

Tim's chest swelled. "So you're attracted to me too."

"You know I am, you big lug." She gave him a playful slap on his coat-clad arm, then grew serious. "How are we going to do this tomorrow? I figure you'll want to talk to Officer Chapline and come up with a plan."

"Yes, though I don't want us to go in there guns ablaze. I'd really like to take Frank Smith alive."

Ginny stepped over a dead log. "What are we going to do about April?"

Tim shook his head as he pushed a low-hanging limb out of their way. "I don't know. I take it you aren't calling social services."

"No." Ginny met his gaze. "It would be great if you could locate her mother, though I don't know how to feel about a woman who would walk out on her daughter. I mean, is that the kind of person you'd want to leave your child with? I wish she could just stay with us. At least I'd know she was being cared for."

They reached another small clearing. Despite the cold, the thick carpet of ivy was a lush green. "Does she have an idea where her mother is? It seems her mother would want to keep in touch."

She shook her head. "April never speaks about her, but then, she was so young when her mother left. You can't miss what you've never had."

He had an idea. "Do you know her mother's name? I've got contacts around the country who would help me find her. At least then, April wouldn't be alone."

"You would do that?" Ginny looked dumbstruck, then flung herself into his arms, raining kisses on his cheeks, nose, anywhere but his lips. "You are the most wonderful man."

Who was he to argue? Tim folded her into his arms, then nuzzled the soft shell of her ear while she continued to press kisses to his cheek.

"Hmmm." She breathed out on the sigh.

The tiny moan sent him over the edge, and he turned his head for a kiss. Her lips were soft and slightly open, an invitation to deepen the kiss.

A twig snapped, and he reluctantly lifted his head from hers.

Tim glanced at her, his breath caught in his throat at the dreamy look in her eyes. He lowered his head again but then he felt it—the barrel of a pistol pressed to the back of his neck.

"You've made a new friend, I see. And I'd hoped you would have died in the attack."

Tim's heart slammed hard against his ribs.

They had found Rolf.

The sight of a gun held to Tim's head made Ginny stiffen in terror. One slight move and the man she had come to love would be murdered right in front of her. They needed help, but who would come for them? Murph thought they were on their way home, and Belle wouldn't step foot in these woods, not this late in the day.

That left it up to them to figure out a way to escape. She glanced over Tim's shoulder at the brute. He was tall like Tim, but wirier than Tim's muscular build. Considerably older than her, if the gray hair at his temples was anything to go by. His clothes were plain, but he carried himself like someone in a higher class, a member of the long-removed German royalty perhaps. Or maybe it was just his smug expression.

"She's a lovely fräulein, Elliott. Such a waste that she should die alongside a piece of English garbage like you."

Her eyes shot open when Tim chuckled. "You're not going to shoot us."

Ginny almost swallowed her tongue. Of course Rolf was planning to kill them. She had no doubt of it. There were so many things she still had left to do, like finish college and start her nursing career. Images of chubby babies with Tim's vivid blue eyes and her sweet smile came into focus. A lifetime of love and friendship unfolded before her. She'd only known him a couple of weeks, but her heart knew he was her life. Her love. She wanted to grow old with him.

Which wouldn't happen if Tim kept talking. Well, she wasn't ready to give up just yet.

Ginny stretched to her full height. "Why do you say that, darling?"

She felt his smile all the way to her toes. Tim turned and faced the German. "If he discharges his gun, someone in town would hear the gunshot and the coast guard would investigate it. Isn't that right, Rolf?"

The man laughed, but Ginny saw the truth in his eyes. He wasn't sure his plan would succeed. Rolf turned the gun on her. "Maybe I should shoot your lady friend, Tim, and show you I have no qualms about pulling the trigger. But no, I think a burial at sea would be a more fitting end to our acquaintance. You may have survived it once, but I doubt you'll fare as well this time. Now, move."

Tim darted a quick glance at her, and she understood. His rash confrontation was meant to comfort her. For the moment, they weren't in any danger. Forcing herself to relax, Ginny fell in behind the captain, with a verse she'd learned as a young girl early in her faith repeating over and over in her mind. *If God is for us, who can be against us?* Wave after wave of peace drifted through her, shoring up her faith. She released the breath she'd been holding and relaxed. This was just the first of a lifetime of hills and valleys she and Tim would have to face. God was with them too, the third strand of an unbroken cord.

The path narrowed into a forest of dense underbrush and trees that forced them to walk single file. Prickly vines scratched against her denim-clad legs, the thorns piercing the heavy fabric and prickling her skin. Tree limbs caught on her wool scarf, tearing it from her head, leaving her face and ears exposed to the bitter cold. She tugged the pins from her snood and stuffed it in her coat pocket, praying that her hair would provide some warmth. Tim glanced back and gave her a wolfish grin, and despite the dire circumstances, she found herself grinning.

How would they get out of this? Every escape route led to the same conclusion—first one, then the other would be shot. At least that way, her parents would have closure. If Rolf went through with his plans to drown them in the ocean, their bodies might never be found.

The path ended at a small spit of land surrounded on three sides by the sound. Brush and dead logs were piled high along one side of the fishing shanty, probably to camouflage it from the boats passing on the sound. The rest of the place resembled Murph's place, only smaller with one or two rooms at the most. A thin steady stream of smoke poured from the flue, the only sign that it was something more than a run-down shack.

"Franco." Rolf prowled around them like an alligator playing with his meal. "Come, brother. We have guests."

Ginny flinched as he called out to Frank again, this time directly behind her. She turned to glare at him. "Don't do that again."

Surprise sparked in the man's eyes, and he laughed as he came to stand in front of her. "I can see why you like her, Elliott. She's spirited." He stroked his finger down her cheek to her chin, then tilted her head back, but she jerked away. "You don't like that. Well, maybe you'll like this more." Grabbing a handful of her hair, he yanked her head back, then ground his mouth into hers. Fear and anger spiraled through her. Her boot came down on his foot, and he broke the contact, giving her time to gouge at his eyes. He ground his lips into hers again, the metallic taste of blood filling her mouth as the assault continued. Placing her hands on his chest, Ginny shoved him as hard as she could.

Rolf didn't move.

"Let her go!" Tim roared as he plowed into the man's side, sending all three to the ground.

Dazed, Ginny sat up, then spat a mouthful of blood into the vines. Her stomach roiled, and she wiped the imprint of his assault away with her hand and then her sleeve, until her mouth felt bruised and raw. Glancing around, she saw Tim, his fists crashing one after the other against the German's battered face.

She shoved her hand into her coat pocket and froze. Where was her father's pistol? Tim had Schmidt pinned, his arms locked beneath Tim's knees, his hands empty. There were two guns missing, not just one. She scoured the area. A small indentation in the ivy a few feet from the men caught her attention. Her knees almost buckled as she hurried over and dug both out of the vines. She slipped hers into her pocket but held tight to Rolf's gun.

"Put the gun down, Miss Mathis. I don't want to hurt you."

A little too late for that. Through watery eyes, Ginny jerked around to find Frank standing at the corner of the rickety porch, his German-made Luger aimed at her. She tightened her fingers around the grip of the gun. Daddy had made her practice shooting every week as a teenager, aiming at everything from tin cans to oyster shells. But could she get off a shot before Frank did? Her finger settled over the trigger.

A piercing blast ripped through the silence. "I'm running out of patience, Miss Mathis. Put it down. Now."

Rolf's gun made a soft thud as it hit the ivy.

Frank turned his gun on Tim. "Rolf has been expecting you ever since he learned you had survived, Mr. Elliott. I wasn't so sure. These woods can be a bit tricky to navigate even for the natives." He glanced at her. "I am surprised to see you here, Miss Mathis. You're not the type to get involved in something like this."

"You mean defending my country?" Ginny snapped.

Frank chose to ignore her. "How is my daughter? Is she all right?"

Such an interest in his child surprised her. April had said that she was certain her father loved her, but what kind of man would bring this kind of evil into their home? Ginny met his gaze. "She's worried sick about you."

His bushy brows knitted together as the barrel of his gun dropped to his side. "Just like her mother, that one. Always worried about something."

"She wouldn't worry if you'd give up this notion and go back home." Ginny slowly took a step toward him. "She needs you, Frank."

"I know, but I have to be able to take care of her." He drew in a deep breath, then lifted the gun toward Tim again. "Once we have successfully landed our troops, my brother and I will be considered heroes in our country. I will be able to give my little April everything she rightfully deserves."

"Not if you're in Leavenworth," Tim said as he joined her, shaking his bloodied fist. A quick glance over her shoulder found Rolf laid out as if in a sound sleep, his face bloodied and bruised. Ginny slid her hand into Tim's. A journalist? The man could give Joe Louis a run for his money.

Tim gently squeezed her hand before turning his attention back to Frank. "You seem to love your daughter, Frank. Do you have any idea what this is doing to her? She's terrified to go home, afraid of what she could find there. And how do you think people will treat her, knowing her father is a traitor to the country that took him in? Right now, she relies on the kindness of others for food and shelter."

Ginny held her breath as Frank shook his gun at them. "I provided for her. The house is in her name, and she has money for food and clothes. What more could she need?"

"Frank, those things don't matter. You matter to her," Ginny answered softly. "She's afraid she's going to lose you and be all alone in this world. She loves you."

He lowered the gun to his side. "I only want the best for her—"

A gunshot rang out, cutting Frank off. Ginny jerked around to see Tim grab his arm as he crumpled to the ground. Dropping to her knees beside him, she focused on the growing stain on the sleeve of his right arm. She tore her gloves off then opened his coat. Blood completely soaked his shirtsleeve. "Tim?"

He drew in a shuddering breath. "I'm fine."

Ginny wasn't so certain. It looked like the bullet had nicked an artery. If she didn't slow the bleeding down, Tim would bleed out in a matter of moments. She opened his shirt, then pushed her gloves down the sleeve to the wound, but that was a temporary solution. A tourniquet would buy them some time until help could come. Ginny began to unlace her shoes.

"Brother, there was no need to do that," Frank barked. "Miss Mathis is good people."

"These people are our enemies, Frank. They deserve no mercy from us," Rolf bit out as he scrambled to his feet. "What we do, we do for the fatherland."

Ginny barely slipped the laces under Tim's arm and tied them off before Rolf grabbed her by her hair and yanked her to her feet. Tears welled in her eyes, but she refused to cry, not in front of this man. Shoving her, he suddenly let her go and she stumbled to keep from falling.

Rolf walked over to Tim and kicked him in his injured arm, causing Tim to shout in pain. The man bent over him, a smirk on his face. "Goodbye, Elliott."

No, this couldn't be how it ended for them. She wanted time with Tim. Years, decades. *Please, Lord, give us time together.*

Rolf stalked toward her, grabbing her by the arm and jerking her close until his gun was pressed against the back of her head. Pushing her across the short yard to the edge of the porch, he glanced up at his brother. "Take her inside and tie her up. Make sure the ropes are tight."

Frank nodded, then held out his hand to her. "Miss Mathis."

Ginny glared at his hand, then walked past him into the shack.

≣ CHAPTER 19 ≣

"I've never made fried peach pies before." April speared the browning dough, then flipped it. "Daddy thinks baking anything but bread is a waste of time and money."

Belle just nodded as she loaded another spoonful of batter for the frying pan. How many other simple pleasures had Mr. Smith kept from April? Over the past few days, she'd discovered a lot of things about April. Like she didn't have a Bible to take to church and she missed her momma more than she let on. Despite everything, April still loved her father, so Belle had kept her mouth shut. No sense hurting her friend when she was already down.

The batter sizzled as Belle poured it into the pan. Having April here had made her realize how blessed she was with her own parents and Ginny, no matter how crazy they made her at times. She'd never take their love for her for granted again.

A loud banging at the front door made Belle drop her spoon into the batter. A quick glance at April showed the effects of her father's treatment—indescribable fear of being pulled from a place of safety and comfort. Turning off the stove, Belle grabbed the girl's arm, then pulled her across the room and into the pantry. She flicked on the overhead light, then turned to April. "There's some comic books and a chair behind the back shelf. Lock the door and don't open it for anyone except me."

April nodded.

Once she heard the soft click of the lock, Belle pressed herself against the door and drew in a deep breath. With Momma visiting family in Ocracoke, and Ginny and Tim off to talk to Mr. Murphy, she was the only line of defense her friend had. Belle closed her eyes. *Lord, help me keep April safe. Be with her in her time of need. And thank You for the family You've given me. They're the best, Lord. Amen.*

Grabbing a kitchen knife out of the drawer, Belle walked through the hallway into the living room as the pounding at the door grew louder. Steeling herself, she pulled back the curtain and glanced out the window. A sigh of relief tore through her. Rushing to the door, she flung it open. "Mr. Murphy, I wasn't expecting you. I thought you'd be with Ginny and Tim."

"I was." He glanced nervously around the living room. "Is your momma here? I need to speak to her."

"No, she's out of town," Belle answered, noting the worry lines around his dark eyes and mouth. Something wasn't right. The last time Mr. Murphy came to town was when he almost died after a cottonmouth got him. Before that, she didn't know. "What's wrong, Murph? Why isn't Ginny with you?"

"That man got her."

"What man? Tim? No, he's her..." She wasn't sure what Tim was to her sister. It might be love, but...

Murph took her arm and shook her gently. "No, Miss Belle. That man got him too. You know, the one they came to see me about this morning."

Belle's heart tumbled into her stomach. After weeks of looking, they'd found the German. Only now, they might be in danger. "What do you mean he took them? Took them where?"

"That's what I'm trying to tell you. After your sister and her friend left, I remembered I had an empty soup jar from your momma. Ginny promised to bring me another one, but I felt kind of bad, thinking about having two of your momma's jars. So I went after them." He stopped to take a breath. "That's when I saw them. He had a gun to Mr. Tim's head and was leading him off to that old shack I sold Mr. Smith." He shook his head. "I knew I should have never sold him that place."

Belle forced herself to breathe. Ginny and Tim were in trouble. "Did you notify the coast guard? Or the police?"

Murph sucked on his lower lip. "Officer Chapline is the only one of them folks who'll talk to me, and he's in Kill Devil Hills. I tried to find someone else, but they just ignored me, Miss Belle. You know how folks are. They don't like to talk to folks like me."

"They don't like to talk to people like me either, Mr. Murphy, which makes them dumb as rocks in my book." Now wasn't the time to try to solve the problems of the world. That would have to come later. They had to find Ginny and Tim before they were hurt or. . .Belle couldn't think about that now. She needed to get her sister and Tim home. "We need to round up the girls and see if any of their dads or brothers will help us. You know how to get to this shack?"

"Know it like the back of my hand."

Belle flashed him a smile as she tugged him inside the house. "Then let's get moving."

It took less than fifteen minutes for Belle to alert the other girls. By the time Mr. Murphy had finished the fried pie and glass of milk April had prepared for him, there were thirty men, women, and boys with every type of weapon at their disposal gathered in their backyard. Baseball bats and golf clubs. BB guns and rifles. Mr. Hamby had even brought the small harpoon from his boat. Now all they needed was a plan.

"The walls of the shanty are paper thin, so we can't be firing any weapons, or we risk hitting Ginny and Mr. Elliott," Ruthie and Clara's dad explained. "Our best hope is to draw the Germans out."

"How are we going to do that?" Mr. Rutherford asked, taking the last fried pie Belle offered. "It's odd for one person to be in that part of the woods this time of year, much less a small army."

The men were still working on a plan when Belle and the other girls slipped inside the back door to get more pies.

"This is the last one." Belle forked it onto Lucy's plate, then turned to face them. "What are we going to do? We can't let them go into the woods without something in their bellies."

April glanced at the area beside the refrigerator. "What about the cookies? We'll have to take money from our troop fund, but this is a worthy cause."

"Cookies," Belle muttered to herself, an idea forming. She jerked her head around. "April, didn't you say your dad has a sweet tooth for Girl Scout cookies?"

"Yes, but what has that got to do—"

Belle interrupted. "Didn't he also tell you he wanted to be the first to know as soon as they came in?"

"Yes, but—"

"Oh no." Crossing her arms, Lucy shook her head violently. "We are not going to use cookies to get those men to come out of that shack."

"Why not?" Belle asked. "It's a better idea than anyone else has come up with, and Mr. Smith isn't going to let anything happen to us." She turned to April. "Not as long as you're with us."

Ruthie wrapped her arm around Belle's shoulder. "It's a brilliant plan. The adults can surround the place while the six of us 'sell cookies.'"

"That's not much of a plan," Lucy stated, shoving back her

chair. "You're pretty much giving them the chance to shoot at us."

"Not if I'm there," April replied. "I know my dad isn't a good man, but he is a good father. He wouldn't let anything happen to us. Plus, he's been wanting some cookies ever since last year. I promised him I would get him some. He knows I'll keep my promise."

"Come on, Luc." Clem kneeled in front of her. "It won't seem as suspicious with all of us there."

Lucy shook her head. "I understand that, but my momma has already sent her only son to fight in this war. She shouldn't have to worry about her daughter too."

"We understand, Luc, but everyone is making sacrifices. Think of Ginny and Tim," Clem continued. "They were only trying to keep the island safe for us. This is small compared to what they're doing."

Lucy scrubbed her face with her hands. "Oh, all right. Our parents probably won't let us do it anyway."

"I'll protect you with my softball bat." Clem grinned.

Lucy rolled her eyes. "You can barely hit a ball, so sure, go ahead."

Belle grinned. "Good. Now, someone grab those boxes and let's get going."

When they presented their idea to the group, the majority thought it too risky, but the girls were adamant. It was a known fact the troop visited each house on the island to sell cookies. Why not include the shanty? By the time they had finished talking, a plan to keep the girls safe as they "sold cookies" was in place.

By the time they reached the woods surrounding the shack, Belle's nerves were a tangled mess. What if the Germans had already done something to Ginny and Tim? How would she live without her big sister if the worst had happened? She prayed, then prayed again, the peace she sought just out of reach.

"That looks like a person," Ruthie whispered beside her.

Belle jerked her head up. "Where?"

Her friend pointed toward the middle of the weedy postage stamp yard. "There, and they're moving this way."

"It is someone, and it looks like they've been hurt."

Before anyone had time to react, Clem shot out of the tree line, crouched low to the ground. Grabbing the person by his arm, she dragged him back to their post. Flipping him over, Belle's heart caught in her throat as she kneeled beside Tim.

"He's been shot in the arm." Clem wiped her face against her coat sleeve. "Ginny must have seen it because she tied off the blood supply right above the gunshot."

Which meant Ginny was alive, or at least she was an hour ago. Belle opened Tim's coat, her stomach roiling at the sight of so much blood. "He needs a hospital."

"I'm on it." Clem snaked her way through the trees to a group of older boys who looked interested at the opportunity to see a real gunshot wound. Soon, Tim along with Clem and the boys were on their way.

"Ready, girls?" Mr. Hamby asked, his harpoon aimed at the front door.

The girls glanced at one another, then Belle whispered, "Let's pray before we go." Each girl lowered her head as Belle began. "Lord, we're here today asking for Your protection. Put a hedge around us as we protect our homes and our way of life. Be with Ginny, Lord. Keep her safe, and help Tim, please. Heal him." Belle hesitated, then continued. "And Lord, be with Mr. Smith and his brother. Let them surrender without any more bloodshed. All this in Jesus' name I pray. Amen."

"Amen," the girls responded.

Picking up a sack containing cookies, Belle smiled as she took Ruthie's hand. "Make new friends but keep the old."

"One is silver and the other, gold," Ruthie answered as she took Clara's hand.

By the time they reached the shack's door, they were singing and laughing at full voice. The door swung open, and Frank Smith stepped out on the porch. "Girls, what are you doing here?" His focus turned to April. "Daughter, I wasn't expecting you."

April held up the box of cookies. "You made me promise I would bring cookies to you as soon as they came, and I always keep my promises."

The man's expression softened as he stepped toward the stairs. "You always have."

"Brother, who are you talking to?" Rolf Schmidt, the man Tim had spent weeks looking for, stepped outside and surveyed the scene. Eyeing the girls, he glared at his brother. "I thought you said she didn't know where we were."

"It's just the Girl Scouts, brother. They go to every door on the island to sell their cookies this time of year." Mr. Smith came down the steps, not noticing Lucy's father behind the thick bushes until the man held a shotgun on him.

Rolf turned to retreat, but Mr. Hamby charged up the stairs, pushing the German against the wall while holding his weapon on him. Once the men were tied up, Belle dropped Ruthie's hand and tore off toward the shack's door. She bumped into a table, and a large box with a microphone fell to the floor. Going farther into the room, she saw Ginny tied to a post, her mouth gagged.

Belle fell on her knees in front of her sister and started working on the handkerchief. "Are you all right? I've never been so scared in my life. I thought I'd lost you."

When the knot loosened, Ginny spat it from her mouth. "Where's Tim? Is he okay?"

April worked on the ropes that held Ginny's legs together, while Ruthie sawed through the ones at her wrist with her daddy's pocketknife. Lucy held up a container of water as Ginny drank. "He's lost some blood, but Clem took him to the hospital."

Ginny sagged against the post and sucked in great breaths as she began to weep. Belle wrapped her arms around her, whispering words of comfort, lifting broken prayers as her big sister clung to her. One by one, the other girls joined in, nursing Ginny the only way they knew how.

With love.

⟨CHAPTER 20⟩

Nothingness.

Tim drew in a breath, then another, the heaviness lifting from him in small degrees. The emptiness threatened to pull him back under, into the void between sleep and alertness, but a distant voice, so sweet and gentle, called to him. A growing ache settled over his right shoulder, and he tried to move but couldn't. Why did his arm feel so cold and heavy? The question floated around his thoughts. There was that voice again, begging him to wake up, to come back to her. He recognized it this time.

Ginny.

He forced his eyelids open, blinking against the bright light as his eyes adjusted. Starched sheets crinkled beneath him as he stretched, the smell of antiseptic jarring his brain. Tim lifted his head as much as the bandaging would allow but couldn't find her. Had he been dreaming the sweet words she'd whispered to him? If so, he wanted to sleep forever.

A warm hand clasped his, and he knew it wasn't a dream. She was there, her head bowed over his hand, her features relaxed and quiet in rest as she prayed over him. His Ginny truly was the most beautiful woman he'd ever known, inside and out. Her sweet spirit calmed his restless one. The life he'd planned was an empty one without her in it.

For now, he needed to heal, and the best medicine for him would be a glimpse of her glorious smile. "Ginny." Her name came out as a raspy whisper, so he tried again. "Sweetheart."

"Tim?" Her eyes flew open, and she lifted her head. Her lips quivered, then with a little hiccup, she smiled, her eyes drifting over his face as if she were putting it to memory. "Tim."

His name sounded like a prayer on her lips. "I'm sorry I scared you, Ginny. Are you okay?" His last thought before losing consciousness had been of her. "I didn't want to leave you."

She grasped his hand to her breast as her tear-rimmed eyes met his. "I thought I'd lost you, you big lug."

"Never, darling." It was the truth. If Ginny would have him, he'd spend the rest of his life by her side. "What happened? Rolf didn't. . ."

She shook her head. "No. Mr. Smith kept an eye on him. They'd barely tied me up when the calvary arrived."

His thoughts felt fuzzy. "The calvary?"

She gave him that sweet quirky smile that made his heart trip in his chest. "What do you think?"

Tim thought for a moment, then shook his head. "The girls. Are they all right?"

"Good as gold." Ginny nodded. "But it wasn't just them. Murph was the one who sounded the alarm. He had one of Momma's quart jars and wanted to return it. He saw us with Rolf." A shadow fell across her eyes. "He tried to get both the police and the coast guard to listen to him, but they wouldn't. So he ended up at our house. He told me Belle was on the phone to the other girls in the troop before he was even finished with the story." She gave him a glorious smile. "She had a small army coming for us by the time she was finished. Mr. Hamby even brought his harpoon, which he used to keep Rolf in line."

Tim laughed, then grimaced, clutching his shoulder. "We'll defeat Hitler in no time with people like you and your troop around."

She tightened her grip on his good hand. "Don't forget yourself in that mix, Mr. Elliott."

He leaned his head back against the pillow. "Belle really is something."

Her soft chuckle warmed him. "Don't tell her that. She's got a big enough head as it is. The local papers are eating the story up. There's even a reporter coming from Raleigh to interview her and the other girls."

He could see that. A Girl Scout troop exposing a German spy would be a front-page story any other time. It was an interesting angle. "Too bad they won't be able to publish it."

"Why not?"

"If folks knew how close America came to being invaded by the Germans, it would send the public into a panic." He shook his head. "Roosevelt can't afford that, not after Pearl Harbor."

Ginny sat back in her chair. "I never thought of it that way, but you're right. Poor Belle. She'll be so disappointed."

Tim closed his eyes, exhaustion pulling him down again. "I hate that. They're really good girls, you know."

"Yes, I know." He could hear the smile in her voice as she stood and tucked his arm under the covers. "Just rest now."

He forced his eyes open again to find Ginny hovering over him. Worry clouded her clear blue eyes, and he wanted so much to comfort her. "Did you mean what you said about loving me?"

Surprise replaced the concern in her eyes. "I wasn't sure you could hear me."

"I did." He studied her face. "How did you get that small scar on your forehead?

Ginny reached up and skimmed her fingers over it. "I fell and hit the corner of a coffee table when I was eleven months old. Why?"

"I just wanted to know." He skimmed his lips against it. "So do you love me?"

She nodded. "I do."

"I do too, you know. Love you, that is."

She laid her head on his good shoulder, and he used the opportunity to kiss her forehead, cheeks, anywhere he could reach. Then she lifted her face and pressed her lips to his in a tender kiss. When she moved away a few minutes later, her glazed eyes met his. "Now, rest."

"And you? When will you rest?"

She struggled to smile. "You know I don't need much sleep."

"You're dead on your feet, sweetheart." He lifted his hand to her face, watching as her eyes closed and she leaned into his palm. "Why don't you lie down beside me?"

Her eyes flew open and she stared at him. "I can't do that. What will people think?"

"That we've been through a horrible experience and need some rest, and they'd be right." He caressed her cheek with his thumb. "I don't care what people think. All I care about is you. Come. You can lie on top of the covers if it will make you feel more comfortable."

Ginny hesitated, glancing at the closed curtain and then back at him. "If this hurts you, I want you to tell me."

"Of course," he lied. It didn't matter if his arm fell off and rolled around on the floor, he wouldn't tell her. Having her near would be worth it. He scooted over to give her room.

She toed off her shoes, then climbed up on the bed and stretched out beside him. He wrapped his arm around her as she curled into his side. She felt soft and feminine as she rested her head on his chest, the slight scent of lavender clinging to her. This was the closest thing to heaven on earth.

"Close your eyes," Tim whispered. "I've got you."

"And I've got you." Tension slowly released its grip on her muscles until she felt completely relaxed in his arms. "This feels lovely."

"Shhh. . ."

Ginny breathed a little sigh, then snuggled closer. Within a few seconds, her soft, even breaths told him she was asleep. With a gentle kiss to her brow, Tim closed his eyes and followed her into oblivion.

———————— ≈ ————————

Belle slipped out of the curtain and pulled it closed behind her, her lips twitching, ready to burst out in laughter. She'd always wanted a brother, though she knew they could be a nuisance at times. But a brother-in-law was even better, especially when it was someone like Tim.

After stopping by the nurses' station to tell them Tim was asleep and shouldn't be disturbed, she hurried to the reception area where the rest of the troop waited. Belle had barely pushed open the door when she was accosted by Ruthie.

"How's he doing? Is Ginny with him?" Ruthie's ponytail flicked from side to side as she shook her head. "Was he pale? I've never seen that much blood in my life."

Belle grabbed her friend by the shoulder and gave her a gentle shake. "He's fine, though he's real tired."

"The doctor said that was normal considering how much blood he'd lost." Clara snaked her arm around her twin's waist. "Once they stitched him up, he was fine."

Lucy joined them, then glanced around. "Where's Ginny?"

Belle smiled. "She's asleep."

"Poor woman," Lucy sighed, leading them over to a group

of chairs. "She's been at Tim's bedside for the last two days. She really ought to go home and rest."

"I think she's quite happy where she is." Belle told them about finding her sister and Tim asleep. "Do you think she'll have a June wedding? Maybe they'll have it on the beach."

"Ewww!" Ruthie cried out. "With all the oil and stuff? I don't think so."

Belle grimaced. "Yeah, I'd forgotten about that. Then maybe they'll get married in the backyard. We could fix up that old trellis and decorate it with flowers and some of the English ivy that we found in Buxton Woods the other day. You know, in honor of Tim's country."

Ruthie's eyes went wide. "What if they decided to get married in England? What would we do then?"

"I doubt they'd do that considering the bombings going on there," Clem reasoned, then turned to Belle. "Where's April? I figured she'd be in the middle of this."

"You didn't hear? The police located her mother. It seems her father had threatened to kill both her and April if her mother tried to take her when she left. April was talking on the phone with her mother when I left." Belle choked up thinking about the happiness in her friend's voice as she spoke to her mother for the first time in years. "Hopefully she'll be reunited with her mother very soon."

"So how did Tim propose?"

Belle shrugged. "I don't know."

Lucy glared at her. "What do you mean you don't know? They told you they were engaged, didn't they?"

"Calm down," Ruthie said, eyeing the receptionist as she stared at them over her wire-rimmed glasses. "Miss Perkins won't think twice about throwing us out of here if we don't quiet down."

"Ruthie's right." Belle glanced from one girl to another. "You're my dearest friends in the world, well, you and April. If we can't get along, how can we expect to win this war? We've got to stand united. That means no more name-calling or bickering between us. Understand?"

The rest of the girls nodded, and then Lucy held out her hand to Belle. "I'm sorry. I just got caught up in the moment, I guess."

"And I got caught up in the thought of having a brother-in-law." Belle took her hand and pulled her into a hug.

"It's going to seem kind of strange not fighting at times," Clem said, smiling at them. "But I think I can get used to it."

"I know." Belle scrunched up her nose. "But with everything else going on in the world, it seems wrong to bicker over silly little things."

"She's right." Ruthie put her arm around Belle's waist. "Look at what we're able to do when we work together."

"We did kind of save Tim and Ginny the other day," Clara said, holding out her hand to Clem.

"And we found Tim and took care of him after the tanker was bombed," Clem added.

"Not to mention, we caught an honest-to-goodness German spy," Lucy said. "I wonder if the Girl Scouts have a merit badge for all of this?"

The girls laughed, drawing Miss Perkins out from behind the counter. Watching her, the group moved to the farthest corner of the room where they sat down.

"Let's not forget April. Without her telling us about her father's plans, we could have been invaded by now," Clem said softly. The girls had voted to keep Mr. Smith's part of the Germans' plans between them for April's sake. German hatred was already high on the island, and they didn't want April to bear the brunt of it.

"Has she seen her father yet?" Ruthie asked.

Belle shook her head. "He's refused to let her see him. Her mother is supposed to be here in a few days, so I'm hoping she can see him by then."

"Well, she can stay with me until her momma gets here." The girls turned and stared at Lucy. "I can be nice when I want to be."

The room erupted with laughter. It felt good to laugh after the last few weeks. And there'd be a wedding to look forward to in the months ahead. Glancing at her friends' smiling faces, Belle remembered something her father had said once—a person is blessed to have one truly good friend in life. And she had five. One day, they'd grow into women, marry, and have children or even a career, but they would always have each other.

She'd pinkie swear on it.

Dear Reader,

I hoped you enjoyed getting to know Ginny, Tim, and the girls as they fought to protect their home during the Battle of the Atlantic. Until a few years ago, I believed the war raged only in Europe, parts of Africa, and the Pacific. After a trip to the Graveyard of the Atlantic on the Outer Banks, I learned about Torpedo Junction, the name given to the area off the Outer Banks during the war and realized how close the fighting came to our own shore. Between January 1942 to August 1942, almost four hundred ships were sunk off of Cape Hatteras and surrounding areas, most witnessed by the islanders. Five thousand civilians and merchant marines were killed due to the unorganized and sloppy defense system of an unprepared United States, yet the public was unaware of the battles. In 1942, the war effort wasn't going well for the Allies so to keep spirits up, news stories about the attacks were squashed. There are many great books about the Battle of the Atlantic, but the two I found most helpful are both called *The Battle of the Atlantic,* one by Jonathan Dembleby, and the other, by Mark Milner. You might also like to read *Taffy of Torpedo Junction* by Nell Wise Wechter. It's a children's book written by a teacher who lived on the island at the time.

I became fascinated with Girl Guide/Girl Scout history after a visit to the Girl Guide Museum in London. As a former Girl Scout myself, I spent the next few years researching the organization's history and made a trip to the Girl Scout house in Savannah, Georgia. Between the Girl Guides across Europe who formed troops in German concentration camps and worked with the French Resistance to the Girl Scouts in the states who spearheaded drives, planted Victory gardens, and filled civilian positions to free up fighting men, these brave trailblazers played a huge part in the Allies victory. Doors that had been firmly closed for young women were cracked open by the Girl Guides/Girl Scouts' work during the war. If you'd like to read more on the Girl Guides/Girl Scouts of that time, I highly recommend How the Girl Guides Won the War by Janie Hampton. I'd also recommend the Girl Scout's Handbook from that time period.

Any mistakes are mine. I did take some literary license at times to make the story gel so please forgive me.

Until next time, I will keep you in my prayers.

Patty

ABOUT THE AUTHOR

Multi-published author Patty Smith Hall lives in the North Georgia mountains with her husband of thirty-nine years, Danny. When she's not writing at her kitchen table, she's playing with her grandsons, visiting her family, or serving in her church.

HEROINES OF WWII

They went above the call of duty and expectations to aid the Allies' war efforts and save the oppressed. Full of intrigue, adventure, and romance, this new series celebrates the unsung heroes—the heroines of WWII.

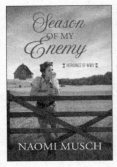

Season of My Enemy
By Naomi Musch

Only last year, Fannie O'Brien was considered a beauty with a brain, and her future shone bright, despite the war pounding Europe. With her father's sudden death and her brothers overseas, Fannie must now do the work of three men on their 200-acre farm—until eight German prisoners arrive and, just as Fannie feared, trouble comes too. Someone seems intent on causing "accidents," and Fannie is certain the culprit is one of the two handsome older Germans—or possibly both. Can she manage the farm, keep the prisoners in line, and hold her family together through these turbulent times?
Paperback / 978-1-63609-291-1

Escape from Amsterdam
By Lauralee Bliss

Helen Smit is finally realizing her dream of working with children by entering university to pursue a teaching degree. But life takes a drastic turn for survival when Nazi Germans occupy Amsterdam, and Jews, who are rounded up across from the university, begin to be deported. Now all she can think of is helping all the kids escape before it's too late. Her friend Erik Misman is aware of underground efforts to help Jews, but joining them would mean risking everything Helen holds dear. Can she smuggle at least some children from the city, and will there be any safe haven left in the country?
Paperback / 978-1-63609-376-5